The Mystic Cipher

A Story of the Lost Rhoades Gold Mine

The Mystic Cipher

A STORY OF THE LOST RHOADES GOLD MINE

By

Dennis L. Mangrum

Bonneville Books
Springville, Utah

ISBN 13: 978-1-59955-219-4

Published by Bonneville Books, an imprint of Cedar Fort, Inc., 2373 W. 700 S., Springville, UT 84663
Distributed by Cedar Fort, Inc., www.cedarfort.com

LIBRARY OF CONGRESS CATALOGING-IN-PUBLICATION DATA

Mangrum, Dennis L.
    The mystic cipher : a story of the lost Rhoade's gold mine / Dennis L. Mangrum
        p. cm.
    ISBN 978-1-59955-219-4 (acid-free paper)
    1. Rhoades, Thomas, 1794 or 5–1869—Fiction. 2. Gold mines and mining—
    Fiction. 3. Treasure troves—Fiction. 4. Uinta Mountains Region (Utah and
    Wyo.)—Fiction. I. Title.

    PS3613.A537M97 2008
    813'.6—dc22

                                2008043658

Cover design by Jen Boss
Cover design © 2009 by Lyle Mortimer
Edited and typeset by Allison M. Kartchner

Printed in the United States of America

10 9 8 7 6 5 4 3 2 1

Printed on acid-free paper

The True Hero

The credit belongs to the man who is actually in the arena, whose face is marred by dust, and sweat, and blood; who strives valiantly; who errs, and comes short again and again because there is no effort without shortcomings; but who actually strives to do the deed, who knows the great devotion; who spends himself in a worthy cause, who at the best knows in the end the high achievement of triumph and who at worst, if he fails, while daring greatly, know his place shall never be with those timid and cold souls who know neither victory nor defeat.

—Theodore Roosevelt

Other books by Dennis Mangrum

Seasons of Salvation
Diamonds are Forever

Acknowledgments

This page is usually where an author thanks those who helped along the way. I guess it could be analogized to a pitcher thanking a catcher after throwing a no-hitter. He couldn't have done it without his catcher or the shortstop that made the diving backhanded grab or the centerfielder who caught a fly ball just before it went over the fence.

I had one of each: my daughter, the catcher, Nichole Jones, who read and suffered through countless changes and gave invaluable help in forming the story and characters. The center fielder, Tristi Pinkston, who made the game winning catch not once but twice; and last but not least my brilliant shortstop, Allison Kartchner, my editor at Cedar Fort who makes her living saving pitchers' hides.

The story was born and written—well kind of written. It could be compared to a rough stone that needed to be rolled down a long, long stream to knock some very rough edges off.

Tristi (of Precision Editing) put her heart into polishing the manuscript—knocking off a lot of jagged edges—polishing it. Without her you would not be reading this story. She was a brilliant editor probably because she put more into editing than just changing words and dotting the i's. She tried to feel what I felt when writing the story.

Allison is an editor that every publisher should wish they had. She cares; she is smart; and she is not afraid to suggest changes that will make the story better. I've worked with a number of editors, some I hope to never hear from again, but Allison is my first choice every time I choose my team.

Thanks also to Indiana Jones, my daughter's daughter. She is the only person that I know who is now a certified translator of the Deseret alphabet, and she's only fourteen. If you need help, you can contact her at Pleasant Grove Junior High.

Thanks also to my readers and critics: my lifelong friend Laurin Rackham and my brother Collin Mangrum for their thoughts, directions, encouragement, and for adding energy to complete this story.

.

Chapter One

A single rifle shot pierced the tranquility of the afternoon calm. Birds instantly abandoned their chirping trill—even the crickets were hushed as the forest and its inhabitants perceived impending danger. Every living creature went to instant alert. Dirt flew as a bullet plunged into the earth. Carver instantly recognized the sound of a rifle and took control. He dived away from the direction of the shot and rolled to the left. His sixth sense drove him to the closest cover, a man-sized granite boulder. The bullet seemed lost or misguided when it plunged into nothing but the soft earth a few feet from where Carver had been standing. The shooter was either a very bad shot or very good shot—bad if he had intended to hit Carver, good if he had only meant to send a calling card. But why was someone shooting at him? Was someone trying to scare him off? But from what? Why? He had no clue.

He scanned the immediate area, trying to locate any movement—a glimpse of motion, a shadow that wasn't there before. He listened for even the slightest sound, anything that would provide him location or direction of the shooter. Even his reliable intuition failed to provide him any information.

Stealth soon put him past the tree line and into cover. He didn't stop, but now was not the time to run. Now was the time to turn the tables take the offensive, attacking when it was least expected. He was back in the battle zone. His instincts and senses were on battle-red. Hopefully, the shooter would make one mistake.

While Carver moved his eyes were focused—searching, never stopping. He scoured the surrounding vicinity, an eagle searching for a rabbit while constantly and silently moving. For him there was no retreat, only advance.

Thirty minutes later Carver had completed a perimeter reconnaissance of the area and had been unable to find any trace of the shooter. It was as if no one had been there—a mirage. There weren't any footprints or vehicle tracks, nor could he even find a spent bullet casing. Whoever had fired the shot was good, professional.

Carver had only recently resigned his commission with an elite Army Ranger unit. He was a seasoned combat veteran who had spent most of his time ahead of the front line. He knew his stuff and all the tricks, yet he couldn't find a trace of the shooter. Even more perplexing was why someone would be taking a potshot at him. Maybe it had just been some redneck out having some fun. But anyone good enough to escape his detection wouldn't have missed the shot. Consequently, Carver assumed the shot had a message attached to it—he just didn't know what it could be or who was sending it. It had been an intentional signal, a warning. Maybe it was related to his recent legal action against the Forest Service. He had been awarded some twenty acres of land that the Forest Service had wrongfully claimed as its own.

After he made sure no one was in the vicinity, he strode back to where he had been digging fence-post holes along his newly claimed boundary line. He wanted to find out what his posthole auger had struck in the bottom of that last hole. It had sounded and felt like metal.

As he walked back to his work, he heard something moving

toward him. Whoever or whatever was not attempting to conceal its presence. His keenly alert senses took control as he started moving towards the sound.

"What's all the shooting about? You woke me up from my nap," came a distinctive raspy voice. It was Rylan Edison, Carver's closest neighbor and perhaps his best friend. Carver was the antithesis of sociability. Rylan, on the other hand, was a true good ol' boy, so unlike what one would think of as a retired attorney. He had lived in Marion, Utah, in the same house for the past thirty years. Carver liked Rylan and trusted him implicitly, and there weren't many that slid into either of those categories. Carver was a loner, avoiding relationships of any kind, except for Rylan, that is.

Rylan had been Carver's grandfather's best friend. Rylan had also represented Carver against the Forest Service. In fact, it had been Rylan who had discovered the boundary problem and goaded Carver into the action. Carver had inherited this ranch only three years ago from his grandfather. He had recently returned from the Army and was now trying to resurrect the old ranch and turn it into his retreat, his hiding place from the world. Rylan thought of himself as Carver's social chairman; at least, he had felt that way since Carver had returned to Marion. Carver repeatedly reminded him he already had a mother and didn't need another.

"I was hoping you could tell me," replied Carver as he appeared out of the trees and resumed his trek back to work.

"It wasn't you?" questioned Rylan.

"Nope."

"Do you know who it was, or who or what they were shooting at?"

"Don't know. I couldn't find any signs or tracks."

"That's strange," commented Rylan. "We don't have many people taking pot shots around here except during hunting season."

Carver returned to the fence line and started digging in the post hole again. Rylan came over and sat beside him.

Clunk, clunk

"That doesn't sound like dirt to me," exclaimed Rylan as he stood to see what was in the bottom of the hole. "What do you have in there?"

Carver enlarged the opening. Rylan got on his knees and brushed the dirt off of what looked like a metal box, maybe nine by twenty inches. Finally Carver got two edges of the box unearthed and reached down to try to lift it from its burial place. There weren't any handholds, and try as he might, he couldn't budge it. He picked up a shovel and went back to digging, trying to make the hole bigger so he could get his hands under the bottom of the box.

"It looks old," said Rylan. "Maybe there's some of that legendary Spanish gold in it. Wouldn't that be a hoot?"

Carver rolled his eyes as if to say Rylan was certifiable, and kept digging. Rylan reached down again and dusted off the top of the box. It was definitely old. Carver knew Rylan was a history buff, particularly in early Utah history. He prepared himself to hear another of Rylan's lost gold mine stories; Rylan knew a million of them. Sure enough, Rylan began.

"Thomas Rhoades, the central figure in many of the legendary stories of Spanish gold, had his home just down the road a piece. Matter of fact, this very land was part of the original Rhoades' land grant. Did you know that?"

"Never heard of him," said Carver.

Rylan watched Carver continue his excavation. "Have you ever heard of the Lost Rhoades Mine?"

"Nope," replied Carver.

"Glad you asked, because it's a great story," Rylan said. "You see, when the Mormons first came to the Great Salt Lake Valley, they were very poor. They didn't have any way to acquire wealth, yet within a very few years they had built a thriving metropolis, purchased land, were minting their own gold, and had paid cash for the emigration of over 100,000 Saints."

Carver shrugged. If Rylan noticed Carver's apparent lack of interest in his story, it didn't affect him as he continued. "The emigration itself would have cost nearly $2,000,000, and in those days that would have been a king's ransom. The Church also paid $12,000 in gold for Fort Bridger within two months of reaching the valley."

Rylan stood up and stretched, adding, "It has also long been rumored that the angel Moroni atop the Salt Lake Temple was plated with Rhoades' gold, as well as the twelve golden oxen holding up the baptismal font inside the temple. Some even say the oxen are solid gold. You wonder how the Mormons did it? I'm glad you asked."

Carver glanced up at Rylan and asked, "Are you going to talk all day, or are you going to give me a hand?"

Rylan said, "Hey, I'm just about through. Now pay attention." Then he continued as though he were reading from a script. "The legend began when Isaac Morley secretly introduced Brigham Young to his blood brother and friend, the powerful Ute Indian Chief Wakara. Wakara had never seen Brigham Young face-to-face until that secret meeting and was surprised to recognize him. You see, at eight years of age, Wakara had seen Brigham Young in a vision. He had seen Brigham wearing a tall formal hat. In that vision, the great Indian God Towats had instructed Wakara to help the High Hats with the gold."

Carver finished digging around the box. It was no longer wedged into the compacted soil. He tried to remove it by reaching down into the hole with one hand. He couldn't get both arms into the hole to get a good grip on the box, and one hand was not enough to extricate it from the ground. Rylan watched out of the corner of his eye, pretending to ignore Carver's efforts. He leaned back and continued with his narrative, obviously waiting to help until he had finished his tale.

"Wakara told Brigham Young about this fabulous sacred mine full of gold, and that he had been instructed by Towats to assist the Church with gold from the mine. In short, Brigham chose Thomas Rhoades to be his emissary with Wakara because Rhoades knew the Ute customs, spoke their language, knew the Uintah Mountains, and Wakara liked him. Wakara eventually took Rhoades to the secret mine, although it wasn't really a mine. It was more like a sacred ancient Indian gold repository. It may be undocumented and impossible to prove, but I say the historical facts speak for themselves. The Church became financially solvent in a very short time with no apparent means for doing so. Wakara allowed Rhoades to take gold out of the mine for use by the Mormon Church."

Carver held up his hand for Rylan to stop. Rylan stopped, but held his mouth open as if he were frozen.

"Do you really believe this fairy tale?" Carver asked.

Rylan looked shocked. "What do you think is the point of this whole story if I don't believe it?

"Now let me finish. Wakara's help came with serious strings attached. First, Brigham could only send Rhoades for gold; second, it had to be needed by the Church; third, Rhoades was only allowed to take the amount of gold he could carry; and last, neither Rhoades nor Young could ever tell anyone anything about the gold, or its location. These promises were made by Rhoades, under penalty of death with Wakara and by covenant to Brigham Young. And of course I can't prove one word of what I am telling you—it's all hearsay and undocumented legend.

"Be that as it may, neither Rhoades nor the Church has ever acknowledged acquiring gold from Wakara. But that doesn't mean it didn't happen."

Rylan got down on his knees to look in the hole so he could see what Carver was doing to rescue the box from its burial place, shrugged, and went on with his story.

"In my opinion, Wakara's gold mine provided the financial assistance that the struggling Church so desperately needed, even though outsiders think the legend is allegorical and typical of many lost treasure stories.

"Anyway, Rhoades never broke his promise to Wakara or his oath to Brigham Young. Well, that's not technically true, because he did tell his son Caleb. As the story goes, after a few years, Thomas Rhoades got too old to make the trip. He talked to Wakara and Brigham, who both allowed him to tell his son, but only after Caleb took the same oath and covenant."

Carver tried to wrench the box from its resting place. He didn't need Rylan's help—he would do it himself.

Rylan leaned back against a tree and continued, "The Church's need for assistance diminished and Caleb's trips became less frequent. After only a few years of service, Caleb was killed in a dispute related to the mine. Supposedly, Caleb left two maps for his wife, from which numerous other maps have sprung, purportedly describing the location of the fabled Carre-Shin-Ob, or the Lost Rhoades Mine. Supposedly, with Caleb's death, the location of the mine was lost, except to certain few Ute Indian guardians.

"However, that's not the end of the story. It seems that from time to time, a few privileged individuals have been allowed to not only see the mine, but to remove additional gold to aid the Mormon Church. Again, the Church has neither admitted nor denied that fact."

Carver finally broke his silence. "How come no one has ever been able to find it?"

"Someone did. Their names were Thomas and Caleb Rhoades," replied Rylan.

"If you're through talking, why don't you quit resting and get over here and help me?" grunted Carver. The hole was bigger and he told Rylan to get on one side while he got on the other.

"It's heavy, so when you're ready, we'll both lift at the same time," directed Carver.

"So, you were actually listening to my story," replied Rylan.

Carver ignored the statement and said, "This thing is either glued to the ground or very heavy. Okay now, lift—when it's high enough, try to get your other hand under it." Rylan strained. When they got it high enough, they slid their hands under it and were able to lift and push it out of the hole. It came to rest, teetering on a pile of loose dirt. Carver examined the box closely, but couldn't find any way to open it.

"By darn, Carver, this just might be an old Spanish box. Legend has it that the Spanish only stored valuables in metal boxes such as this. See this cross marked on the top?" Rylan brushed dirt off the top corner. A double-lined cross was clearly marked.

Rylan pointed at the box. "That cross means this is a box of Spanish origin. Carver, do you have any idea what a stir this will cause?" Rylan wasn't through with his story, of course. He was never really through talking or telling stories.

"Legend also has it there's a spirit who guards the sacred gold. Maybe that's who took the potshot at you." He laughed.

"What if the box is just full of dirt?" asked Carver.

"Admit it. The story captured your fancy, didn't it?"

Carver didn't acknowledge the question. He stood and slowly did a 360 degree turn, carefully scanning his surroundings. Even though he had cleared the area, he had an uneasy feeling in his gut, like someone was watching. "We've got to get out of this clearing," said Carver.

"But I'm dying to open the box," Rylan said impatiently.

"We're not doing anything until we find some cover. Help me drag this over out of this meadow so we aren't exposed."

Carver stopped behind a big pine. Rylan said, "We need to get that box into your cabin before someone sees it, and we're not going to be able to lug it by hand. I'll mosey down to your place and fetch your four-wheeler. You wait right here and don't get shot while I'm gone."

With that, he turned to head towards Carver's cabin and said over his shoulder, "That was a joke, Carver." Carver didn't laugh. He was lost somewhere in his own world.

Carver checked the area again but didn't see any sign of unnatural movement. Even though the birds had commenced chirping, things didn't seem right. He bent down and examined every inch of the box, dusting off the dirt. He felt something near the top and brushed the dirt until he could see a pencil-thin etched line. If he had a knife, he might be able to fit the blade into the joint and pry the chest open. He wondered why it was so heavy. It must weigh well over a hundred pounds.

Suddenly the hair on the back of his neck rose. He stood and carefully surveyed the area again. He resolved to start carrying a handgun as well as the knife. He didn't like being unable to protect himself or his friends.

It took them nearly two hours to discover how to unlock the metal case back at Carver's cabin. The box had some sliding pieces like a Chinese puzzle, and once they were slid into position, the lid easily lifted open on inside hinges. The metal case was a marvel. There was no evidence that moisture had ever seeped into the case.

The box was lined with about fifty 1 x 1 x 3-inch square rods or bars that were extremely heavy for their size. Carver lifted one of the blackened bars out of the box and examined it. Rylan picked up another of the metal bars, scraping a corner with his knife.

"Dang, these are pure gold bullion," exclaimed Rylan. "Each of them must weigh close to a couple of pounds. If each is about two pounds, that's thirty-two ounces. Times that by $800 per ounce, which is what gold is going for these days. They're each worth about $25,600. If there are fifty of them in the case, I'd say that you have about 1.3 million dollars sitting there on your floor, my friend."

Each of the metal rods appeared to be almost black. Upon examination, Rylan found stamped on each bar a double-lined cross, a letter *V,* and the phrase "Anno. Dom. 1675."

"Good criminey," exclaimed Rylan. "I was just talkin' about the legend of Spanish gold hidden in these parts. I really didn't believe your little box would actually have some of it inside. Can you imagine the value of these gold pieces to collectors? Maybe two, maybe five times actual value. I mean, this is the real deal, my friend."

"I wonder who it belongs to?" asked Carver.

"Haven't you been listening to a word I said?" exclaimed Rylan. "This may be the biggest find of the century around here. You are looking at proof of the Thomas Rhoades legend. Do you have any idea how many people will go absolutely bananas when they hear about this?"

"You didn't answer my question."

"It's yours! Who else do you think it could belong to? It was buried on your land and you found it. By law, it's yours."

Carver was silent, thinking about the implications and said, "No one's going to hear about this, Rylan."

"You don't understand, Carver. This is . . . well . . . this is an incredible discovery. I mean, not only are you a multi-millionaire, just think about it. This is proof, evidence so to speak, that Thomas Rhoades actually had access to Spanish gold bullion. See that letter "V" stamped on each bar? That means tax has been paid to the King of Spain, and that cross means the gold was refined from a Catholic mine, and . . . and . . . it was minted in 1675." Rylan was almost speechless—almost.

"Just because the law says it's mine, doesn't make it right," replied Carver. "It either belongs to Rhoades or the Church, but not to me."

Carver didn't care about ownership of the gold. It wasn't his, regardless of what Rylan said. He lifted the gold bars out one at a time. Between layers of gold, he found an old leather satchel. Rylan was still discussing ownership of the gold when Carver handed it to him.

The leather bag was also made to withstand the elements, particularly water and moisture. Rylan painstakingly cut the stitching that sealed the packet with his knife. Inside he found some very old handwritten documents.

While Rylan was examining the contents, Carver lifted a round rock that looked like quartz out of the case. The orb was laced with pure gold. It must have been one of Rhoades' personal keepsakes.

Rylan exclaimed, "See these initials 'TR' carved into this pouch? It must have belonged to Thomas Rhoades. Imagine! Forget the gold, Carver. This case could prove to be more valuable than all of that gold together. This could be your ticket to fame and wealth."

Carver wanted to forget the metal box and all its contents. He wasn't looking for fame or money. He didn't want a bunch of crazies tromping all over his property looking for gold. He finally told his friend, "I don't want the problems the gold or this pouch will bring. We should just take the box and its contents to Church headquarters and let them solve the problem."

"Don't be so hasty, Carver." Rylan was looking at the old satchel, overwhelmed. "All my life I've heard stories of this legend. I kind of believed them, but there was never any proof. This . . . this . . . means it wasn't just a story, it was real. This could be the single most significant archeological find of the century. I mean, the local historians will have a field day and the treasure hunters . . . well, they'll probably start looking for the mine again. These mountains will be turned inside out by gold seekers."

Carver paced across the floor. He looked at Rylan and said, "Don't you understand? That's exactly what I'm trying to avoid."

Rylan looked at him like he had totally lost it. "Don't you understand what this could mean to the Utes? To say nothing of vindicating a whole slug of historians as well as putting to rest one of the most significant legends of the West."

Rylan opened the pouch and removed a document, carefully touching only the edges. He set it on the floor and slid the document into a plastic cover sheet.

Carver knew Rylan would die to be the one to analyze the document and contents of the box. He would want to publish a paper and connect all the dots that had for so long been scattered. This would put Rylan's name in the history books. Oh, he knew Rylan wasn't looking for fame or glory. He wanted the truth known, not perverted or hidden from the population. "Carver, this note is written in some kind of foreign language, or maybe code. Maybe it's Latin, or a combination of Latin and hieroglyphics."

Rylan was transfixed, in another world. He showed the document to Carver:

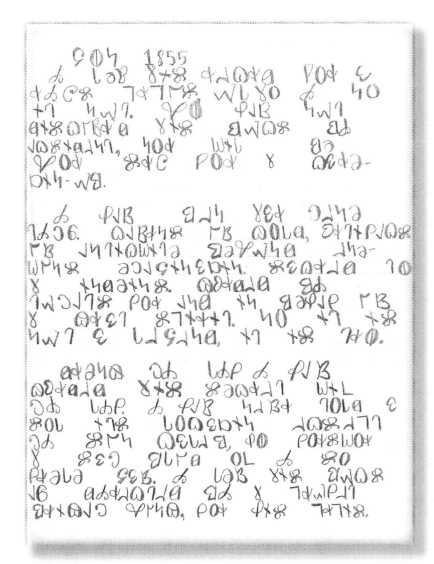

Following the hieroglyphics a second encrypted message was written, different from the first:

PWHV TFCEHXHRLNXRCSAXRGPGWX
CIOYHTERDAIIFZOUWCBTWJCYROJKLBTVFPVTV
AIHMLXKVAOUXVLAGVCDGJMRLYDYFMLXKVA

Carver had no idea what either of these missives said or meant, and he didn't really care. Rylan spoke softly, almost silently, to himself, and then lifted his head. His eyes were ablaze. "This is getting juicy. We have the framework for another National Treasure movie right here in our own backyard. Isn't your curiosity aroused just a little?"

"Nope."

"We've got to decode this document before we make any decisions," Rylan stated emphatically. "This document could be the biggest blockbuster to hit this state since polygamy. Carver, you've got to give me time to try to figure out what this document says. I don't want to give it to someone who will sweep it under the carpet and cover up the truth."

Carver didn't want to see his friend get involved, but he had to admit, Rylan's motives were just about as pure as they came.

Rylan continued as he studied the document, "The Spaniards were in Utah between 1500 and the mid-1700s. It's irrefutable that they mined and smelted gold all over this territory. Some even say Montezuma shipped all his gold northward, maybe even as far as Utah, to hide it from Cortez in the 1520s. This one document could provide us with information to conclusively vindicate the Rhoades legend."

When Carver didn't reply, Rylan asked, "Do you mind if I take this document, make a copy, and try to decode it?"

"Sure, you can have it, with one stipulation—you don't tell anyone. I don't want a bunch of lunatic gold diggers around my place."

"I have a suggestion," said Rylan. "Why don't we just hide the gold in your basement safe? I won't tell anyone what we found today. Once I decode this document, you can determine what you want to do."

Rylan would do anything he could to uncover this information, and Carver wanted his friend to have that opportunity. But he didn't want the world to know where it came from. "Why don't we take it to someone in the Ute Tribe or to the Church and see if you can get some help?" he suggested.

"Umm . . . I don't want any help right now," Rylan said.

Carver shook his head. Rylan was stubborn, that was for sure. "Okay, Mr. Edison, we have a deal. You take the same oath Thomas Rhoades took, and you can have all the time in the world to figure out what it says."

"Thanks, Carver. But there might be one person I need to call."

"I thought we had a deal," said Carver. "You can't tell anyone."

"Well, this isn't just anyone. You remember my daughter, Cassandra? She might be able to help, but I can promise she won't tell anyone anything."

Carver remembered Cassandra, vaguely. She was somewhere near his age but he couldn't recall any specifics about her. "I'm not sure about this, Rylan."

"The last time you saw her, she was a kid, but not anymore. She's a returned missionary and she's working on her doctorate at Yale."

"Missionary, huh? Where did she serve?"

"Not too far from here, actually. She went to the Ute reservation near Duchesne."

Rylan's eyes lit up and Carter recognized the expression all too well.

"I'm not interested, Rylan. Me an' women just don't mix."

"Hmmm," Rylan said. Then he smiled and added, "Well, if you're not interested in marrying my daughter, you shouldn't mind if I invite her to help me decode this message."

Rico pulled out his two-way radio. "It has been found," he said.

"And has it been opened?" The heavily accented voice spoke on the other end.

"It was taken inside. I could not see the contents."

"Keep to your post," came his instructions. "And remember, you will be rewarded."

That afternoon Carver deposited the gold in his secret basement safe. He had constructed it to be big enough to hold weapons and other personal belongings. It was hidden behind a wall, and the gold fit easily into one of the compartments.

Rylan had taken the old document and its pouch. Carver figured it would be as safe with Rylan as anyone. Maybe now Carver could relax and get back to putting his ranch into working order.

That afternoon, he went to town to stock up on some provisions. He ignored the nagging feeling that he should stay around his place, but he shook it off, blaming it on his reluctance to go shopping. As he turned off the highway on his way home, he was startled to see a cloud of dark smoke coming from the direction of his cabin. The nagging feeling returned. He gripped the steering wheel and wondered when he was going to start listening to his feelings. He pushed on the gas, knowing that it was too late.

He stopped in the driveway and realized his home was a total loss. There was nothing he could do. That was one of the problems living way out here—the fire department would arrive too late to be of any help.

Carver stood there and watched, helpless to do anything. When the fire department arrived, they couldn't do anything either. His muscles were tight as knots.

The fire chief approached. "Looks like the fire spread very quickly, kind of unusual. Did you store any flammables in the cabin?"

"No," replied Carver. He tried to appear calm and collected, but inside he was smoldering. The chief asked a few other questions and left, advising him they would come back and look around after everything had cooled down.

As soon as everyone was gone, Carver conducted his own investigation. This fire had been intentionally set. He used all his skills, trying to determine how or who had set the fire. He was unable to discover the trace of anyone within a mile of the cabin. He was baffled. Whoever had done it was good.

His grandfather's cabin was gone. The cabin meant the world to him. Daily it reminded him of his grandfather, his favorite person in the world. Someone had just made this very personal.

After the fire burned itself out and the coals cooled, Carver found an access hole through the floor joists to the basement. The fire had not reached the basement nor had it destroyed the joists or the main floor. Carver didn't climb into the basement but saw that no one had tried to enter his secret safe room, not that he cared if he lost the gold, but he wondered if someone had been looking for the gold or satchel, and decided he should pay a visit to Rylan.

"I want you to take extra precautions around here," he said to his friend upon reaching his house. "Whoever torched my cabin didn't find the gold. Maybe they don't know what they're looking for, but if they know about the satchel and documents, you can bet they're going to come looking here. Make sure those documents are hidden in case someone comes around looking for them, and arm yourself."

Rylan responded, "Okay, and I've got a bed and a place for you to stay until you rebuild your place."

"Thanks, I might take you up on that. Someone has caused me a lot of trouble. I want to know who and why, but I won't need a bed tonight. I'm going to be out and about. I am however, concerned about you. I want you to be careful, Counselor. These guys look like they play for keeps."

"You remind me of General MacArthur, one of my favorite people," Rylan told him. "When a reporter asked him why he was retreating he said, 'We are not retreating, we are advancing in another direction.' I assume that you're not retreating, either."

Chapter Two

Placing his radio on his desk, Vincent Vargas leaned back and smiled. Carver Nash would not soon forget the lesson he'd been taught.

Cass shook her head as she tried to explain one more time, wishing her dad could somehow see the expression on her face through the phone. "You're not listening. I have some very crucial research to conduct this summer if I ever want to complete my thesis. I can't spend the summer in Utah."

"Cass, you have to understand. This could be the most propitious opportunity of my life."

"Please speak English, Dad, if you want me to understand what it is you are trying to say. Remember, I hang out with guys that speak in differential equations."

"I need your help and there's no one else I can trust."

"But you won't even tell me what it's about."

"I promised to keep it secret. Besides, this is an open line."

"Okay, Dad, here's what you do. I'll give you the phone number of the pay phone down the hall. You go find a pay phone at the closest gas station and call me from there in fifteen minutes. Then, even if your home phone is bugged, they won't be able to hear when you tell me the secret. Trust me, it'll work. I watch them do it in the movies all the time."

"Cass, I'm not joking . . ." he paused and she knew he was trying to figure out the best way to tell her. "Besides, there's this guy I want you to meet."

"Ah, just what I thought. You're trying to line me up again. Is that what this secret stuff is all about?"

"You've heard of the good-looking, strong, silent type, haven't you? That's him, to a T."

"Dad, I have absolutely no time for a man in my life right now, even if he were James Dean reincarnated with a testimony."

"Cass, this isn't just about a guy. It's about . . . well . . . just do me a big favor and get on the next plane and come spend some time with dear old Dad. Either that, or I just might have to cut off your allowance."

"Dad, you know I would do anything for you—"

He interrupted before she could finish her sentence. "Now that's what I'm talkin' about. I knew you would come if I asked."

Cass loved her father—he'd been her best friend since her mother had died five years ago. He was not ordinarily subject to fits, paranoia, or dementia. If he asked her to come, she knew she would go. It was just very unusual, since he hardly ever asked for favors.

"About my allowance—I haven't received last month's check yet," she said.

"Okay, so I stretched the allowance thing a bit," he said.

"It'll be your fault if I have to come back here for another year just to finish." She paused for emphasis and then emphatically added, "But no fix-ups, understand?"

"Great! I'll make reservations for you in the morning," he said. "Cass, you are the best daughter I ever had."

"I'm your only daughter. But I can't come tomorrow. I think I can get everything ready and be able to leave in about six weeks," she said with a grin he could not see.

"Cass . . ."

"Okay, okay. But I've got to wrap up some loose ends. I'll be there within the week."

Cass couldn't imagine what her father needed that was so urgent. Nothing ever happened in Marion; maybe in one of the neighboring metropolises of Peoa, Kamas, or Oakley, but not Marion. Besides fishing, the next most exciting thing to do was to sit on the porch and wait for the Second Coming.

This guy he'd mentioned had to be part of his anxiety to get her to come. It was such a Utah thing to be married before you were twenty-five. At the upper end of her twenties, her father was the only one who still held out hope she could find Mr. Right. His first comment in every phone conversation was, "So who did you go out with this week?"

She'd never intended to be an old maid. When she got home from her mission and went to BYU, she dated a lot of guys—some of them were even nice, but she never felt fire in the belly around them, just indigestion. Everyone around her was getting married or engaged, so she decided that she needed to get married too. One guy really liked her, and she thought she could make it work. Didn't love only occur in romance novels anyway? She wanted a home surrounded by a white picket fence with a bunch of kids running around.

They talked about marriage and even set a date for the wedding. One night, he took her to a very expensive and quaint French restaurant. The waiter brought some grape juice, and floating in her glass was a diamond ring. When she saw it, she froze. She couldn't get married just for the sake of appearances. She wanted more, and felt he deserved more than half-hearted love too. Since then, she'd hid out in the math department, content to focus on her studies. If she couldn't marry for love, she didn't want to even think about it.

Maybe she'd give it another try after she graduated.

Her thoughts returned to the conversation she'd just had with her father. He had been so secretive, but he just wasn't a cloak-and-dagger type of guy. Sometimes he got really excited about a book he was reading, and he did love to play darts or gin rummy, but he definitely wasn't a CIA operative. The one thing that really got him going was Utah history. He was a confirmed history junky. She wondered why he asked her to bring her old code books. What could that be about?

Now that she had let her father talk her into traipsing back to Utah, she was excited about the trip. Yes, she missed her father, but what she really needed was to get on a horse again, ride up into the mountains, and think about nothing. She loved riding in the mountains—it was somehow mind-cleansing.

She could finish her thesis any time—there wasn't a rush. As far as she knew, her thesis chairman was still traveling around in outer space and wouldn't touch down for some time. Math professors were like that.

"Listen to this, Carver. In 1896 a poor dirt farmer named Jesse Knight was approached by the presiding authorities of the Church. They wanted him to help pay the huge penalties and forfeitures incurred following enforcement of the Edmunds Tucker Anti-Polygamy Act. Now I ask you, why would the leaders go to a man who lived in Manti, Utah, population forty-five, who didn't have a dime, and ask him to help pay an obligation of about $2,000,000, a sum greater than the national debt at that time?"

Rylan paused, waiting for an answer. Carver finally spoke. "When you find out, let me know. I've got to run. See you later." Carver knew Rylan was going to finish his story, but he had to needle him a little. He was exhausted, having spent every night for the last week outside, watching for uninvited guests. He had set up a hammock thirty feet off the ground in which he occasionally slept. He had also set up an electronic perimeter to detect anyone who came snooping around. Nothing had triggered the system, though, except for a few deer. Rubbing his eyes, he decided he could listen to Rylan for a minute. No longer.

Rylan continued as if he had not been interrupted. "Apparently, Knight, or some other unnamed person, was miraculously able to provide over $2,000,000 to rescue the Church. Of course, everyone assumed it had been Knight and that he had access to gold from the Carre-Shin-Ob, but he never admitted that fact."

Rylan paused to give Carver a chance to speak. When he didn't say anything, Rylan asked, "So why did they come to Jesse Knight? What did they know?"

Again Carver didn't have any guesses.

"Well, I forgot to tell you one significant piece of information," Rylan added. "There was an unconfirmed rumor that Knight had seen a vision about the same sacred Indian gold mine, located high in the Uintah Mountains that Thomas Rhoades had visited. In fact, he wrote down the substance of his vision." Rylan read from the book he had in his hands.

> Inside the tunnel he saw piles of gold and silver bars stacked high and rotted leather bags of gold nuggets spilled across the floor. A vein of pure gold crossed the end of that chamber while artifacts of ancient design were piled against its walls. The walls were made of gold-gilt, engraved with strange hieroglyphics, similar to those he had seen in the book of Mormon.
>
> While at the treasure repository he was visited by the angel Moroni. He showed him precious artifacts of purest gold, including records on plates of gold.
>
> He told him that in the days to come the church would face financial ruin and when that time came, Knight would be allowed to return to that place and take enough gold so that he would be the means of saving the credit of the church.
>
> He said that Indians guarded the place, not because of the gold which is there, but because there are artifacts of great religious significance to them.
>
> He claimed that he had been to the tunnel after the vision.[1]

Carver didn't disregard the story, but then, he didn't jump up and down and give Rylan high fives, either.

Rylan continued, "Apparently the leaders of the Church placed some significance on Knight's story, or they wouldn't have visited him. In fact, they may have had some knowledge of the existence of the mine from Brigham Young. Anyway, no one has ever admitted where the money came from to pay all the fines, but within months of the leaders' visit to Jesse Knight, the entire amount was paid.

"Coincidentally, the Prophet Wilford Woodruff thanked Jesse Knight in a letter dated November 22, 1896, just after the debt had been paid. Let me read you the letter he sent.

> Dear Brother Knight:
> I feel that this kindly act is an answer to my prayers, to open some doors of relief whereby we may meet pressing demands upon us. May God bless and prosper you.
> President Wilford Woodruff [2]

"It's interesting that President Woodruff didn't say what he was thanking him for. Don't you think that is a little strange? A little too coincidental? I do. Particularly since the letter is dated right after all the debts and fines had been paid."

Carver stood up, intending to leave. Rylan reached over and pushed him back down in his seat. Carver inwardly groaned. Who knew how long this was going to take.

"During the next two years, the Church continued to experience financial problems. Yet again, the Church mysteriously found a source of funds and was able to finance its continued operation. Almost two years later, the First Presidency wrote Jesse Knight another brief letter.

> September 3, 1898
> Brother Jesse Knight
> God Bless you and yours forever. May you have a great abundance of peace and prosperity, and an eternity of bliss in the life to come; this is the prayer of your brethren in the Gospel.
> Joseph F. Smith, Lorenzo Snow, Heber J. Grant [3]

"Again, there was no explanation of what Knight did to warrant thanks. But if I were a guessing man, I would say Knight was allowed to visit the mine. He would have been the third man so chosen—the first being Thomas Rhoades and the second his son Caleb."

Carver could tell Rylan's spring was wound tight. He initially thought the story was not a big deal. Every country he had been in seemed to have a legend of a secret gold depository. Nevertheless, he had to admit Rylan spun a very convincing tale supported by numerous details, some of which seemed to be authentic. But gold or no gold, it bothered him that he could wake up and find the hills around his home thronged with gold seekers. And he hadn't had trouble from anyone until he discovered that box.

Rylan's voice interrupted his thoughts. "What if this document we found leads us to the Lost Rhoades mine? Can you imagine?"

Carver finally spoke. "Your coded message doesn't appear to be a treasure map, Counselor."

"What else could it be? Why else would Rhoades bury a box loaded with gold and an encrypted message?"

"There you go again, making an assumption that it was Thomas Rhoades," Carver pointed out.

"Well, it must at least intrigue you. I haven't heard you use more than three words in a single sentence in a long time." Rylan stood and paced. He scratched his head and said, "I think that box belonged to Thomas Rhoades. First, your land once belonged to the Rhoades family. Second, the initials 'TR' on the satchel must stand for Thomas Rhoades. Third, there was Spanish gold bullion in the box, which is the same kind that Rhoades purportedly delivered to the Church, and fourth, there is a quartz crystal laced with gold which is similar to the gold orb Rhoades was reputed to have discovered in another separate Spanish gold mine. Coincidence? It would be like filling an inside straight with a one-card draw. It just doesn't happen."

Carver nodded, but didn't say anything. Rylan continued, "Now, let's look at the document we found. The first part of the message is written in an unknown language. The second part is definitely written in code. Why? Why would Thomas Rhoades go to the trouble of burying a box of gold with an encrypted message?"

He added almost matter-of-factly, "That's why I asked my daughter to come out and help. She had a few classes on encryption. By the way, she should be here in a few days. Maybe you can take her riding or to dinner or something?"

"That almost sounded, and I add *almost*, like you were trying to set me up with your daughter. I don't date, remember?" replied Carver. "Women are nothing but trouble."

"You would be doing me a big favor, Carver," Rylan said deliberately. "Besides, you might be good for her. Cass is a great gal, but she has your attitude about dating."

"And you think I can persuade her that I'm Prince Charming?" questioned Carver.

"Well, that may be stretching it just a wee bit, but if you don't say anything, she might think you are really smart. I'll consider us even, if you take her out. She really likes to go riding in the hills."

Carver was perplexed, wondering when he had become indebted to Rylan. He tried to remember Cassandra as a child. She had been tall as a young girl, gangly, and almost blonde. She took after her mother, which was good because Mrs. Edison had been a fine-looking woman. However, he hadn't forgotten that Cass was feisty and smart. She would argue with anyone about anything.

"Carver, I need some time to decipher this message from Thomas Rhoades." He nudged Carver with his elbow. "You just haven't caught the vision yet. This may be my most exciting opportunity to do something, make a lasting contribution—and at my age I won't get many more chances. This message has my name on it—I can feel it in my bones. Work with me until I decipher the message. Then we can make a decision as to what to do with it. Okay?"

"Rylan, I don't have a good feeling about any of this. It looks to me like you're running right into the briar patch. Besides, the gold doesn't belong to me." Carver added as an afterthought. "But if the message leads me to the guy that torched my cabin, well then, that's a whole 'nother story."

Rylan's enthusiasm couldn't be squelched. "But think about the significance of such a find. What if there really are pre-Columbian golden plates in the mine containing a history of the Ute Indians?"

Carver just wanted to be left alone. "Then let someone else go find the mine, the gold, and the plates. Let them deal with the Ute Tribe, the gold diggers, and those trying to find a get-rich-quick scheme. I don't want to have to fend off reporters, television cameras or anyone else looking for a story. My privacy and solitude are my most valued possessions."

"But if the Church gets hold of this, it may end up buried in some vault in a granite mountain. It's too important for that, even if it encourages more gold seekers."

Rylan sorted through a bunch of papers and stopped when he found the one he wanted. "All kinds of beliefs swirl about the legend of the Lost Rhoades Mine. They should stir some interest. Listen to this statement made in *The Utah Gold Rush*, a book published by the Borens.

> The genesis of the Lost Rhodes Mines lies in the tale of an ancient source of gold predating even the Ute Indians, stemming from their ancestors whom the Utes called 'Old Ones'. The 'Old Ones' were undoubtedly the Aztecs, because the Utes owe their origin to the Uto-Aztecan ethnology.
>
> The Aztecs mined gold in ancient times until about 1169 A.D. when they left the Utah region. They left the Utes in charge of protecting the sacred mines.
>
> Before Montezuma was killed he loaded the bulk of the great Aztec treasure and took it northward. Some believe it is this treasure that is in the cave that Wakara took Thomas Rhodes.
>
> They named the place Carre-Shin-Ob, or where the Great Spirit dwells. Chief Wakara was shown by Towats a vision of the great treasure and named him the caretaker. Towats told him that he was to reveal the secret of the sacred gold to no man, except the High Hats. That he must give the secret to one great man among them.[4]

"Wouldn't you like to be involved with something that establishes a whole new threshold of knowledge?"

"I'm not sure I believe all this stuff about visions of mines filled with golden plates, carvings, and the like. I guess it's possible the Utes did have a cave where they stored some old Spanish gold and they allowed Rhoades to use the gold for the benefit of the Church. That's about as far as I'll go," replied Carver.

"What if there are golden plates and other ancient Aztec golden artifacts buried there as well?" Rylan probed.

"I think it's going to lead you directly to trouble and you won't even get to pass GO."

While Rylan wasted his time working on the Rhoades document, Carver kept himself busy rebuilding a new cabin. He intended to make it a replica of his grandfather's. He ordered new rough-sawn timbers from the local sawmill and started cutting, notching, and fitting them together. Building a log cabin today wasn't nearly as hard as it had been for his grandfather.

Rylan had summoned Carver for what he claimed was an emergency, but he wanted to feed him first, probably to soften him up. It appeared Rylan hadn't slept in three days. Carver guessed he'd been up every night trying to make some sense of the document. His lack of sleep hadn't affected his ability to cook a good meal, though. He was without peer when it came to cooking, at least around these parts. Rylan had something on his mind, but he wasn't saying anything yet.

He finally spoke. "Are you doing anything in the morning?"

"What do you have on your mind, Rylan?"

"I need some help, or more like a favor."

"Name it."

"Can you drive me to the airport?"

"Are you going somewhere?"

"No, I need to pick up someone."

"Let me guess—your daughter?"

"Yeah, but my car's in the shop."

"Take mine."

"Um, that won't work. I need you there with me."

"Why?" The suddenly innocent look on Rylan's face was a dead giveaway. "Are you still trying to set me up with your daughter?"

"No, no, nothing like that, although I am going to hold you to your promise to take her riding."

"I didn't make any such promise," Carver protested, throwing down his napkin.

"Sure, you did. I heard you. But I want to run some ideas by you and Cass and it's easier with the two of you in one place."

"Has she agreed to help you in your crazy search for the Lost Dutchman?"

"It's the Lost Rhoades, not Dutchman. And not exactly—but that's where you come in."

At 6:00 AM the next morning Carver picked up Rylan in his ten-year-old Land Rover. It wasn't much on looks, but it was mechanically sound. Carver took care of it himself and he knew it inside and out.

Once they arrived at the Salt Lake International Airport, Rylan had Carver drop him off at the terminal and told Carver to go to the park-and-wait area. He would call him as soon as he had his daughter and baggage in tow and then Carver could come pick them up out front. Carver was not looking forward to the hour-long drive back to Marion—Rylan was devious sometimes.

Rico scanned the area with his binoculars, noting with satisfaction that both Carver and the older man had climbed into the Land Rover. He waited until they had pulled out onto the road, then picked up his radio.

"The house is empty," he said.

"You know what to do," came the reply.

Cassandra ran over to her father and threw her arms around him.

"Dad, it's so good to see you."

He whispered in her ear, and she took a step back. "You did what, Rylan?" She called him Rylan when she was upset.

"My car's in the shop, so Carver had to drive me."

"He wouldn't let you take his car?" Her father was playing matchmaker again, but it didn't appear there was anything she could do about it. She shook her head, wondering what kind of redneck her father had picked out for her this time.

"He's not like anyone I've ever introduced you to before. Besides, he's probably my closest friend."

"Great! That means he's at least thirty years my senior. I told you, I don't date older men."

"Cass, all I ask is that you be nice to him, as a favor to your dear old dad."

She looked into his eyes and felt her irritation melt away. She loved her father and never could stay mad at him for long. Deciding to change the subject, she asked, "Are you ready to explain what all the cloak-and-dagger stuff was on the phone?" She had watched him scrutinize the airport like he had been looking for someone and couldn't find him.

"As soon as we get in the car," he said.

"Are you serious? Are you afraid someone might be listening right now?"

"No, it's not like that. Just wait until we get in the car."

She grabbed his hand and led him towards the baggage carousel. "That's my suitcase right over there."

He grabbed the bag. It was heavy but not big compared to the bags he remembered his wife had taken on overnight trips. Cass picked up an additional suitcase, and they made their way out the sliding glass doors.

The Land Rover pulled up in front of them. As soon as it came to a stop, Cass watched as a big man slid out of the car, grabbed her luggage and stowed it in the rear, and then almost glided back to the driver's seat, all without saying a word.

"Nice to meet you too . . . what did you say his name was?"

"It's Carver Nash. He doesn't talk much, especially when he's upset."

"Why is he upset?"

"He thinks I tricked him into coming to pick you up."

"So he's not in favor of any setups either?" She hadn't even met him yet, but already they had something in common.

"You could put it that way. We better get in or he just might drive away and leave us."

Cass wouldn't have blamed him if he did drive away. If his hatred of blind dates was anything like her own, it would be natural.

She climbed into the backseat, letting Rylan sit next to Carver. They'd all feel more comfortable that way, she thought. Plus, she could look him over without being obvious about it. He wore loose-fitting clothes, but they didn't hide his well-defined muscles. He looked like a man with a purpose, so different from the men her father usually introduced her to.

She could tell he spent a lot of time outdoors. His skin was so tanned he could pass as an American Indian—a look that she liked. He had sharp blue eyes and light brown hair that was just tousled enough, she knew he didn't spend any time in front of a mirror. He was different, all right, but she wasn't ready to leap into anything just yet. Instinctively, she raised her barriers.

"It's nice to meet you too, Mr. Nash. What do you do when you're not driving my father on errands?"

Carver cast a quick glance in her direction. "I'm a rancher."

Rylan leaped in. "Carver, this is my beautiful, smart, and single daughter Cassandra, but everyone calls her Cass. You probably remember her as a kid, right?"

"Well, thanks for helping my father in his time of need, Mr. Nash. I feel much safer with you behind the wheel. My father talks all the time and never looks at the road." She smiled and poked her father in the shoulder. Carver gave a slight nod of his head, but didn't utter a word. She wasn't going to get anywhere with him, so she decided to go after her father.

"Okay, Dad, now that we're in the car, which I assume has been swept for electronic listening devices, will you let me in on the big secret?"

"Don't you want to wait until after breakfast?"

"I think right now would be a good time."

"Okay, Cass. About two weeks ago, Carver was out digging a fence line on his property. Carver inherited his grandfather's ranch right next to our property. Anyway, I heard a single rifle shot coming from that direction and went over to see what was happening. Apparently someone took a potshot at Carver but missed. Anyway, he found an old metal box of Spanish origin buried in the ground. We got it back to the cabin and opened it. It was filled with gold bullion and one document in an old pouch. I think the document was written by Thomas Rhoades."

"Sure. Don't tell me you think your box has something to do with the Lost Rhoades Mine." That old mine had been one of her father's obsessions for years.

"That's exactly what Carver said. In fact, he doesn't want anything to do with the message or the gold, but I figure there's got to be around 1.3 million dollars in gold in that box."

"I don't know too many people who would just walk away from that kind of money," said Cass. "Why don't you want it, Mr. Nash?"

He didn't reply. No surprise there.

"I've spent the last week reading everything I could get my hands on about the Lost Rhoades Mine," replied Rylan. "There are still people out looking for it, and books written about it. Some people have speculated that the ancient Seven Cities of Cibola and the Carre-Shin-Ob are one in the same. Some old Mormon historians have even speculated that the mines are repositories of the wealth of the people in the Book of Mormon."

"Really?" Cass interjected, leaning forward a little.

"Let me read you a statement from Kerry Ross Boren, a Ute Indian who was also a distant relative of Chief Wakara. He claimed to have been made the guardian of the famous mine and was allowed to visit it one time.

> Knowing that I could walk right to the sacred mine of Carre-Shin-Ob, instead I approached the Elders of the Ute Tribe by way of family inter-marriage with the Reeds. After a great deal of deliberation and discussion, I entered into the same blood-oath that my 3rd great grandfather and both Thomas and Caleb Rhoades swore to.
>
> Upon that promise never to reveal the location of Carre-Shin-Ob, never to return there, and not to remove or disturb anything—I entered into one of the most fabulous and probably richest mines in the world. My time spent in Carre-Shin-Ob consisted of 6 hours—not enough but certainly more than enough to change my life forever. While hundreds of people have searched for the Rhoades Mines and the rumored fabulous wealth that the Utes and the Uintah Mountains keep secret, I can honestly say that it does exist.
>
> Within the caverns of Carre-Shin-Ob reposes the semi-mummified bodies of great Utes such as Old Chief Sanpete and Chief Wakara, as well as many others. It is an eerie feeling when your flashlight goes out momentarily and you feel the walls come alive—as though all of those Great Ones were watching every move you make. Carre-Shin-Ob is composed of a series of caverns with connecting tunnels formed through a series of active volcanoes, thereby forming lava-tubes that honeycomb the Uintah range.
>
> My own eyewitness to the astounding secrets that Carre-Shin-Ob revealed sounds to the laymen to be too fantastic to be true. However, the Sun Chamber (as I dubbed it) was an Aztec Temple. In the center of this immense room were nine great stone pillars, too large in circumference for a man to encircle his arms. This entire chamber—walls, ceiling, floor, and pillars—were plated with what appeared to be pure gold!

In fact, as I have since thought, it might not have been plated with gold so much as the interior was solid natural gold, from which the center had been excavated, leaving a certain amount of thickness around the exterior walls. If so, the amount of gold once filling this chamber staggers the imagination.

On the other hand, the amount of gold still in this chamber surpasses anything ever yet discovered, enhanced by the additional number of gold artifacts stored therein. For instance, there were two gigantic solar disks, each taller than a man and several inches thick, they were apparently of pure gold and must have weighed tons each.

The disks represented the sun, with rays emanating from the center outward, and between the rays were intricate carvings of signs and symbols of a peculiar nature. In the very center of each disk was a carved cross, very much like the Celtic cross of Ireland (or Wales), with ivy vines woven around the design.

Furthermore, there were golden masks and statuettes, and many stone boxes filled with treasure of another kind: gold plates with hieroglyphic writing on them! There were smaller stone boxes, too, and these contained an assortment of precious stones—emeralds, rubies, turquoise, sapphires, and strangely, sea shells—and others contained gold bracelets, circlets, rings, earrings, and other ceremonial jewelry. Together with the masks, disks, statuettes, and other artifacts, the caverns were a treasure trove like something out of A Thousand and One Arabian Nights. [5]

Cass didn't say anything, wondering if her father's dreams were suddenly coming true. She was glad he'd waited until she was seated before telling her everything that had been going on.

"Cass, the document we found is written in some kind of code. I've tried to figure it out, but I have no idea where to start. That's where I need your help. You took a couple of classes on encryption, right?"

Before she could answer, they pulled into Rylan's driveway and stopped. Carver retrieved her suitcase, she grabbed her satchel, and they all walked up to the porch. She stopped and turned around to look at the mountains, the forest, and her home. She tried to breathe it all in. She loved this place.

"It's gone!" she heard her father yell.

Chapter Three

Carver changed like flipping a light switch. Cass could almost see his senses flare to instantly on. She watched as he entered the home with the skill of a trained professional and cleared each room. He moved purposely, quickly, and quietly. "What did they take?" Carver asked Rylan in a clipped tone.

"They got a copy of the Rhoades Document, but I don't think they got anything else."

"How do you know someone took it, and you didn't just misplace it?" Carver's eyes never stopped moving, even while interrogating Rylan.

"I know because I kept it right here in page 113 of my copy of *Faded Footprints*. I don't leave it lying around."

Carver left the house without another word. It was like he was there and then he was gone, and she never heard a sound.

"Where did he go?" Cass asked.

"I imagine he went out to check the grounds. He was a Ranger in the Army. He can track anything that moves."

Suddenly Cass felt uncomfortable. "Are you sure he's on our side?"

"You don't meet many people like Carver, Cass. He's not a big talker, never says much about himself. He's especially quiet about his life in the military—he won't say a word. But I've known him since he was a kid. I trust him with my life and I know he would do anything for me. With him around, I don't even need guard dogs."

Rylan turned on his computer while he talked with Cass. Carver returned, looking agitated.

"I couldn't find any signs of unwanted visitors and there wasn't a forced entry. Does anyone have a key to your house besides me?"

"No."

"Are you sure they didn't they get the original document?"

"No, I put that away in a safe deposit box. They only got a copy."

"Have you talked to anybody about the document, Rylan?"

"I haven't spoken to a soul except Cass, and I didn't even tell her about the document until she was in the car with us."

"I take it this isn't the first time something strange has happened to you two since your little discovery," Cass commented.

Rylan handed a copy of the document to her. "When we found this, I scanned it before putting the original away for safe keeping. Then I emailed it to myself. What do you make of this?"

Carver interrupted. "Rylan, your home was just broken into, and you're not the least bit concerned? I've been shot at and my house burned to the ground. I think it's time you took this business a little more seriously."

Cass watched the interplay between the two men. Carver was either paranoid or he knew something she didn't. Her father, on the other hand, didn't seem particularly concerned with his own safety. It was apparent the only thing he cared about was finding the mine. She wondered about both of them.

She turned her attention to the document and focused, hardly breathing. Everything was quiet as she read.

She finally broke the silence. "Well, the first part of the document doesn't look like a coded message. My guess is that it's written in a foreign language. However, I've never seen anything like it. It may have its origin in Latin. The second part is definitely an encrypted message."

"See, Carver, I told you she was smart," said Rylan, smiling smugly.

Cass gave him a look, then changed the subject. "Dad, didn't Brigham Young try to start his own alphabet when the Saints settled in the valley?"

"Dang! You're right, Cass. He called it the Deseret Alphabet. Let me look it up on the Internet."

A few minutes later he said, "Here it is! I'll enlarge it so we can read it." Rylan printed the alphabet and then started comparing it to the document.

"They're the same," he said excitedly.

Carver stood and walked over to Rylan. "I'll be going, unless you need something else. You make sure this place is locked up when I leave, and if you need anything, call my cell. Make sure Cass also has my number so she can call if necessary."

Then he was gone.

"Friendly sort," Cass said.

Rylan muttered something conciliatory, but he was deeply involved with analyzing the document. He was lost to her, so she went to her room to get settled in and then to find something to eat. It was apparent her father had no intention of helping her.

Cass woke up the next morning to the sounds of her father performing a war dance of some kind. Suddenly her door burst open.

"I've got it!" It was her father. He obviously hadn't slept, shaved, or showered. He looked like he had been dragged through a rat hole, but he was definitely excited. She smiled. She hadn't seen him this excited since the last time they had ridden "The Drop" at Magic Mountain.

"Listen to this, Cass. I think I've finally translated the message." Rylan began to read his translation.

June 1855

I leave this record for a righteous purpose, although I know it not. You have not discovered this box by accident, nor will be your search for the Carre-Shin-Ob.

I have been there many times: caverns of gold, artifacts of antiquity beyond anyone's wildest imagination, sacred to the Indians, guarded by Towats for and on behalf of the Great Spirit. No, it is not a legend, it is true.

During my life I have guarded this secret with my life. I have never told a soul its location except my son Caleb, who foreswore the same blood oath I so freely gave. I leave this box as directed by the Prophet Brigham Young, for his purpose.

I have held true to my word and oath. The gold freely given from Carre-Shin-Ob was always provided and directed by Wakara, "to be given to the Tall Hat, Brigham Young." I have seen many other mines and much gold, some Spanish and some with richly laden ore. I have been permitted to use that for my own, but that from the Carre-Shin-Ob was reserved for only Church use.

Remember that the secrets of the Carre-Shin-Ob belong to our Indian brothers and the Old Ones who have always proven to be watchful and faithful guardians of the secret for the Great Spirit. They were never tempted to use the riches for their own gain.

Accept this quest only with a pure heart; and then beware, for not all guardians of the Carre-Shin-Ob are aligned with the Great Spirit.

Thomas Rhoades
I, Caleb Rhoades, add my testimony to the

statements of my father. I have left two maps: one is useless without the other. Your quest is to find the two maps and follow the trail to the Carre-Shin-Ob. Indian or trapper, we were never sure.

Caleb Rhoades

"I told you, Cass, this will lead us to the Carre-Shin-Ob. I knew it. I knew it!"

"Dad, before you get any more involved with this, you must consider what you're doing. There are still people who are obsessed with the search for that mine. If any of them hear you have a document from Thomas Rhoades, you won't be safe."

Cass's excitement was turning into concern. "Then there are the Utes. Some of them would like to get the gold to help their people, others believe the mine is sacred. Some consider themselves to be the guardians of the mine secret. And you know some very strange things have happened in these mountains over the years."

"It's all easily explained, Cass. I'm not worried about it."

"Dad, someone already knows you have an old document. They may not have translated it but they are certainly working on it."

"They will never figure it out," he said.

Cass shook her finger at him. "Tell me how you account for the things that have already happened to you and Carver since you discovered that buried box?"

"But what if the mine really does exist?"

"Why don't we turn this over to the Church authorities or the Ute tribal council?"

"That's what Carver suggested," replied Rylan, looking like some wind had gone out of his sail. "If I give this to the Church, it will be lost forever, buried in the archives. I'm not sure who the gold in the mine belongs to. But can you imagine being the one to find the mine?"

"This may be bigger than we can handle."

"We can keep it secret," he said. "No one needs to know."

"Like you and Carver have done a great job of keeping it secret so far." She hated the look of disappointment on his face, but she couldn't bear the thought of something happening to him.

"Cass, I need your help decoding the directions to the mine."

At that moment both heard a loud knocking at the door. "I've got to hide my work notes. Will you get the door, Cass?"

"Dad, I'm not even dressed," she said as she grabbed her robe.

"Give me one full minute before you open the door. I'll hide my notes and call Carver. Then I'll grab my pistol."

"Someone knocks at your door and your first instinct is to grab your gun? What have you gotten yourself into, Rylan?"

As she got near the door, the fear factor dramatically increased. The person who had burned Carver's house to the ground might be on the other side.

Cass waited the minute, and when she didn't hear anything from her father, she reached for the door. At that instant, someone started pounding again.

"Cass? Rylan?"

She took a deep breath, recognizing Carver's voice. She unlatched the dead bolt, and then turned the handle. Carver stood there, looking apprehensive.

"I was worried about you two. Is everything okay?"

Cass slowly exhaled and motioned for him to come in. At the same time, Rylan walked into the living room carrying his pistol.

"At least you're armed, but next time you probably shouldn't send the lady to the door," Carver said sarcastically.

"Do you think I'm not capable of opening a door?" she asked, folding her arms.

Rylan tried to speak over her. "I couldn't answer the door because I was hiding my documents."

Rylan went over to his study while Cass glared at Carver.

"If you weren't afraid of who was behind the door, why were you holding your breath with your father standing in the next room holding a gun?" Carver said.

"You said we should be careful." She didn't like it that he knew she'd been holding her breath.

"Carver, you've got to hear this." Both Carver and Cass turned and went into Rylan's study. He looked like the absent-minded professor. "You know, the Rhoades message turned out to be written in the Deseret Alphabet. It took me almost all night, but I was able to translate the message. It's just like I told you—it's a map to the Carre-Shin-Ob."

"Not quite so fast, Father. I'm not sure it's a map—maybe an invitation to begin a quest, but not necessarily a map," added Cass, glancing back at Carver to assess his reaction. It was like trying to read the face of a rock. How did he do that? She didn't like that she was so transparent, while she didn't have a clue what he was thinking or feeling.

Rylan read the translation to Carver. "Well, what do you think, Carver?"

"I think this has gone far enough. Your lives are worth more than any gold you might find at the end of your quest. I don't feel good about any of this."

"Carver, you've got to be a little intrigued. Imagine the gold—wealth greater than maintained in Fort Knox. Think about finally proving the existence of a legend. Maybe even proof of the Book of Mormon. Maybe it's time for this stuff to come forth out of its hiding place into the light."

"Rylan, you've told me all the stories of people ending up mysteriously dead or missing while searching for the lost mine. Even your message warns you. You could be placing your daughter in danger. Are you willing to assume that risk?"

"To be honest, until you knocked on my door, I really hadn't considered the possible danger to Cass. I'll send her back to school. If I need her help, I can always email her."

Cass held up both hands. "Oh, no, you don't. You can't drag me out here, tell me all about this incredible quest, and then send me back home. I'm in it for the long haul. Besides, I'm a pretty good shot. I can handle myself."

Two hours later they all sat around the dining room table. Rylan had fixed a wonderful conglomeration of sausage, hash browns, and Swedish waffles, covered in homemade strawberry jam. Both men had hesitantly agreed to let Cass stay. She knew they were just trying to protect her, but she could take care of herself. Plus, she couldn't let them have all the fun.

After breakfast, they decided to brainstorm about the translated document and throw out any and all ideas that came to mind, no matter how outlandish. Rylan had made a copy of the translation for each of them to mark, study, and use to make comments.

Rylan started the discussion. "It's clear that both Thomas and Caleb claim to have been in Carre-Shin-Ob. They claim the mine has 'artifacts of antiquity beyond anyone's wildest imagination.' Obviously there were things they saw that they considered more valuable than gold, that they considered sacred. I don't know what that could have been except for golden tablets."

"Why do you think Brigham Young directed Rhoades to leave this message?" asked Cass. She was interested in the fact that it seemed the finder of the letter, her father, had been known to Brigham.

"Maybe he knew it would be discovered in a time when the items in the mine would be of great worth," answered Rylan.

"I want you to take notice that Thomas and Caleb Rhoades pointed out four times that the mine is well guarded," noted Carver. "And not by good guys. Rylan, I thought you told me once that the present day Utes don't know the location of the mine, that the 'Old Ones' didn't pass along its location. How could anyone be guarding the mine now if they don't know where it is?"

"Maybe they know generally but not specifically," suggested Cass.

"If that's the case, do we have to worry about the Utes interfering with your search?" Carver asked.

Cass changed the subject. "What's this about one map being

public, or at least known to others?"

Rylan replied, "Before Thomas died, legend has it that he drew a map for his wife and she used the map to try to find the mine for over two years. There are many maps floating around today purporting to be official. Many have their genesis in the map Thomas drew for his wife."

Cass decided to get down to details. It was possible she would not be able to decode the message, but she wanted to give it a try.

"Somewhere in that box, there's a clue that will provide directions to at least one of the two maps. The key to breaking the cipher can be anything," she said. "More likely than not, it will be related to those things you found in the box—the gold, the quartz-gold orb, the pouch, the box itself, or this document. If it's not, then we could play the guessing game for years without success. Are you sure there weren't any secret compartments in either the box or the pouch?"

Carver replied, "I doubt the box has any secret compartments. It's still in my safe—how about I check it tomorrow?"

Rylan had already left to retrieve the pouch. He inspected it closely while everyone watched. He couldn't find any secret compartments.

"I don't want to take it apart unless I have to. Let's see if we can find the keyword using other information."

"Well, that leaves us with the quartz-gold orb or the document itself. Why do you think that gold orb was left in the box?" asked Cass.

No one had any comment or thought concerning the gold orb.

Finally Cass said, "We need to consider everything from Thomas's viewpoint. There are many different methods of writing codes that date back long before his day. I think we're dealing with a substitution cipher, but I'll have to do some studying on it to be sure. You solve a substitution cipher with a ring made of concentric rings with letters of the alphabet disposed around the outside in some random manner. Once the key is known, the two wheels can be aligned and a code written using the letter substitution method. The code written in the Rhoades document could be such a message, but we don't have a cipher ring."

Rylan hastily took notes while Carver leaned back and closed his eyes. She decided to continue, if only for her father's sake.

"Regardless of what type of code is used, you need the key, a word or phrase, which should be somewhere in the message itself, the pouch, or in the box. The best key is hidden in plain sight. Which means, we probably have it, we just don't know we have it."

Rylan, who had been studying the document very closely, suggested, "Maybe the key is 'TR,' the initials on the pouch."

Carver opened his eyes and added, "I'm stuck on the last sentence of Caleb's words. 'Indian or trapper, we were never sure.' They seem out of place and meaningless. What do they have to do with the rest of the message?"

"You might be on to something, Carver. What do the words mean? Are they trying to tell us the key? On the other hand, he could simply be saying that he didn't know whether we should beware of a trapper or an Indian," said Rylan.

Cass said, "Maybe the clue has something to do with the 'Old Ones.' We believe the 'Old Ones' refer to the Aztecs."

Carver said, "Maybe we should think about these things, let them roll around in our heads for a day or two, and then get back together. In the meantime, I'll go have a good look at the box and the gold and see if there is anything there. We didn't look at each gold bar."

Rylan added, "I'll go over the pouch more closely."

Carver came to attention as if he were listening to something. Quick as a cat, Carver was at the window, then the door. Cass was again shocked at how quickly he could move without making a sound. Rylan picked up his pistol but looked at Cass as if to say, "What was that all about?" Carver opened the door and was gone.

Ten minutes later he returned.

"I'm sure someone was on the porch listening to our conversation. I suggest you burn all of the notes you've made or lock them away in a safe. I'll be outside tonight, but make sure you lock the doors and windows and keep yourselves armed."

Chapter Four

Cass was shopping in the Smith's store in Heber, pushing her cart down the aisle when she heard a familiar voice.

"Sister Edison, is that you?"

The reference to her missionary name brought back a flood of memories, all good. She had just enough time to turn before she was engulfed in some very large arms.

"Reber, is that really you?" Cass exclaimed as she returned the hug from her old friend Reber Kolb, a full-blooded Ute Indian and her former antagonist. She had participated in more religious discussions with him than anyone else on her mission. He had never joined the Church, but he had listened to every gospel principle and seemed to understand them. Oh, he had asked questions about everything, more often than not just to harass her.

He was physically bigger than Carver—not taller, just bigger—and had a heart to match his size. He was a good man, although a little secretive, maybe even mysterious. To the best of her knowledge, he now had some position on the Ute Tribal Council.

"Did you ever join the Church, Reeb?" she asked.

"I've been waiting for you to come back and baptize me. All the missionaries around here have been afraid to teach me. I thought maybe you told them I was cursed."

Even though he'd let her go, he continued to look into her eyes and held them with his willpower. She believed he had always liked her more than just as a teacher. Finally he looked down at her left hand.

"It doesn't look like any guy has claimed your heart yet. What's the problem? You scare them all off?"

"Nah, I don't have time—too many things to do. What about you, Reeb?"

"Me? I'm still waiting for a Sister Edison look-a-like who wants to go up in the hills, live in a teepee, have a bunch of kids, and start our own tribe. And you promised you'd come looking for me if you weren't married by the time you were thirty."

"Hey, it could happen. I just turned twenty-nine. But I have a problem relating to men, unless we're talking in number theory, prime number generators, or differential equations." She didn't mind being honest with Reber—it was like talking to a brother.

"You relate to me, and I guess you could always use math for something practical, like counting cows or kids."

Cass wanted to get out of the riptide and decided to take the offense.

"If I remember right, you promised you would join the Church if I ever came looking for you." She smiled at the flustered look on his face. "How about we drop the Sister Edison stuff? You can call me Cass." She knew she was blushing. His sudden reference to marriage had caught her completely off guard. What happened to the brother-sister relationship she'd thought they had?

They decided to finish their shopping and meet in the park down the street. Cass watched him leave the store without purchasing anything. It had been a long time since she had been excited to spend any time with a man, even if he was just a friend. She hurried to complete her shopping, anxious to be finished and on her way. She couldn't deny the instant chemistry that had sprung up between them, and she wanted to investigate it further.

They talked for over an hour, reminiscing about old times. She promised to come out to Duchesne and go riding with him before she went back to school. She remembered the freedom of riding the ridges, the beauty of the mountains, combined with the thrill of sitting on a horse. There was something very personal to her about sharing these joys with an old friend. She liked him, but for that matter, everyone liked him. He was the center of attention everywhere he went, not only because of his size, but also because his personality was infectious. She made him promise to start reading the Book of Mormon again.

"Tonight," she had told him before he left. She wondered why she felt her voice catch as she spoke to him. She shook her head. Maybe I'm catching a cold, she thought.

"Whatever," he replied as he climbed into a beat-up old Ford pickup. "If you don't show up at the reservation soon, I'm going to come looking for you."

After seeing Reber, she felt better than she had in days. There were so many memories associated with him, and her mission. She didn't know what she would do with the romance he obviously wanted to foster. She was somewhat distracted because of Carver.

Before she left Heber, she had a few errands to finish. When she left Heber Valley Mercantile and turned to hop in her car, she happened to glance back. The same car that had pulled out behind her when she had left Smith's was parked only a space behind her. She glanced in her rearview mirror to see who was driving the black Ford, but the windows were tinted and she couldn't see anything. Her heart skipped a beat and her palms got sweaty. She watched as the vehicle pulled out and slowly drove past her to continue up the road. Maybe it wasn't the same vehicle she had seen earlier. She felt neurotic for being so suspicious, but then, some pretty weird things had been happening back on the ranch.

After two stops, she picked up Highway 40 and started heading back towards Marion. Once or twice she thought she saw the same black Ford just turning a corner, but it was so far behind her and she couldn't tell for sure. She wiped a bead of sweat from her forehead as she sped up on a straightaway. Once, she pulled over to let it catch up with her so she could check it out, but no car ever passed. She wondered if she was slowly losing it, or becoming paranoid over too many lost gold mine stories.

Rico cowered before Mr. Vargas, whose face was contorted with anger.

"Have you been unfaithful to me?" Mr. Vargas demanded, his fingers clenched to his sides. "Ramon tells me you haven't been very diligent in your work lately."

"I am faithful, I swear it," Rico said, stammering out the words. "I've done everything you've asked. I set the fire, I followed the girl . . ."

"Ramon says you hope to gain more for yourself," Mr. Vargas said.

"I have worked for you many years. Who would believe Ramon over me?"

"I would." Mr. Vargas nodded, and the silent henchman behind the door pulled out his gun.

That evening, after Cass, Rylan, and Carver ate dinner, Carver dropped three tiny electronic objects on the table and asked, "Do you guys know what these are?"

Rylan picked one up, turned it over, and put it back on the table. "I don't know, but they could be pieces of a computer."

Cass shrugged. "I don't have a clue. I stay out of the insides of computers."

Carver said, "These are listening devices, bugs. I found one under the dining room table, one in by your computer, and the other in your phone."

"My house has been bugged?" asked Rylan.

"Yes, and with state-of-the-art equipment," replied Carver.

"Maybe they were left here the night someone stole a copy of your document," Cass suggested. "You know, a funny thing happened to me today. While I was shopping at Smith's . . ."

Carver interrupted her, almost rudely, and asked, "You were shopping? Where? When?" He gave a sharp glance in Rylan's direction.

"You heard me, Smith's in Heber."

"Were you by yourself?"

"I couldn't stop her, Carver. She just left," admitted Rylan.

"As I said before I was so rudely interrupted, I went shopping and accidentally bumped into an old friend from my mission days. His name is Reber Kolb and he's a great guy, a full-blooded Ute Indian."

Carver again interrupted her: "Had you planned on meeting him?"

"I'm not sure I'll ever get though my story at this rate," she said, "and no, I hadn't planned to meet him." She continued, "Anyway, I was thinking back to the conversation I had with him. He said something that didn't bother me at the time, but it does now. He knew I'd been home for a week. How could he have known that? I haven't spoken to him in years. Then something else—he left the store without purchasing anything. Why was he in the store if he wasn't shopping? Maybe bumping into him wasn't as accidental as I thought or he pretended."

"How well do you know this guy?" asked Carver.

"Well, I told him I would marry him if I didn't find someone else before I was thirty."

"You what?" said Rylan. Carver felt something in his stomach twist, maybe it was the dinner they'd just eaten. An awkward silence followed.

"So, what does this guy do for a living?" asked Carver.

Cass didn't want to answer a bunch of meaningless questions about Reber. "All I know is that he once had some ties to the Ute Tribal Council, but I don't have any idea if he still does."

Her frustration with Carver's protective demeanor and Reber's mysterious appearance was evident. "Anyway, on the way home I thought I was being followed. I stopped to let the car I thought was following me catch up, but it never did. I don't know. Maybe I'm just being paranoid."

Carver was frustrated. Cass couldn't go wherever she wanted, whenever she wanted—not without some protection. He thought he had explained this to Rylan, but then, Cass was pretty bullheaded.

He'd been conducting some of his own research and discovered there were several radical, hard-core groups involved in a determined search for the mine. They were hardened men, only concerned with one thing—gold. And they were capable of committing any act to achieve their goals.

The situation had suddenly become more complicated with the information Cass just divulged. Someone with connections to the Ute Tribe had taken the effort to learn that Cass was home. Coincidental? Could be. But not on top of everything else. Someone had tied her to Rylan and possibly Carver and their discovery of the box. That someone arranged a chance meeting at the grocery store. Someone had the property under surveillance and knew when Cass left the property and where she had been going. He couldn't attribute those coincidences solely to someone's romantic interests.

If it had been Reber, why would he try to follow her home? She said he knew where she lived. Why not just call? And why was he so anxious to get her to visit the reservation? Nothing added up. He somehow needed to convince both Rylan and Cass to be more careful.

He decided to probe just a bit. "So, do you like this guy?" he asked.

"What does that have to do with anything? He's a nice guy."

"Didn't your father tell you not to leave this house alone?" Carver continued.

"Cass, you don't understand the situation. Carver is just looking out for you," said Rylan.

"Yeah, and next he'll be asking if I'm dressed warm enough." She rose from the table, feeling as though both men were ganging up on her. She was sure she could find something to do in the other room.

"What chance do you have of getting her out of here and back East before she gets hurt?" asked Carver.

"None whatsoever," Rylan said, pushing back his chair from the table. "While you're trying to protect her, I think she's trying to protect me. She won't leave until this whole thing is resolved."

Carver went back to the beginning: the discovery of the buried box. If someone knew it was buried there and didn't want it discovered, wouldn't he have just dug it up before it was found? Whoever had done the shooting hadn't known the box was there. But why had someone taken a shot at him the minute he had found it? And why plant the bugs, and follow Cass? Reber's sudden appearance didn't sit right with Carver.

He would have to insist on much stricter house rules, particularly for Cass, the vulnerable link. She was so obstinate. She wouldn't like him hanging around every time she went anywhere. Maybe he would have to shadow her to see who else was following her, but he didn't like using her as bait.

He could always try being nice to her, maybe even become her friend. Fat chance of that, he thought. Rylan was controllable, but Cass, she was a problem. The best thing he could do would be to talk Rylan out of continuing this ridiculous search for the mine.

"How did you know to look for bugs in our house?"

"What?" Carver had been so deep in thought, he hadn't been paying attention to what Cass had said.

"You came in here and looked around for bugs. What made you think to do that? Are you some kind of anti-terrorist detective?"

Carver didn't intend to answer her. The issue right now was keeping her safe, not satisfying her curiosity.

"I don't like you leaving the house by yourself. Too many strange things have been happening," he said.

"Do you intend to become my personal bodyguard? Or are you proposing I stay locked up?"

"Look, Ms. Edison. If you and your father continue this unfortunate quest, you're going to have to allow me to set up some ground rules or I can't protect you."

"You're the only one someone has shot at."

"Listen to me, will you? Someone broke in here and took a copy of that document. That means they have what you have. If their intention is to find the mine, then they have to find the key to the encrypted message, just like you do. They may not want us breathing down their necks. If they figure we're interfering with them, they may decide to do something more serious than just take a warning shot at us."

Rylan finally tried to intervene. "Cass, he's right. I don't want to put you in jeopardy. Maybe it wasn't such a good idea to bring you back here."

"Dad, you're all I have left," Cass said, turning toward her father. "I'm not going to let you do this alone, if you're so determined to go ahead with it, after all that's happened."

Her voice was soft as she spoke to her father, but then she turned back to Carver. "And I can take care of myself, you know."

Carver arose and walked towards the front door. "If you need me during the night, blink any light in the house three times. And call my cell if anything unusual happens, and I mean anything."

"Yes, Sir," Cass shot back.

Carver left and pointed to the door lock as he passed.

Rylan said, "Cass, why do you bristle every time he says anything? He only has our best interest at heart."

"I don't know, Dad. He's just so bossy."

"He might be, but he's always been right. Why don't you try being nice?"

She shrugged. "He just gets my hackles up, that's all."

Rylan raised an eyebrow, but didn't say anything. She was grateful when he said, "Have you figured out the key to break that code yet?" And even more grateful when he didn't mention Carver again for an hour.

Carver activiated the electronic warning system around the Edison home. Twice during the last night, the warning had gone off, but Carver had not been able to find anything except signs of a deer and a skunk. Lights stayed on in the house until about three in the morning. He assumed Rylan was trying to break the code, and wondered if Cass worked alongside him.

He found an ideal location in a tree on a hill, which gave him a view of the entire house. He constructed a belay line that would allow him to slide out of the tree and directly in front of the house in a matter of seconds while maintaining full sight of the house during the entire ride. He also had night vision gear, his sniper rifle, and a listening device, most of which was stuffed into his backpack.

At 5:00 AM the lights in the living room flashed three times. Carver was at the front door just as Cass opened it. He had his rifle slung over his shoulder and his pistol in his hand. She closed and locked the door behind him.

Rylan said, "Cass just received a text message on her cell phone. The message was clear: 'Forget the gold mine or the next bullet won't miss.' "

Carver looked at Cass. "Did you get a number on caller ID? And who has your cell phone number in the area? Did you give it to Mr. Kolb?"

"The caller ID showed 'restricted number.' I don't know anyone in the area that has my number. It's a new one—I just got it a month ago. And I can't remember if I gave my number to Reber, but I don't think so."

Rylan said, "Come in here, Carver. We've spent some time on the cipher. Let us tell you what we think we know."

"Someone just threatened to kill you and all you want to do is talk about the cipher. How about we get the police involved in this right now?" Carver asked.

Rylan rubbed his chin, the night's stubble thick. "You know we can't do that. We'd have half the world breathing down our necks looking for the gold. Someone is just trying to scare us."

"Well, they're doing a pretty good job," Carver replied.

Rylan either didn't care about the threats or was so caught up with the quest he couldn't be bothered. "Tell him what you think about the cipher, Cass."

Cass gathered her notes together. She had a stack of books with notes and papers poking out in several locations. "I've been working on this for a while, and I have a suspicion our cipher is a Vigenere Cipher. In order to break it, we have to know the keyword. Or, the code could have been written using a pair of cipher rings, but that would require us to have both rings in order to break the code in addition to the key."

She stood as she flipped through a few pages. She reached back on her desk and retrieved a sheet of paper. She looked at Carver. If he had been in the military, he knew something of codes. She wondered if she was boring him.

She found the information she wanted and continued. "On the other hand, it could be a transposition cipher, or the Gronsfeld cipher, where a number is used as the keyword. After looking at all these possibilities, I'm fairly certain we're looking at a Vigenere cipher."

Cass reminded Carver of a porcupine, but at the moment, she was a cute porcupine. He moved over to the window while she talked, just checking the outside perimeter.

Rylan added, "Something has been bothering me about the Rhoades cipher. The last phrase, 'Indian or trapper' is not only out of place, but I've heard it before. I've tried to remember where since I first read the document. It's such a contrived statement, it should be easy to remember."

Cass replied, "I've tried that statement. It doesn't work. However, other possible keywords could be Towats, Carre-Shin-Ob, Wakara, Aztec, Old Ones, or maybe even Rhoades or Brigham Young."

"Can you explain the Vigenere Cipher in a little more detail?" asked Rylan.

"The cipher text is created using a twenty-six-row and twenty-six-column fixed array, each row of which contains the entire alphabet. The rows of the array are labeled A through Z as are the columns. The first row is A through Z in alphabetical order. The second row starts with B and goes to Z, adding A at the end. Each row thereafter is displaced one letter.

"In order to create the cipher text, you would write the message, the plain text, in a single word without spaces. Directly beneath the plain text word the keyword is repeated so as to match the number of characters of the plain text without any spaces."

Cass held up a sheet of paper that displayed the array she was describing. "The cipher text is created immediately below the keyword text. For example, let's say the first letter of the keyword is C and M is the first letter of the plain text. Looking at the array, one would find the column labeled M and the row labeled C. The letter in the array at the intersection of the M column and C row becomes the first letter of the cipher text.

"It sounds complicated, but it's fairly simple and I've devised a short program on my computer that will produce a plain text message using the cipher text we have by inserting any keyword. So I need some time to try these keywords."

Twenty minutes later Cass had tried every keyword they could come up with. Nothing produced a plain text message. She looked dejected and said, "Either it's not a Vigenere cipher or we don't have the keyword. Carver, you know you could help us here. You haven't offered anything."

Carver smothered his irritation with her abrupt tone. "I've been thinking since Rylan mentioned the Indian or trapper phrase. I don't know for sure, but it seems I heard that phrase related to the naming of the town of Peoa."

Rylan jumped in. "You're right Carver. That's where I heard it. Legend has it the name "Peoa" was found carved into a tree that had fallen over the creek in the area. It was assumed that it was either the name of an Indian or a trapper."

Cass typed the name "Peoa" into her program. "Nice try, you two, but it didn't work."

"How did you spell Peoa?" Carver asked.

"I spelled it just like it is, P-E-O-A."

"That may be a problem, because I think it was originally spelled P-E-O-H-A and got changed somewhere along the way."

Cass typed in the new keyword. "Hey, I think we might have something here." She printed out the message and handed a copy to Rylan.

ASTONEBOXHIDDENINPLAINSIGHT
NEARTHEHEADWATERSOFTHESOUTHFORKOFTHEWE
BERRIVER
LETTHEFLIGHTOFTHEARROWGUIDEYOURFLIGHT

After scribbling on it a few times, Cass said, "I think I've got it." She handed the new sheet of paper to Rylan. Carver looked over his shoulder.

A/stone/box/hidden/in/plain/sight
Near/the/headwaters/of/the/south/fork/of/the/Weber/River
Let/the/flight/of/the/arrow/guide/your/flight

"Good job, Carver. We never would have figured it out without your help," Rylan said.

A loud *twarp* reverberated in the house. Carver threw Cass and Rylan to the floor and went to the front window, searching the area. Nothing!

He opened the front door. There stuck into the wood was an old red arrow with a message tied around the shaft. Carver retrieved the message, closed the door, and read in scribbled, barely legible handwriting.

Stop your quest for the mine.

Tomats

Chapter Five

Carver handed the arrow and note to Cass. "Lock up when I close this door. Same protocol." He slipped out into the world of darkness and whatever else existed beyond the light.

"Does he think he's bulletproof?" she said to no one in particular. She slammed and locked the door. Suddenly finding the mine seemed a lot less important. In fact, she didn't care what the cipher said. Someone had just shot an arrow into their front door. Carver had gone straight out, directly towards whatever trouble was out there. Because he was out there, she felt safe, but she disliked his superior attitude and the way he treated her as though she were helpless. She knew she didn't have the survival or tracking skills he had, but she wasn't about to simper and swoon at the first sign of danger, either. She wished he'd give her just a little more credit than that. And to top it all off, he was frustratingly noble and honor-bound.

She showed her father the arrow. "Dad, maybe we ought to listen to Carver. There are too many weird things happening, and even this note seems to escalate the threats to a new, personal level."

"Cass, that's why I want you to go back to school." Rylan turned from looking out the window. "I don't want to have to worry about you. I know we've gone over this before, but now you really need to listen to me. You've already done your job and decoded the message. You don't have to hang around here anymore."

"I'm not going anywhere until you agree to stop this irresponsible treasure hunt," she told him, tears stinging her eyes. "It's simply not worth it. Besides, you don't believe this fabled mine really exists, do you?"

"Cass, you know I do. There's a reason I was present when Carver discovered the box. I feel it's my responsibility to keep the treasure from falling into the wrong hands." He ran his hand through his hair, making it stand on end. "I can't just walk away—besides, Carver's house was torched. I've got to help him find the responsible party, even if it's just some crazy out there trying to scare us."

"I'm glad you're able to look at it rationally, but what's the worst thing that could happen if you turn your information over to the Church, or even the cops?"

"No one will ever hear of it again."

"And, that's bad?" she replied. She knew it was a losing battle to dissuade him, even worse than trying to get him to stop singing "The Impossible Dream" in the shower as part of his morning ritual. She had never seen him so consumed. It was time to change the subject. Maybe now was a good time to ask him some questions that had been on her mind, but that she'd been hesitant to ask because of the implications he would draw. She asked in a softer tone, "Dad, tell me about Carver."

"What do you mean?" Rylan had a look of studied innocence on his face, and she knew exactly what he was thinking. He was going to tease her about this for the rest of her life, but she had to admit, against her better judgment, she was starting to get curious about this silent friend of her father's.

"You know—like where he grew up. If he pulled the hair of the little girl who sat in front of him in school. If he played football in high school. Or, why he won't ever talk about himself. For that matter, even talk."

"Sit down, Cass." Rylan sat down in a chair facing her on the couch. She curled her feet under her, grabbed a pillow, and waited.

He wasn't teasing her—in fact, he suddenly seemed very serious.

"He's an only child, born and raised in Randolph, one of the coldest places in the country. His parents owned a small cattle ranch from which they barely eeked out a living. I'm sure he played every sport the high school had, including rodeo. After high school, he went to Utah State University in Logan and got involved in the ROTC program to help him pay for school. After finishing two years of college, he served a mission in Arizona, on the Navajo reservation."

She was stunned. They seemed to have a lot in common, but she never would have guessed. "He served a mission?" She tried to picture him in a suit with a missionary haircut, but she couldn't quite complete the mental transformation.

"When he got back from Arizona, he completed his degree at Utah State and got a BS in Agriculture Science. He wanted to help his dad run the ranch, but right after graduation he had to serve his time in the military. He was immediately accepted into an elite Ranger unit and went through their intensive training. To the best of my knowledge, he served in Afghanistan and some other very hot spots. He won't talk about his time there."

Cass wasn't sure how she felt about the war, but she did appreciate the servicemen who put their lives on the line for their country. She felt a wave of pride wash over her just knowing Carver had been one of them.

"How do you know so much about him, Dad?"

"His grandfather was my best friend. He loved Carver and talked about him incessantly. I know all about his early life, but after his grandfather died, the information stopped. He doesn't talk about himself. He's a very private person."

"What about women?" she winced, barely daring to ask the question, fearing to expose too much of herself.

"Ummm?" He looked at her with a twinkle in his eye. "I don't know if he's ever had a serious relationship, but don't tell me you have some interest in him?"

"I don't have time for romance, Dad. You know that."

"But you say it with such passion, Cass."

"What happened to his parents?" She was going to make him finish his story.

"His father was involved in some kind of farming accident and died while Carver was in the military. His mother couldn't or didn't want to hang around without him. She died of natural causes within the year. The farm was lost to foreclosure and the only family Carver had left was his grandfather."

Three quick knocks sounded from the door, Carver's code. "Dad, don't you say anything about, well, you know."

"About what?" Rylan grinned at his daughter, and she wasn't sure if she could trust him not to spill the beans to Carver the first chance he got.

Rylan opened the door. Carver came in, and after fixing the deadbolt said, "I found some tracks just outside of my electronic perimeter. They obviously discovered my defense and avoided it. That means we're not involved with some two-bit drugstore gangsters. However, I don't think whoever fired that arrow was a ghost, even though they didn't leave any prints. They had a vehicle parked down the road a ways and used it to make their escape."

His tone was a little bit melodramatic and for a moment, she pictured him in a superhero costume. That was easier to imagine than him as a missionary. Squelching down the urge to address him as "Captain America," she said, "Tell me who you think is trying to scare us off. That is, if you have an idea."

"Someone is trying very hard to make us believe the Ute Indians don't want anyone traipsing down the trail towards the Carre-Shin-Ob."

"How they do they always seem to know what we're doing before we do it?" She thought back to her meeting with Reber. He seemed to know too much. Maybe she needed to take him up on his offer to go riding. If she did, she couldn't let her father or Carver know—they wouldn't let her go. But if she had the chance to glean some information that might keep her father safe, she'd do whatever she had to do.

Two days later, early in the morning, Cass called her father from her cell phone. "Dad, don't get mad and don't tell Carver, but I set up a date with Reber to go riding. I'm just about to drive into Duchesne. He has a couple of horses here and we're going to spend the day out riding in the hills."

"Cass, we had an agreement." Cass had not heard the steel in his voice before. She knew she should have told him. Sometimes she knew she was not only impulsive but also a little too independent. "You weren't supposed to go anywhere without one of us."

"I know, Dad, but Reber would never harm me, and besides, I may be able to get to the bottom of some the problems we've been having."

"Carver will string me up for letting you get out of here alone."

"What he doesn't know won't hurt him. Just don't tell him. Maybe I'll be back before he realizes I'm gone. By the way, I'm sure my cell will be out of range, so don't panic if I don't answer your calls."

Carver spent the morning working on his cabin. He had the walls up and part of the roof in place, and was pleased with his progress, but he couldn't wait for night to fall. He wanted to catch their unseen predators in his crosshairs, tired of being a victim. As soon as dark descended, he was going to lie in wait, and this time he would catch them.

He wished Cass had just listened to her father and gone back to school. He knew he spent too much time checking on her safety. He could be much more effective if he didn't have to worry about her.

She intrigued him, and he had to continually remind himself that feelings created weakness. Caring interfered with operational decisions. He had been there before and he wasn't going to be hand-icapped again, and yet he was tied to Rylan and well, yes he had to admit it, to Cass. He wasn't going to lose either of them.

Carver didn't believe there was a cave filled with bullion or golden plates. He wouldn't have been surprised if the Utes once had a mine in the area where they stored stolen Spanish gold. He knew the Spanish had established over thirty-two smelting cites in the area. They could have produced a mountain of gold with thirty-two smelters operating. History noted that the Utes did get fed-up with the Spanish and rebelled by stealing their gold on at least two occasions in the 1700s. Surely most of that gold would have been exhausted by this time, if it had been given to Thomas Rhoades and Jesse Knight. However, he knew he would never convince Rylan that his quest would be fruitless.

He also had no doubt there were certain present-day Ute Indians who believed they had the absolute right to keep gold seekers from looking for the lost mine, and would feel justified in using any force necessary, including shooting. There were too many stories of people ending up dead or missing for the stories to be make-believe. He intended to keep Rylan safe, which meant, in part, keeping him off Ute land.

He decided he needed to have a little talk with Rylan and Cass. He wanted to implement some safety protocol, maybe use tracking devices to ease their ability to locate each other quickly. He got cleaned up and made a quick round of the property, just to insure there weren't any undesirables hanging around.

The bad guys now had a copy of the Rhoades cipher. If they hadn't been able to crack it, they would be coming back to see if Rylan had. If they had figured it out, they didn't need an attorney and his daughter hanging around to cause complications.

He knocked three times and Rylan let him in the house. "Come over here, Carver. I've been studying these maps with the information we have from the cipher."

"Where's your daughter?" Carver asked.

"Umm . . . she went out for a bit. Look at this map," he said, trying to avoid Carver's question.

"Where did she go? I thought we had an understanding." Carver wasn't going to let Rylan redirect his question that easily. He knew Rylan would try to cover up for Cass, but he would never lie to him.

"She went out for a bit."

Carver felt the agitation rise in his chest. "Where did she go, Rylan?"

"She went out on a date," Rylan answered.

The answer caught Carver by surprise. He hadn't even contemplated the idea. He didn't know what to say or do. He was mad, but then, he knew he couldn't control her life. He shifted his feet, knowing he had to ask but not wanting to worm his way into Cass's life. "With whom, and where?"

Cass enjoyed riding with Reber. So far he had been a perfect gentleman and she chastised herself for questioning his motives. He was good-looking, laughed at her jokes, and leaned toward suave. Of course, her recent encounters with men were either in the math department or Carver, and Reber shone in that light. He had an endearing personality that invited her to trust him. She felt entirely safe around him and sorry for anyone that crossed him. He had been raised in the ways of the Ute.

She felt at home in the saddle and they talked and laughed as they headed into the foothills. He took extra care to make sure she was safe, leading the way when the grade got steep. He hadn't known she was such a good rider and constantly commented on her natural ability to handle the horse.

"I didn't think the white men let their women ride horses or get their hands dirty. I thought you had to stick to BMWs," he teased.

"Yeah, well, I can drive one of those too. Race you to the top." With that, she took off at a full gallop.

They stopped by a small stream and Reber retrieved a lunch he packed. "You're crazy. What if your horse had stepped into one of those prairie dog holes?" he asked.

"I'm not blind."

They sat on rocks in the middle of the stream with the water slowly ebbing and bubbling around them. It was beautiful, and she felt at peace, something that had escaped her since she left New Haven. She was in the mountains with a man she liked. She felt content and relished it.

Reber brought her out of her dream world with just a few words.

"What do you know about your new neighbor?"

"You mean Carver Nash?" Her defenses instantly flared. How did he know about Carver and what prompted him to ask her?

"Yeah," he replied.

She studied him, trying to see what lay behind those dark brown eyes. "Why do you ask?"

"Oh, no reason in particular. I've just heard stories about him."

"What kind of stories?"

"Well, you know, he beat the Forest Service out of a bunch of land in court. I think your dad represented him. What kind of guy is he, anyway?"

It was a weird question. He probably knew more about Carver than she did. And why would he be interested in land disputes in Marion? The more she thought about it, the madder she got. Then she remembered where she was—a long way from nowhere.

"He's a nice guy. Helps my dad a lot, but he doesn't say much."

"I heard he's some kind of Army hero."

"Maybe. I don't know," she replied. "He never talks about himself or his time in the Army."

"Maybe he's got something to hide," he said.

Again her defenses arose. She felt her palms become sticky and she was sure that he would see some smoldering in her eyes.

"Reber, I don't know what this is all about, but Mr. Nash has treated me and my father better than anyone else ever has." She thought now would be a good time to start heading back, and nervously wondered just how good an idea this little excursion had been.

Almost immediately, Reber turned back into the perfect gentleman. "I'm sorry, Cass. I didn't mean to offend you. The only thing I really care about is you. Tell me about your school, when you'll graduate, and what you are planning to do when you're done."

The conversation shifted to a familiar, easy back-and-forth discussion. She really believed he was concerned for her—well, more than concerned. He wanted to develop a relationship. "Maybe we'd better start back towards town." He helped her on the horse and they rode leisurely back the way they had come. Cass had forgotten the reason why she wanted to come and as a result, she had not gotten any answers to her questions.

They came out of the mouth of a canyon, riding next to a small tree-lined stream. It was beautiful and Reber, well, he was nice. He constantly teased her but made her feel beautiful at the same time. His attention was infectious.

Reber had stopped his horse to let it drink. Cass climbed down and Reber stuck a beautiful Indian paint flower behind her ear. He put both hands on her shoulders and looked into her eyes. She shuddered and felt a strange warming sensation spread through her. She thought he was going to kiss her and she didn't know what she would do if he tried, but she didn't turn and run either. At that instant a bullet struck a tree not ten feet from them.

Reber grabbed her hand and pulled her down behind a large rock. More rifle shots rang out. They seemed to be very close. She was scared and tried to make herself as small as she could. She noticed Reber didn't appear afraid. Maybe he was used to this kind of stuff. He turned to face her and said, "Keep down. I'm going to get my rifle from the horse." With that he was gone.

The shots stopped and Reber returned. He leaned the rifle against the rock and lifted Cass to a standing position. He drew her against him and hugged her softly. He spoke to her, trying to soothe her nerves. "I'm sorry. Some hotheads on the reservation have gotten upset because they heard that some new interest in the mine has surfaced and they think you may have something to do with it. I think those shots were just a warning and weren't meant to hurt anyone."

Cass accepted Reber's hug, trying to still her nerves. His calm voice was a stark contrast to the terror that raced through her. She didn't know how close those shots had come to hitting their mark, but she wanted to get out of there, and fast.

"She went riding with Reber Kolb," replied Rylan.

"She did what? Rylan, once those guys decipher the document, they won't have need for any of us. In fact, we'll complicate their life a great deal. For all we know, they already have the location of the mine and are on their way right now to do away with us. And Cass is out who knows where."

Carver wondered why he was so upset with Rylan. He should be giving this lecture to little Miss Muffet instead. He'd told her to stick close by—why did she have to be so stubborn?

"I didn't know she had gone until she called me on her cell phone from Duchesne. I tried to talk her into turning around and coming home, but she had no intention of listening to me. She thought she might be able to get some information."

"Information? So, now she's Nancy Drew? Try calling her cell phone."

Carver fumed while Rylan punched the numbers into his phone. He had done everything he could to keep that girl safe, and she had taken off the minute his back was turned. Didn't she understand what he was trying to do? She was probably trying to figure out if Reber Kolb was involved in the problems they'd been having. Smart, real smart. Let's just go up to him and ask him if he's the bad guy or not.

Rylan folded his cell phone and said, "All I get is her voice mail. She told me she would be out of range." He slid his phone back into his pocket. "I don't know what else to do, Carver. I called you as soon I hung up with her."

Carver walked out of the house and slammed the door.

It was twilight when Rylan's car pulled into Carver's driveway. Cass was driving and appeared to still be breathing. Carver felt a weight lift from his shoulders, but not entirely. Even though he was glad she was home, he wasn't in any mood to talk to her, not right now, maybe never. He stepped back into the trees, not wanting to be found.

About an hour later, his cell phone started vibrating. He figured it was a call for help and set off for the house. He hit the porch, Colt .45 in hand, the same time as the door opened. She stood there, waiting for him. He lowered his gun, turned and started walking away, convinced she had just called wolf.

"Carver, don't walk away from me," she yelled into the night.

He stopped and turned around. "Come in and talk," she said, holding the door open wide.

He couldn't think of anything to say to her that would be polite. She'd gone against all his safety precautions and now she wanted to talk? He was going to need some time to cool down before he'd even be able to form a sentence. He was furious. He squeezed his hand into fists, clenched his jaw, and walked away without looking back.

Cass got out her cell phone and called him again. This time he did not respond at all. Rylan said, "Give him until tomorrow. Maybe he'll calm down by then."

She went up to her room and slammed her door, not sure why she was so angry. Okay, she'd done something really stupid. She'd left the house alone. She'd been out of cell phone range, and, she'd had the life scared out of her. Reber had been there and he'd comforted her, but strangely, all she'd wanted at that moment was Carver.

When she called him, she'd hoped he'd be glad to see her. But the look he'd given her was almost one of disgust, and that made her feel ashamed of herself, like a little girl who'd broken the rules and gone running off. And that's exactly what she'd done.

She'd wanted to prove that she was independent, that she could provide some valuable information to help in their treasure hunt. Wanting Carver as badly as she had made her feel vulnerable, and she didn't like that at all. It certainly wasn't what she'd been aiming for, and the realization that she just might need someone after all . . .

If he had just given her a chance . . . a chance to explain . . .

"Carver won't even answer his phone. It's been two days of the silent treatment—why is he being so stubborn?"

"Sounds familiar, don't you think?" Rylan smiled at her, but she waved off his comment.

"I'm starting to wonder if I even want him to come back."

"We need Carver to find the mine, Cass."

"Maybe we should just give it up. We've had nothing but trouble since you found that box." She decided it was time to tell him about her little adventure with Reber.

"Dad, the other day when I was riding with Reber, someone started shooting at us."

Rylan dropped the documents he'd been holding, his face suddenly ashen.

"Dad, it's okay—they didn't come close to hitting us. In fact, they seemed more like warning shots. Reber thought so, too. If they wanted us dead, they wouldn't have missed."

Rylan passed a hand over his face and sat, staring at his daughter with stricken eyes.

"Reber told me there's a rumor going around that we're looking for the mine. There's a group of radicals on the reservation who've taken a blood oath to protect the mine and will do it, at any cost."

"Why didn't you tell me about this?" He looked like a ghost.

She felt a guilty twinge in the pit of her stomach.

"Dad, I didn't want you to worry." She stood and began pacing the room. "But Reber clammed up every time I asked him a question.

"I asked him how anyone could know we were out riding. He didn't have an answer. I asked him why anyone thought we were looking for the mine. He said it was just a rumor. He skirted every question I asked. I wonder if I should have been more afraid of Reber, or the guy taking shots."

"Maybe we should call the police," suggested Rylan.

"Maybe I should go try to apologize to Carver," replied Cass.

"I'll go with you."

"No, this is something I have to do by myself."

She watched Carver straddling a timber on the roof—he looked like he knew what he was doing. He almost had the house closed in. He didn't look her way and she wasn't ready to let him know she was there, but she had the sneaking suspicion he knew. She wanted to watch him a little longer, and she didn't know quite what to say.

"If you've got something to say, then come up here and say it," he said without looking at her. She reluctantly walked out of the trees and sat on a log lying near the cabin.

"Well?" he said.

"If you can come down here, I'd like to talk to you."

He turned to look at her. She couldn't tell whether he wanted to strangle her or turn her over his knee and give her a good spanking. He climbed down and crossed the yard, taking a seat on a log facing Cass. He looked directly into her eyes and she didn't turn away. He didn't say anything and she knew it was her turn.

"Listen, Carver, I'm sorry." She struggled as her emotions began to take control, and she had to blink to avoid tears. She was sorry. She had put herself in a position beyond his protection and she had been terrified. She had gone against his instructions and suffered the consequences. She didn't know how much more serious the consequences could have been, and thinking about it upset her even more.

She didn't trust Reber any longer despite his claim of innocence. Carver, on the other hand, she would trust with her life. She didn't know why she felt so sure about him, but she did.

Carver didn't respond to her apology, but he wasn't looking into her eyes anymore, either. He looked at the ground, the trees—anywhere but at her. She wished she knew what was going on inside that head of his.

She regained control and continued, "You have a right to be mad at me." She turned her gaze away from him, not wanting him to see her emotion. She wiped her eyes and sniffed.

He reached over and tilted her chin so he could look into her eyes. "Once, I lost some people I cared for very much. I can't, and won't, do that again."

"What?" Before she could ask him any further questions, he responded in a quiet, forceful voice.

"You go home now. I'll come by tonight."

With that he rose, grabbed the overhanging timber, and levered himself back up on the roof to finish his work.

Did he mean he would never care about anyone again, or that he didn't intend to lose anyone again? Trying to be logical and reasoning it out didn't keep her heart from thudding. She knew what he meant—she just wasn't sure if she liked the effect it was having on her. She stood and began to move away.

"Cass, be careful."

She turned around—he was looking at her, and she felt safe. She liked the way he spoke her name. She knew nothing would happen to her, not now.

"I want more information," Vincent Vargas fumed. He rolled down the tinted window of his car and looked out across the hills.

"The mine is out there somewhere. Why can't anyone find it?"

No one answered him. His driver had learned the hard way that his opinion was not to be shared.

Vargas rolled the window back up and told his driver to head home. "I will have that gold," he fumed.

Three days later at 4:00 AM, Carver, Cass, and Rylan walked their horses off Carver's property toward the headwaters of the south fork of the Weber River. Carver had scouted the area the day before and knew where they were going, but he didn't think there could be a mine anywhere in the area. He also knew the best locations for sniper hideouts along the trail. He had muffled the horses' hooves with gunny sack material and intended to stay off the road, hiding in the timbers. It would make the trek harder and slower, but safer. He had a long-barreled rifle in his saddle and a large pistol in a shoulder holster.

Once they entered the tree line, they mounted their horses and rode without speaking. Carver could tell Cass was nervous because she kept fussing with her hair, something she didn't usually do. Rylan beamed like a kid on the way to Disneyland for the first time.

Several hours later, they crossed the road and headed straight for a draw that went to the top of the mountain. Once they lost sight of the road, they stopped behind a grove of scrub oak.

Carver motioned for them to climb down off their horses. "If we wind our way up this draw to the top of the hill, we'll be within walking distance of the headwaters. Now listen—this is important. If anything happens and we get separated, head for that road below, and follow it back home. Do not stop under any conditions, for anyone. If one if us is not back within three hours, call the police and Forest Service. Cass, you follow me and stay close. Rylan, you bring up the rear and keep your eyes and ears open." Carver reached over and touched Cass's arm. Her tension was apparent. Even the muscles in her arm were rigid. He gave her a gentle squeeze as if to assure her everything was going to be okay.

They stopped again at the top of the hill and Carver pointed out the approximate location of the headwaters. They were on Forest Service land, not close to reservation property. They started down into the valley. The sun was up and the day was bright and warm. They had not seen or heard anyone during their entire trek. It was, in fact, a beautiful day in the mountains.

Once they rode into the valley, they followed the stream until it became a rivulet. Cass quoted aloud from the cipher, " 'Let flight of the arrow guide your flight.' What do you think that means?"

They all looked around. "It could be something that looks like an arrow—a rock formation, a misshapen tree, an unusual growth, anything out of the ordinary that looks ordinary," Cass said. They got off their horses and looked around. The ground was covered with thousands of rocks spread throughout the sandy soil. The tops of the rocks were encrusted with a thin film of white alkali as a result of the seasonal moisture in the form of rain, snowmelt, and flash floods.

They all searched but they couldn't find anything that looked like an arrow. At mid-afternoon, Carver suggested that they eat their lunch. They each picked out a rock to sit on, all wondering what the coded message could possibly mean. Suddenly, Carver stood up and dusted the alkali off of his pants. He looked at the rock he had been sitting on and the one Cass was using.

"What?" she said.

He glanced around the area and said, "Follow me." They quickly climbed a knoll. It was steep and rose above the valley floor. Cass was a step ahead of Rylan, who struggled to catch a breath. Once at the top, Carver pointed back to where they had been sitting.

"What are we looking at?" asked Cass.

"If you notice, almost all of the rocks in the valley are covered with white alkali. However, there are a few, like the one you were sitting on, that aren't white. In fact, there are several more like that. Do you see them?"

They looked down. It was clear as day. The dark stones formed an arrow pointing to an odd rock formation. They scrambled down from the knoll, racing for their horses.

Cass and Rylan rode as quickly as possible to the rock outcropping. Carver checked out the area before following, tired of reacting defensively instead of being on the offense.

When he was sure they didn't have any company, he rode up to Cass and Rylan. They had been examining the rocks, Cass muttering, "A stone box hidden in plain sight."

Rylan found a round stone about the size of his car tire with an unusual line running around its perimeter. It looked almost like a cut line, not a jagged freeze-thaw crack line. He picked up a rock as big as his hand and started banging it against the round rock. Then he hit another rock nearby. They didn't sound the same.

Cass and Rylan moved closer, their attention fully trained. Carver felt uncomfortable, though, as if someone were watching them. He looked around, but couldn't see anyone. That didn't lessen his anxiety, however, and he knew he'd better keep his eyes and ears open.

Rylan found some handholds on top of the rock and tried twisting, pulling, and pushing, but nothing happened. Carver positioned himself across the rock and suggested they try turning it together. It moved.

The horses raised their heads and one neighed. Carver immediately went to red alert and waved Cass and Rylan behind the rocks.

"We can't go now," said Rylan.

"Do you think someone's out there?" asked Cass. She had been very quiet all day—well, quiet for her.

Carver got out his binoculars and scanned the area. He couldn't find anything and the horses had gone back to grazing, not bothered any longer. Maybe it had just been a deer or elk. As soon as he had the thought, though, he discarded it. Someone was out there. He was sure of it.

Chapter Six

The terrain was much more precipitous going out than coming in. Cass kept her horse close to the tail of Carver's horse, just as he'd ordered. He had been strung tight as stretched wire since the horses caused a commotion at the rock outcropping. She had known from the look on his face that he wanted to get them out of there, now. She had never seen him so focused.

With Rylan and Carver working together, they had been able to remove the top of the rock, which had been hollowed out. The seal had been an incredible engineering feat—everything inside was absolutely dry. Carver would not allow Rylan to inspect the contents there. Instead they put everything straight into Carver's saddlebags. Carver then quickly replaced the top of the rock, covered all their tracks, got them on the horses, and headed back towards home.

There had been some thirty-odd gold bars inside the rock, and they were a lot heavier than Cass had imagined. There was also an animal hide case containing documents, and a wooden box containing a cipher wheel.

Rylan had desperately wanted to examine the documents on the spot, but Carver said, in a tone that didn't invite any question, "When we get home," and that was that. He had them moving quickly and quietly back the way they came.

Rylan had whispered to her that the gold was similar to the Spanish gold they had previously discovered. Cass had recognized the cipher ring the minute Rylan opened the wooden box. She had tried to explain how it worked, but Carver kept pressing her to hurry and to keep quiet. She wondered if he knew something he wasn't telling them.

Rylan and Cass both held their comments, knowing Carver would not tolerate sound. Once they were back in the saddle he had them on silent, running.

He stopped them at the top of the hill. He had his binoculars out, constantly scanning the area behind and in front of them. Finally he said, "Something's not right. I want you two to follow our trail back down this draw. If I haven't caught up with you by the time you hit the road, then stay on the road and make for home as fast as you can. Do not come back here or stop for any reason."

"We're not leaving you here alone." Cass felt like a Private First Class telling her fire-breathing drill instructor what to do.

He didn't even respond to her comment. "Go. I'll be right behind you. Rylan, you lead." He didn't brook any interference with his orders today. She could tell that now was not the time to argue, so she bit her tongue and did as she was told.

Cass continued to glance over her shoulder as she moved down the draw. They were approaching part of the trail that crossed an old rockslide. Rylan continued and didn't notice that Cass had stopped to try to locate Carver. She was sure he wasn't safe, even if he did think he could handle everything.

At that minute, she heard a noise that sounded like large rocks bouncing down the draw. She glanced up to see half of the mountain coming down toward them. She screamed and was about to take off after her father when she was lifted from her saddle.

"Follow me, quick!" Carver said as he lowered her to the ground, grabbed her hand, and started to run.

"What about my father?"

"There's nothing we can do right now," he said.

At the last instant he pulled her into a hollow formed by a vertical rock formation. The air was filled with choking dust, and the noise was deafening. All she could think about was her father somewhere down below, and she started to cry. Carver reached over and pulled her against him. Strong arms encircled her as he held her.

At thirteen, she had dubbed her father Sir Rylan. He had always been there for her. He was all she had left. Her sobs became more severe as she imagined what might be happening to him out there, and she couldn't stop crying. But Carver was there. He was whispering to her and stroking her hair. His arms were so strong and yet his voice so gentle. She didn't want him to let go. In the midst of her darkest nightmare, she saw a light she knew would never go out. She clutched herself tightly to him, trying to fight the darkness.

The word *exquisite* described the texture of her hair. She was so vulnerable, so lovely, so much more. A moment he would never forget. He wanted to make it all better, everything. She didn't deserve this, and Rylan, he only prayed that he might survive. He didn't want to let her go but he knew he had to get her out of there. She stopped crying and suddenly went limp. She must have passed out, but had a steady pulse and normal breathing. He gently picked her up and started down the mountain. He had to get her to safety; that was all that mattered.

She didn't know how long it had been since the rockslide. The next thing she knew, she was sitting on Carver's horse as he led it through the trees. They were in the bottom of the valley and getting close to his ranch.

Then she was lying on her bed in her father's house. Someone pulled a cover over her and placed a pillow under her head. She heard the door close as she slipped back into her darkness, somewhere where there wasn't any pain, any memory, any feeling.

She felt someone kiss her forehead. He was also holding her hand and softly speaking to her. She didn't want to listen. She didn't want to even know who was trying to comfort her. He shook her gently, but insistently. She wanted to scream at him to go away. One eye fluttered open, closed, and then opened. She was staring into her father's eyes. She knew she was dreaming.

"Cass, I'm okay. I'm back."

She struggled to open her eyes again, blinking to focus her vision. It was her father, and he wasn't a ghost. She wondered if she were dreaming as she tried to sit up and almost passed out again.

"Take it easy, young lady."

"Dad, what happened?" She remembered the rockslide. She wondered how he could have survived. She remembered Carver dragging her to safety, his powerful gentle arms, sitting on a horse.

"Cass," her eyes fluttered opened. "Are you with me?" She wrapped her arms around her father and held on for dear life.

After long moments, she drew back without letting go. "How? I mean, I saw the rocks bouncing down the draw straight toward you."

"Cass, after my horse pitched me off, I fell into a shallow crevice and that darn horse fell right on top of me, shielding me from the onslaught. He was crushed, but he protected me from the rocks. I lay there for what seemed like forever, unable to move, until I heard a noise. Then I started yelling for help. Carver spotted my horse and heard me shouting. He dug me out."

He pulled her back into his embrace. "I came out of it with nothing but this broken leg. The whole time I was lying under that horse, all I could think of was you. Cass, I was so worried. When Carver hauled me out of the rocks I kept asking about you. After Carver quieted me down, he carried me down to the Land Rover and took me to the hospital. He told me you were safe—in shock, but okay."

"So he saved you, huh? Where is the big lunk then? I guess I need to thank him, again."

"If I didn't know better, I would think you cared about him."

"Who?" she asked. Without waiting for him to answer, she asked another question, "Well, where is he?"

"I'll tell you in a minute but first, I have something else I have to tell you. Before I tell you, though, you have to promise not to say a word to anyone. Okay?"

"Umm . . . okay . . ."

"No. No umm's. You have to agree to tell no one or I won't say another word."

"Okay, Dad, but what could be so serious?"

"Well, you know how claustrophobic I am. It was a strange sensation, but while I was lying under that horse, I felt a perfect calm. I wasn't worried about anything. I was praying like crazy and thought

I was being watched over and blessed in my time of need. When the rockslide was over, for a brief second I thought I was hallucinating due to a whack on the head, but at the time I saw many generations of Utes and other tribes, some had already lived on this world and some had not yet been born. I don't know how I knew the difference but I did. Anyway I felt a kinship with them that I have never experienced with anyone and as sure as anything each spoke to me. Now you know, I have many Indian friends, but this was different."

"And so . . . I can't tell anyone because?"

"I don't know Cass. It seemed sorta spiritual, but I can't really explain what it was all about. It doesn't make any sense."

"That's it? There's nothing else?"

"Nope, but you know how you can't remember most of the goings on of your dreams and very little of the details? Well, the strange thing is I remember every face, everything they were wearing, every expression, and every word they spoke. And now that I think of it, there was something else. I didn't realize it then, but each spoke in their own native tongue and I understood every word they said."

"Dad, your dream is really cool and all but it is a little weird, even for you. Are you sure you don't need to see a shrink?" She winced when she said it but then a sly smile stole across her face. "By the way, where is our resident superhero."

"I really don't know where he is. He went outside to make sure no one was prowling around."

Cass turned introspective. "You don't think the rockslide was an accident either, do you?"

Rylan shook his head. "Carver found some tracks on top of the mountain where the slide started. Apparently there were two sets of them."

"Dad, we have to go to the authorities. You could have been killed."

"We'll talk about it tomorrow, Cass. I want you to get some sleep." He rose and hobbled on crutches toward the door, only pausing when she asked, "Dad, who looks out for Carver while he's looking out for us?"

Cass snuggled under a blanket pulled up to her chin while sitting in her rocker. One arm snaked out, holding a cup of hot chocolate. She had recovered from feeling like she had been run over by a Mack truck, and had even showered and brushed her hair. Carver still wasn't anywhere around—she wondered again where he was, if he was safe.

She watched Rylan examine the animal skin pouch they had retrieved from the round rock. He handled it with almost a reverence. Perhaps he had forgotten their little adventure and his near-death experience yesterday, but she hadn't.

His leg was in a cast up to his knee and he had it elevated to rest on his desk. That didn't slow him down a bit as he withdrew a yellowed, brittle page out of the pouch. He handled it with care and spent some time studying it. He then made a copy and put the original away in his safe. It was a letter from Caleb Rhoades, the second member of the Rhoades family to gain access to the mine.

Those that follow my path to the Carre-Shin-Ob do so for a purpose other than riches. Now for your history lesson; The Spanish came to this area as early as 1700. Most came for the King's gold. A Spanish mission was founded in 1831 near the forks of the Whiterocks and the Unitah. An earlier mission was established there before 1762. One named for its founder and one for the area. I have been to both sites. In 1844 the Utes were caught in a battle between the Spanish and Navajos. In retaliation the Utes killed every Spaniard in the area and took all of their gold to Carre-Shin-Ob.

President Young told me to leave this trail, this series of hidden messages for his purposes. I know them not.

Two maps were drawn of the location of the mine, one is no good without the other. One is a key to the other. I gave one to my wife and the other was hidden and its location will be discovered by continuing on the path that led you to this message.

Know this! There will always be men that seek for the sacred gold, men with less than noble goals. There are those who will do whatever they can to hinder your quest and steal from you the secret of Carre-Shin-Ob. Beware!

ECUIKWAEYOUJXHUIFBHVHQR
RBEPRFMBJFBKLBAKVOSIVOWOVODMPSNXIM
SSOMDHBQZSUZHSGXIYFLFF

Caleb Rhoades, 1869

Rylan read the letter out loud, whether for her benefit or his own information, Cass didn't know. However, she suspected he was trying to draw her back into his quest without resolving the problem they had yesterday. He had not addressed her request to go to the police.

Rylan retrieved a second document from the pouch. "Listen to this, Cass. It's an agreement between Brigham Young, Thomas Rhoades, and Chief Wakara. Remember, the Church never officially admitted that it obtained any gold from the Utes or Thomas Rhoades. However, such a deal was rumored on the streets of Salt Lake as early as 1852, but officially no one ever acknowledged its existence. This document proves that there was an agreement and it's signed by the prophet."

June 3, 1849

Towats, the guardian spirit of the Carre-Shin-Ob, showed me in my youth a vision of the scared place. He told me that the gold belonged to the High Hats who would come to my land one day. I was told to give the gold to them if they promise:

Only one person will know the location of the mine. If he tells or shows any man the location: all will be killed.

He may only take as much gold as he can carry each time he is allowed to go to the mine.

Anyone that follows the man will also be killed.

The gold is to be used only for Church purposes and nothing else.

The Prophet Brigham and his man, Thomas Rhoades, agree that by signing this document they are entering into a blood oath, the penalty for breaking the agreement is death.

Chief Wakara

Brigham Young

Thomas Rhoades

Cass found herself again caught up in her father's excitement. She supposed he would start off again on one of his history lessons as he reached up and found one of the books he had been using for source material. He leafed through some pages as he spoke.

"Do you know Wakara became the most powerful Ute Chief because he was such a great warrior? He was also proclaimed the greatest horse thief alive. Later, he became friends with Isaac Morley, who was a Mormon bishop residing in the Manti area. Isaac baptized him in 1850."

"I hope he gave up stealing before getting baptized," teased Cass.

Rylan was in his own world and didn't bother to respond. "Prior to the baptism, Morley had arranged a secret meeting with Brigham Young at Wakara's insistence. Wakara told President Young of the vision he had about the gold mine.

"Wakara was appointed an elder in the Church in 1851, and shortly after that Brigham Young adopted him."

Cass crossed the room and sat next to her father, draping her arm across his shoulders. She hadn't fully recovered from the belief that he had been killed, and loved having him close to prove to herself that she'd been mistaken.

Rylan continued. "I found another curious letter in the Journal of History. It's dated October 22, 1850. It's got a quote here from Brigham Young. 'More gold than has already come to the mint has just been brought in, as well as a box of silver so heavy that it required three men to lift it from the wagon.' "[1]

"This proves it, Cass. It all fits together. The mine is real. This statement about gold being brought into the mint is peculiar because he didn't disclose the source of the gold or the amount. However, he did say that it was more than had already been brought into the mint to that date. That is a lot of gold. I think it's a little too coincidental that Brigham and Rhoades met with Wakara just prior to a boatload of gold and silver being delivered to the mint in Salt Lake."

He paused to let that sink in and then said, "Now, let's see if we can figure out this next cipher."

Cass decided she'd play along for awhile, but they were definitely going to have a heart-to-heart talk before they left the house again. She needed to talk to Carver. Maybe he could convince her father to give up this insane quest. She didn't want to lose him, and the rockslide had been too close.

"The keyword to the cipher has got to be in this letter, or, at the very least, the letter points to the keyword. Cass, can you go run the keywords in the message through your cipher program to see if you get any hits?"

She took the copy of the letter he handed her and started running various words and their combinations through her program. An hour later she announced, "Nothing worked. Sorry, Dad."

Rylan had been studying the letter and said, "Okay, let's maybe try to break the letter down into sections. Maybe we can get some ideas. First, why did Caleb give us a history lesson? Did he simply want to set the record straight, or did he have an ulterior motive?" Cass picked up a copy of the document to see if she could add any insight. As she read, she ran her fingers through her hair, her feelings just as jumbled. She wanted to help her father, but she didn't want him in the danger zone again.

"The next section of the letter indicates that President Young knew someone in the future would be thrown into a quest for the Lost Mine using these ciphers. Maybe he wanted that someone to be able to explain how the Church came into possession of gold from the Carre-Shin-Ob. He also knew there would be those who would try to stop anyone from completing the search. If that's the case, we can't just give up. We have to continue. Seems to me that President Young knew we would be involved in this quest."

Cass jumped in. "I object, Your Honor. That last statement called for speculation and does not accurately reflect the record before us."

"I'm just throwing out ideas," Rylan replied.

After thinking for a minute, Rylan continued, "We need to examine the discussion of the two maps. Everyone knows Thomas gave one map to his wife, and we have a copy. Everyone has a copy, but no one has ever found the mine using that map. He didn't do two maps of the same thing—he made two maps that had to be used together. That's significant, because most of the maps of the Lost Mine today have their genesis in only the first of Caleb Rhoades' maps."

Cass had been reviewing the information in the letter and partially listening to her father. "Let's break the history lesson down into some bite-sized pieces. We need information about two early Spanish missions, one founded in 1831 and one earlier. We need names, founders, events, and locations for any such mission," said Cass.

Rylan replied, "It bothers me that these events occurred long before the Saints entered the Salt Lake Valley. Why are these missions and their formation important? I also think we should learn the location of the massacre in 1884 and the people involved. Any of this information could be the keyword. We should also consider any unique topographical characteristic, river names, mountain names, and so on."

Rylan was already on his computer, chasing down historical data on the Spanish missions.

Cass stood and stretched. "I want to go check on Carver." Maybe she could even entice him into trying one of those hug things again, just to see if it felt as good as it had the first time.

"While you're gone I'm going to try to find out if those Spanish missions provide any help in solving the riddle. And oh, don't stay out too late," he said teasingly.

Cass threw together a sack lunch for two and stowed it in her backpack. Carver hadn't been around much since the rockslide. She knew he was trying to finish the rebuilding of his house, and hoped he would be there today. He was.

As she approached his cabin, she stopped in the trees to watch. The cabin was now closed in and weatherproof. She spread out the lunch on an upturned log and waited. She could wait as long as he could.

He walked along the edge of the roof and looked down at her. "You okay?" he asked.

"Yeah, I'm okay," she said. "How about some lunch?" He climbed down from the roof and sat near her. "Thanks. What's the occasion?"

"Peace offering, or a token of my appreciation."

He nodded and started to eat his sandwich, looking at her. She felt he was examining her from the inside out and she couldn't hide anything.

"You weren't alone, so don't get any ideas," he said after swallowing his last bite.

"Beg your pardon?"

"When I took your dad to the hospital. I didn't leave you alone, so don't start thinking it's okay for you to wander off without me."

"How did you watch me and take care of my dad at the same time?" The question hadn't even crossed her mind, but now that he'd pointed it out, she was curious.

"I have friends."

She waited for him to elaborate. He didn't. She decided to try some other questions.

"I heard from someone that you're a war hero. Is that true?"

She watched him squirm, just slightly. She had taken him out of his arena. So much for the peace offering, she thought. Why had she asked him that question? She knew he avoided speaking about his time in the military. She reached over and put her hand on his arm. She wanted him to know she cared.

He replied, "I've seen some action, but the heroes are those guys who didn't come home, those that gave their lives for us. I'm no hero."

"Well, you did receive some kind of medal or award for your time in the military, didn't you?"

"How's your father, Cass?"

"First, you answer my question."

"Maybe I should tell you this story." Carver shifted a little bit, repositioning his feet. "There was this kid who loved baseball. He was small for his age, but had the heart of a lion. He practiced every day. He worked hard trying to learn the skills to be a ballplayer, a shortstop. Then there was this other kid, big for his age. He never had to work hard. Without any practice, he could hit the ball out of the park. When he pitched, he threw white lightning."

Cass leaned back a little, listening to the sound of his voice. It had a great timbre to it—she could listen all day. She wondered why he didn't talk more—if she sounded like that, she'd talk all the time just so she could listen to herself.

"They both made their high school team. The big kid got all the accolades. He hit all the home runs and was the superstar pitcher. The little kid dove after ground balls, slid into second, and got on base so he could score when the big kid hit the long ball. The little kid gave everything he had and then some. He wasn't mentioned in the All-State selection. The big kid was."

He paused before continuing, "So who should have gotten the recognition? The big kid, or the kid who lived in a shadow and made the big kid look better because he was always there doing the pick-and-shovel work?"

She didn't know how that had anything to do with her question, but she replied, "I guess both of them, because neither would have been successful without the other."

"Good answer. Now, how's your father?"

"Rylan's fine. In fact, right this instant he's trying to figure out the keys to the second cipher. He's not about to let someone stop him from finding that mine. He's obsessed."

Carver volunteered, "I spoke with some people I know. They told me about a professional ancient treasure hunter who has a lot of money to throw around. He's trying to locate the Rhoades Mine. He can't really do much exploration because he believes the mine is on Ute land. Apparently two members of the tribe who were on night patrol were killed the other day. My friend believes this professional or his thugs were responsible. He also thinks this man might have purchased his way into the Ute Tribal Council."

She wanted to ask if Reber's name was mentioned, but Carver wasn't finished. "I found evidence the slide was intentionally started. I still don't know how they knew where we were, but they did. It's probably time to call in the cavalry."

"Dad won't let us," she replied. "But maybe you can talk him into it."

Carver didn't reply, and Cass thought she knew what he was thinking. Rylan was a stubborn man, and couldn't be talked into anything he didn't want to do. She took after him in more ways than one.

Rylan had stacks of documents printed off the Internet and copied from books. "Listen to this, Cass. The Rock Creek Mission was probably the first Spanish mission Caleb mentioned in his letter. There's archeological evidence of deep cellars, canals, cultivated fields, storage sheds, and shelters, dating it in the early 1700s. This mission is located near the confluence of the Duchesne River and Rock Creek. They've also found records of hieroglyphic signs and symbols cut into the rock near the mission. The words are of Spanish origin."

About that time, Carver knocked and Cass let him in the house. She smiled and motioned for him to follow, whispering, "He's in his history professor mode again, so you might get bored real quick."

Rylan picked up another set of documents and continued on with his lecture like nothing had happened. "The other mission Caleb spoke of was probably Fort Robidoux. It was a large structure about 200 by 300 feet, located just above the fork of the Uintah and Whiterocks Rivers. It was established in 1831 by Antoine Robidoux and quickly became a center of trade for Spanish miners and French trappers.

"There were two other forts we should consider: Fort Kit Carson on the Duchesne and Green Rivers, and Fort Davy Crockett on the Green River at Brown's Park. All three of the forts were destroyed by the Ute Indians during the uprising of 1844. Perhaps the Rock Creek mission met the same fate.

"There are a number of geographical locations we should also consider as the keyword, such as Sadie's Flat, the old Black Robe Trail, Dry Canyon, and a place called Utahn. One name associated with the area around Rock Creek as early as 1735 was Adolfo Caiecez."

Cass good-naturedly rolled her eyes at Carver. Rylan was sorting papers and Carver appeared to be paying attention. Occasionally he even took notes on a scrap of paper. That was more than Cass could manage to do.

Rylan continued, "There are all kinds of Spanish artifacts found in the area as well as other Catholic shrines. The old North Trail from Santa Fe went directly through this territory. Names of famous Spanish explorers such as Silvestre Velez de Escalante Francisco Atanasio Dominguez have been tied to Fort Robidoux. Also, a four and half pound gold Madonna was found in the area."

"That's nice Rylan, but why are you still researching this?" asked Carver.

"We're trying to figure out the keyword for the second cipher."

"Haven't you two learned anything from the experiences of the last week? There are some bad people out there who will do anything to stop you from searching."

Rylan asked, "Carver, when you were a boy, what did you do when the kid that was twice as big as you kicked sand in your face? Did you run home and stop going to the beach?"

"We're not at the beach, Rylan, and these guys play for keeps. We've learned that the hard way. At least, I thought we'd learned."

Cass sat down at the computer and started to plug in words from the data Rylan collected. While the words were finite, their combinations were limitless. Rylan added, "It's got to have something to do with either the Rock Creek Mission or Fort Robidoux. Let's try the name of any person, river, mountain, city, artifact, or explorer connected with either location."

"Hold on, guys, I think I've got something here," exclaimed Cass.

Chapter Seven

Two days earlier, Cass and Rylan had cracked the cipher. The keyword had been *Robidoux*, one of the first Catholic missions in the area. Once Cass plugged it into her program, the deciphered message appeared. It read:

Not/a/high/hat/but/a/long/neck
And/horses/racing/near/a/sacred/cemetery
Beneath/a/tree/marked/CR

Cracking the cipher didn't necessarily tell them where the mine or next clue would be. They still had to figure out what the decoded message meant. Since then, they had spent a lot of time researching and trying to make connections to known geographical locations relevant to their search. The message didn't make any sense today, although it probably made sense to those living in the area in the 1800s. Rylan tried to confine his research to articles written in that era.

The "high hat," they figured, was Brigham Young or possibly the Mormons. That was the easy part since Wakara named the High Hats in his vision quest.

The "long neck" was tough and no one had any legitimate proposals. Suggestions varied from a giraffe, dinosaurs, a green heron, maybe a wine bottle, or even a guitar. None of those seemed to connect in any way with the other specified parameters.

"Horses racing" was another problem. It could be a racetrack located near a cemetery, but it had to be there in 1859 and as far as they had determined, there weren't any such things in Utah during that time period. Maybe it related to someone or a group that bred racing horses.

Sacred cemeteries were scattered throughout the area—most were on the Ute Reservation. Cass suggested they perform an exhaustive search on each cemetery that existed in the area in the 1850's. That might connect a dot and lead to understanding the message.

They came up with a dozen or so cemeteries, and they started looking into them.

Carver wandered into the house and found both of them buried in research. Both nodded acknowledgement but went back to their work. He went into the kitchen to find something to eat. He was about to take a bite of his sandwich when he heard Rylan shout, "I think I've got something. Listen to this." He started reading from a manuscript. "'Many old artifacts have been found there (on a vista above the Rock Creek Mission), a place where white men are not welcome. On a bench over looking that vista site there is a very old cemetery, a place sacred to the Utes.'

"Here's the real clincher," continued Rylan. " 'On the flat–top, close to that cemetery, there is a place where Ute Indians once raced their horses. Cut into a ledge rock just below that racetrack is a petroglyph depicting those racers of old.' "

"And there's more." He was really getting excited. " 'Among those stone carvings of Indians and their horses there is another figure, strangely out of place. It is the exact likeness of a giraffe!' "[1]

Rylan was sure they had found the general area described by Thomas or Caleb Rhoades in the cipher message, but the Rock Creek area was on the Ute Reservation, which posed a serious problem to their continued exploration. They were dealing with a cemetery on the reservation—a double whammy, since white men were not allowed on the reservation or sacred ground.

Rylan also added in passing that the Rhoades family had a lot of ties to the Rock Creek area, a region filled with a rich history of intrigue and danger for outsiders. Rylan then read them a fairly recent article about an event that occurred near the Rock Creek Mission.

"Harry Young, a construction contractor, was fishing in the area and found a wooden door leading to a mine. He tried to open the door and was grabbed from the back by two Indians and dragged to a log where the fingers on one of his hands were chopped off. He was sent on his way home and told if he returned, his head would be chopped off next."[2]

The story wasn't verified, but it seemed to Cass someone could verify it by just visiting Harry Young and looking at his hand.

Rylan found another story that occurred in the Rock Creek area that seemed to have a direct bearing on their latest decoded message. He read part of the story. "There was a giant cedar near the cemetery beneath which a tunnel had been discovered. Not far from the tunnel, an old pack saddle buried in a blanket was uncovered. Carved into the wooden frame of that old saddle are two initials, 'C.R.'. There can be little doubt that it belonged to Caleb Rhoades."[3]

"There's no way this is just another coincidence," Rylan almost shouted.

In the heated conversation that followed, Carver told them he would go alone to explore the site. "The only way that's going to happen is if I go by myself," Carver said. He had drawn a big line in the sand and was emphatic that no one was going to step over it. He looked Rylan and Cass directly in the eyes to make sure both of them understood.

"I want to help," Cass said, digging in her heels. "Let me come with you."

"Have you ever been out on night patrol? Do you know how to use night vision equipment? Have you ever lain in the grass for eight hours without moving for anything, including having to go to the bathroom or while a giant centipede crawls down your back? Have you ever pointed a gun at someone and pulled the trigger? Could you do it? What if someone had a gun pointed at me, could you pull the trigger? Do you know how to use a GPS and identify not only where you are going but also how to get back?"

"I don't know," Cass said, looking down, defeated.

"I can do all of that. I've done it. The problem is, I can't lie in the grass for eight hours if I have to worry about you being able to do the same. It makes it almost impossible for me to complete my task if I have to make sure you're safe."

"Okay, tell us what we're supposed to do while you're out there putting your life on the line for us poor helpless slobs," Cass retorted.

"You can arm yourselves, bolt the doors, and be prepared to call in the Rangers if I don't return."

"Oh, sure, you just calmly say, 'If I don't return.' There might be some emotion involved with that, don't you think? Don't you think we might care if you didn't come back?" Cass left the room and slammed the door for emphasis.

The next day Carver went to see a friend that had access to international satellite imagery. He wanted to study the Rock Creek area carefully from the air. Hopefully he could locate the cemetery and maybe even the giant cedar tree. Regardless, the imagery would allow him to get the lay of the land and maybe see what he would be up against.

While he was gone, Cass went out to the barn to feed the horses. "I've missed you," said a warm, distinctive voice behind her.

She almost jumped out of her skin. She hadn't heard anyone come into the barn behind her. She suddenly wished she had the pistol Carver had told her to carry with her at all times.

"Reber! What are you doing here?" Her blood pressure stabilized when she recognized the voice and the man, but she didn't like him sneaking up on her, and let him know.

He held both hands up in surrender. "I'm sorry if I frightened you, but if the mountain won't come to me, then I have to go to the mountain. Besides, I felt bad after our last outing. You wouldn't talk to me when you left for home. If I'm right, you believe I'm responsible for that fracas we had in the canyon."

She didn't know whether she blamed him or not, and that was part of the problem. "How did you find me out here? Have you been watching me and the house? And why are you always so interested in Carver Nash?"

Reber sat down on a bale of hay, delaying his answer. "I didn't want you to think I was spying on you or getting involved in your business, but I didn't know who else to ask. We've had some problems recently on the reservation with some hard-core professionals who aren't Indians. It appears there's a concerted effort by a powerful individual to try once again to locate the Mine. In fact, two Utes have recently been shot and killed in the area. There's no evidence to link the shootings to anyone, so everyone in the area is on high alert and looking over their shoulders.

"I know that doesn't answer your question, but it at least sets the stage. In the past, gold seekers were never considered dangerous, but this new threat is different. They are much more professional and equipped with some real high-tech gear. They don't like people getting in their way. They seem to have the money behind them and possibly have even bribed members of the tribal council. I, of course, told the tribe they had nothing to fear from you or your father, but they are still concerned about this Nash guy. He could be very dangerous."

"Carver, dangerous?" Cass was taken back, then recovered and said, "Well, I guess that depends. I certainly wouldn't like to be on his bad side. But all he really wants is to be left alone to enjoy his grandfather's farm."

"Mr. Nash isn't going to make a living off a poor, run-down farm. How does he plan to support himself? Is he independently wealthy? And if so, where did that money come from?"

"I don't know anything about his personal finances." It had

never entered her mind to wonder, but now, with the seed planted, she did. Just how did he support himself, anyway?

"Cass, he could be CIA, or on a mobster's payroll. Who does he work for? He isn't receiving retirement from the Army."

How did Reber know Carver wasn't taking retirement pay? She nearly asked him, but realized if she did, he might think she suspected him. That might put her in danger. Deciding to play it safe, she said, "I'm sorry, I don't know." Then, determined to lighten things up and bring the tone of their conversation back to its original footing, she asked, "So Reeb, have you taken any more of the missionary lessons?"

"I told you I was waiting until you did the teaching."

"That's just an excuse, Reeb. What happens if I show up next year and you're still not a member of the Church? You know I can't marry someone that's not a member of the Church."

"Look, Sister Edison, you just leave those minor details to me."

"That's what I'm worried about," she said, but she was smiling.

She wanted to ask Reber a million questions. She wanted to trust him. She wanted to know if he was really interested in the Church. She wanted to know about his mother and how he knew about Carver and the Rhoades document. She knew she shouldn't risk it until she knew where he stood, but how was she to learn where he stood if she couldn't ask him questions?

Just then, Rylan hobbled into the barn, looking like Captain Hook with a wooden leg. He had finally talked his doctor into a walking cast and, for an old guy, did pretty well at getting around. His sudden appearance surprised both Cass and Reber. Cass sputtered, "Dad, this is Reber Kolb, my friend."

Rylan stuck out his hand and shook hands with Reber. "Nice to meet you, Mr. Kolb. I didn't hear your vehicle drive up. Did you come on horseback?"

Reber laughed. "No, I walked here from the highway. A friend dropped me off. We don't use horses anymore on the reservation if a truck will work." He glanced at his watch and said, "In fact, I've got to get back to the highway to meet my friend in a few minutes."

"Did you stop by the house before you came out here to the

barn?" asked Rylan. Cass knew Rylan was making it clear he didn't appreciate Reber just showing up at the barn unannounced.

"Umm, no. I saw Sister Edison walking out to the barn, so I just followed her out here," he said.

"Following my daughter, hmm?" Rylan raised an eyebrow. "When you have some time, Cass, I need your help in the house." He turned to Reber. "It was nice to meet you, Mr. Kolb. We'll be going now." Rylan excused himself and went back to the house, his backward glance making it clear to Cass that he expected her to follow him, pronto.

"What happened to his leg?" Reber asked.

Cass opened her mouth, then closed it again. Not sure how much she should say, she replied, "You know when you get old, you fall over everything."

She could tell he wasn't buying into her explanation but he didn't press her. Instead he gave her his million dollar smile, bowed and said, "How about dinner this Saturday at seven?"

Cass was again presented with the dilemma. Maybe she could talk to Carver. Check that. She decided to talk to her father. "Umm, let me think about it. Give me your cell number and I'll let you know tomorrow."

"Dad, why were you so unfriendly to Reber?"

"Was I unfriendly?" Rylan lowered himself into a chair. "I thought I was the picture of hospitality."

"You were pretty abrupt with him."

Rylan fixed her with his gaze. "Are you not the one who told me what happened when you went out riding? And did you not tell me that you wondered if Reber was involved?"

"Yes, I did." She knew she should be more careful, but for some reason, she felt she should defend Reber to her father. Of course, if he turned out to be the bad guy, that wouldn't be so wise . . .

"Cass, your safety is my first priority. When I find a strange man in my barn, visiting my daughter behind my back, I tend to be a little unfriendly."

Carver let himself into the house just then, using the key Rylan had given him. Cass had mixed feelings about that key. She liked knowing Carver would be there for them no matter what, but on the other hand . . . he'd be there, no matter what. Whether he was wanted, or not.

"Rylan called me," he said to Cass's questioning look.

Cass closed her eyes and pinched the bridge of her nose. There was no such thing as privacy, not anymore. Well, she might as well get it over with.

"Reber invited me to dinner on Saturday," she said.

The room went silent.

"I think you should go," Carver said after a long moment. "Maybe we can learn who it is that's been causing us all these problems."

"You mean use Cass as bait?" Rylan was instantly on the defensive.

Cass looked at Carver. "*Now* you're willing to let me do some detective work? I can't do it if it's my idea, but if you think of it, it's okay?"

Carver raised a hand. "I don't think Reber's dangerous. He might know something, but I doubt he's the man we're looking for. Besides, I'd follow you and keep you in sight the whole time."

Cass glanced at Rylan. "I don't like it, but if Carver swears he'll watch you . . ." his voice trailed off. Cass could only hope he was starting to rethink this whole quest from beginning to end.

Rylan then surprised Cass by suddenly jumping to another subject. It was so random, even Carver was caught off guard. "Speaking of Saturday, Carver, would you give me one gold bar from each of the two caches we found?"

"What?"

"I want to get them assayed on Saturday. I have a sneaking suspicion they're going to have the same composition as the early Mormon gold coins, which was almost identical to the early Spanish gold bullion."

Rylan then went off into one of his lectures, trying to explain. "The early Mormon coins were not composed of pure gold. In fact, they contained specific amounts of silver and copper. Mormon coins taken to California by emigrants and traders were discounted twenty percent from their face value because of that impurity. Army troops stationed at Camp Floyd were ordered to not pay more than $4.50 for a five dollar Mormon gold piece."

Cass sat in the middle of the room, wondering how her father could just push her dilemma to the side so quickly. Then she realized what he was doing—burying himself in history to hide his worry. He'd done the same thing when her mother died, delving into books about the settlement of the Salt Lake Valley. It was the only way he knew to deal with his pain.

Rylan continued, "I don't believe it's just coincidental that the Mormon coins were composed of exactly the same minerals as the early Spanish gold bullion. Remember, the Spaniards only had crude mountain smelters to create their bullion, and the Mormons didn't have a smelter. In fact, the closest smelter was somewhere in Colorado."

"Rylan, are you sure you want to have the bars analyzed? If word gets out you've discovered Spanish gold, we'll have more than a few people up here to deal with," said Carver.

"Don't worry, I have a friend in the engineering department at the University of Utah. He won't say a word to anyone. But what I'd really like to do is find a way to have the gold on the angel Moroni on the Salt Lake Temple tested. Legend has it that the gold plating on Moroni is Rhoades gold."

Cass shook her head, but she noticed that Carver was really listening. Maybe her father's stories were finally getting through to him. Either that, or he was being brainwashed. It pretty much amounted to the same thing—it was an obsession, all right.

"Let me tell you another tidbit. I found it the other day while doing some research. If the Mormons didn't get gold from Rhoades, where did they get it? They seemed to come up with it every time they needed some cash. I read this excerpt from a journal entry of a guy named David Horne. He claimed that his grandfather's journal had this entry.

> My great-grandfather was George A. Smith, the famed
> southern Utah colonizer. . . . Soon after the Salt Lake Valley
> was settled, Brigham Young sent my great-grandfather on
> a mission to Nauvoo, Illinois . . . to meet with members of
> the Smith family. He took with him a bag of gold for each
> member of the Smith family, as a token of friendship from
> the church.[4]

How is it possible that the Utah Mormons were able to send
bags of gold to the Smiths when they entered the Salt Lake Valley
poor as church mice? Think about this for a minute because most
historical accounts place Brigham Young and the Utah Church at
direct odds with Joseph Smith's wife, Emma, and the members
of the Church that remained in Nauvoo. Yet here we have a little
known account of the Church leaders sending gold to Emma and
some of the Saints that remained. They wouldn't have been sending gold back to Nauvoo unless they had enough to take care of
themselves."

Cass went into the kitchen, her father's voice becoming a comfortable buzz in the background. She was strangely looking forward
to her date with Reber, even if it might hold some element of danger.
Although, she admitted to herself, maybe that was why she looked
forward to it.

Carver waited in an old Ford sedan that looked like it had spent
some hard years down on the farm. He parked on the side of the
road, which meant Cass would have to drive by when she left to go
to dinner with Reber. She passed him, but he waited for two more
cars to go by before he pulled out to follow her. He wanted to make
sure he was the caboose. As she passed through Kamas, a car pulled
out of an alley right behind her. The turn had been made a little too
quickly. The tail stayed right behind Cass as she took the highway

to Heber and didn't turn to take the more traveled highway to Park City. Carver wasn't close enough to be able to identify the driver but saw that he had a ponytail. Carver got the license number, flipped open his cell phone, and called his friend Lassiter to see if he could identify the owner. He got his reply within seconds. The vehicle had been stolen in Nevada six months ago.

Carver wore bib overalls, a red flannel shirt, and work boots. His old cowboy hat was pulled low on his head and he sported a fake handlebar mustache he'd gotten from the store. He had a boot knife strapped to his leg, and a shoulder holster carrying a specially manufactured Colt .45 beneath the baggy shirt. As additional security, he had placed a tracking device on Cass's vehicle and one in her purse. He didn't intend to lose her, no matter what happened. The receiving unit sat beside him on the seat. She was taking the highway towards Heber.

Mr. Ponytail was good at what he was doing; he knew how to tail someone without being seen. Cass drove into Heber and stopped in front of the Gold Miner restaurant. Ponytail drove down the street, flipped a U-turn, and waited until Cass had entered the restaurant before parking across the street.

Carver stopped behind a semitruck and watched. Ponytail didn't leave his vehicle. Carver exited his car and walked down the street. He found a group of trees that would conceal him and took up a position where he could observe both the restaurant and Ponytail. Adjusting his miniature high-powered binoculars, he discovered Ponytail had a super-sensitive listening device aimed toward the restaurant.

Mr. Ponytail was maybe thirty-five years of age and appeared to have the neck and shoulders of a wrestler. This man had the eyes of a professional—they never stopped moving.

Carver scanned the area, constantly on the lookout for anyone else that might be interested in Ms. Edison. No one appeared to show interest in anyone in the restaurant, but that didn't mean there wasn't someone inside. He would have to pay attention to see if anyone followed when she left.

It was past 9:00 PM when Cass left the restaurant with Reber

Kolb, whom he identified from a photo he had obtained from Lassiter. Reber reached to hold Cass's hand as they walked towards her car. Carver didn't see anyone following them from inside, but Ponytail had his listening device pointed in their direction. He would be recording their conversation, Carver knew that. He would like to hear it himself.

Cass leaned against her car, Reber standing way too close to her. Carver wanted to . . . well, he knew he didn't like Mr. Kolb. Reber bent over to kiss her, but she ducked under his arm and gave him a playful push. Carver felt himself start to move toward them and then stopped, gritting his teeth.

She climbed into her car, rolled down the window, and had some parting comments to make to Mr. Kolb before she drove away. Carver watched as Reber walked over to his truck, turned, and looked in the direction Cass had gone. He then got into his truck and drove away in the opposite direction.

Ponytail, on the other hand, was tracking Cass. Carver didn't want to get too close to Ponytail—besides, he had to make sure Reber was not in the chase. He got back in his car and watched his readout. Cass was moving towards home. After Carver made sure Reber was not coming back, he pulled out onto the highway to play follow-the-leader, making sure he was dead last.

As Cass approached Kamas, Carver watched as Ponytail turned off onto a dirt road and vanished into some trees. Carver intended to find out just who Mr. Ponytail was and why he had been tailing Cass, but first he had to make sure Cass got home safely.

He followed Cass through Kamas, stopped on the side of the road, and called Rylan. "Your daughter should be pulling into the driveway in five minutes. If she doesn't make it, call my cell immediately."

A few minutes later, Carver parked his car in a stand of trees near the dirt road Ponytail had taken. He left the car, following the dirt road while staying hidden.

He located Ponytail's car parked beside what looked like an abandoned home. He sensed a trap. Ponytail must have figured out that he was being followed and pulled off the road to find out who was behind him.

Fearing the worst, Carver flattened himself on the ground. At the same instant, he heard something strike a tree where he had been standing. There was no doubt about it—it was a bullet fired from a silenced gun. Ponytail must have had night vision equipment to be able to spot him. Carver slid down into a dry creek bed and immediately moved out, hidden from the view of the shooter. He had to even the odds. He donned his own night vision gear and soon came out of the creek bed behind his assailant. He was about to go after the shooter when he heard a noise in a tree overhead. He turned and fired, hitting a man who fell from the tree and dangled from a rappelling rope. He heard a thump to his left as the tree man's rifle hit the ground. The dart he fired from his gun had instantly paralyzed the guy.

He turned his attention back to Ponytail, who was almost on top of him, pistol pointed at Carver's center. Carver threw himself to the ground on the left, rolled sideways, threw out his leg, and connected with Ponytail's legs, sending him flying into a tree. He went down in a pile. Carver pulled a roll of duct tape from his backpack, put the guy's arms around a tree and taped them together. For good measure, he ran a strip of tape across his mouth. He then cut the hanging man down and taped him to another tree, gagging him as well.

Carver searched both men without finding any identification, but each had a cell phone. He went to Ponytail's vehicle and removed the listening and recording devices, slipping them in his backpack. He checked the house, which was boarded up and abandoned.

Carver placed a call on his cell phone. "Lassiter, this is Nash. I've got two Johns out here who have been neutralized and are ready for transport." He read the GPS coordinates to the location. "I'll call you with details later. I need information from these guys. Who are they? Who hired them? What are they doing? You know, anything you can get. Each guy has a cell phone in his pocket. Run a check on the numbers. Let's see who they like to talk to. Nash, out." He left the area to make sure Rylan and his daughter were safe, his cell phone ringing as he walked away from his trussed-up victims. It was Rylan. Cass was home.

Cass looked happy as she walked into the house. Rylan asked, "So, how was the hot date?"

"I'm still not sure about Reber. He obviously wants to move forward with our relationship, but I reminded him it wasn't moving off "go" until he becomes a member of the Church. He told me if that was all it took, he'd join tomorrow." She shook her head. "I didn't mention the we-suspect-he's-hiding-something thing."

"Probably wise," Rylan said. "Did you get any information?"

"No, not really. I think from a detective standpoint, tonight was a waste." She paused, her hand resting on the back of a chair. "Although, I did have fun. Strange, but I did."

Chapter Eight

"I've already told you, you can't go. It's simply too dangerous," Carver said in a hushed but firm tone that indicated he wasn't about to change his mind.

"You're not being reasonable," Cass told him. "You need a driver."

Rylan finally tried to act as mediator. "Carver, she's right. She can drive the vehicle, drop you off close to Rock Creek, and then drive on into Roosevelt and stay in a motel until you call. You can't just leave your vehicle parked on the side of the road. That's not a good idea."

"I'll think about it," Carver said, breaking eye contact with Cass. He could have knocked her over with a feather. She didn't believe he would ever give in to anyone, least of all to her.

In spite of all the distractions, Rylan had continued his research. His desk looked like a bomb had exploded in a paper factory. He wished they would get as excited about the quest as he was. He dug out a letter and tried to get their attention. "Hey, you know those two gold bars I took to have tested? I got the results back. Both bars are almost identical: gold 82 percent, silver 17 percent, and copper 1 percent. That's exactly the same mineral percentage of the early Mormon coins. Remember, the Mormon mints didn't smelt any gold, they just took what they had, rolled it, and stamped out the coins. It's not just coincidental that the Mormon gold and the Spanish gold have the same makeup. This is further proof that the early Mormon coins came from gold provided by Thomas Rhoades. Either that, or the early Church found its own cache."

Cass shook her head. "That doesn't prove Thomas Rhoades got gold from a sacred mine. If he put that gold in the box you found. Well, he could have found it anywhere."

Carver noticed it was almost dark outside as his phone buzzed. He walked into the other room, away from Cass and Rylan, and spoke softly. He came back faster than he left. "Lock the doors and don't let anyone in until I return. If I'm not back in an hour, call the police."

He slipped out the back door into the darkness, making sure no light escaped as he went out the door. He had his knife in hand and moved quickly into the trees. He had been told the approximate location of the two men that had the cabin under surveillance, but his night vision gear would greatly assist him in pinpointing their exact location.

He caught the first man by surprise as he fiddled with his electronic listening device and was out cold before he had a chance to defend himself. He never realized Carver had jammed the signal. A quick search and Carver found a satellite phone mixed with the listening equipment. Just as he secured cuffs on the man's hands and feet, Carver heard a car start and drive away. The other man had apparently decided he had something else to do.

Carver placed another call. "Lassiter, one of them got away. He left in a vehicle, headed towards Marion. You can probably see him on the satellite link. The one here can be retrieved at your convenience. There's no rush because he won't be walking anywhere very soon."

He hung up the phone and returned to the cabin. Three knocks and the door opened. Cass stood just inside the house, holding the door. "What was that all about?"

"Nothing. I just wanted to make sure we didn't have any people out there trying to make our business theirs."

"Wait a minute," said Cass. "You're telling me nothing just happened? You had us in lockdown."

"It was the newspaper. They wanted to renew my subscription. I don't understand how they got my cell number or why they were calling so late at night. I gave them a hard time."

"I don't know how you can joke about something like this," Cass said.

Carver wanted them to be cautious, but he didn't want them to worry about being safe in their own house. He was just glad Lassiter had noticed the intruders on the satellite imagery and warned him.

Cass was particularly appealing when she got her dander up. He watched as her expression softened. She appeared to have instantly lost her accusatory attitude. Carver knew she wasn't buying his story, but maybe she would let the subject drop.

"How about we take a little walk? It's so nice out tonight."

Carver was surprised by the invitation and responded with a weak, "Okay." He had no idea what she had up her sleeves, but he didn't think she was extremely dangerous.

"Dad, we'll just be outside."

Rylan was buried in one of his books and nodded his acknowledgment.

Cass was a tall person. She didn't just stroll along enjoying the beauty of the moment—she intended to get where she was going. Carver easily kept up with her but was surprised by her aggressive stride. He noticed the smell of lavender-scented shampoo and liked the clean smell that drifted across as her hair blew slightly in the wind. She was beautiful, and his recognition of that fact didn't make it any easier to find a safe topic of discussion.

It had been a long time since he had really looked at a woman. The last girl that meant anything to him was before his mission. He had believed that she was his soul mate and would be forever. Then he had left on his mission, and the next thing he knew, his forever soul mate had married his best friend. Since then he had purposely avoided any relationship. He still hadn't figured out how something that was "forever" could end.

But Cass, well, she had snuck up on him. Maybe it was her take-charge attitude and her unwillingness to back down. She was willing to meet him eye-to-eye. He couldn't slip anything by her—in fact, he was sure she could see right through him every time he told her a half-truth. It wasn't that he was purposely trying to lie to her. He just wanted her to be safe and not have to worry about certain problems.

She pulled him out of his musings with a question. "I understand why Superman never married Lois Lane. It was because he didn't want her exposed to his problems for the rest of her life. What's your excuse?"

He was surprised by her question and took a minute before trying to respond, "I've never found anyone that would have me. You know, it's hard to take the country out of the boy." It was the best he could come up with on the spot, although he wished he knew how to just open up to her. It would be nice to share his thoughts and feelings with her, but he had to admit, he didn't know how.

Cass wanted to kick herself. Sometimes her mouth just starting working all by itself without first having the approval of her brain. Even though she had known him for more than a month, he hadn't said more than two words about his personal life. So the first thing out of her mouth, she asks him why he's not married. Stupid, she thought, and wondered about finding a rock to hide under.

She was intrigued by Carver. She had heard warnings all her life to be careful of the strong, silent type, and now she knew why. She wanted to know what he was thinking, particularly about her. Maybe he only liked brunets? Maybe she was too tall? Maybe too bossy? Maybe he hated all women? Maybe he really was Superman?

At least a minute of silence had passed. She was struggling to find the right words to cover up her faux pas.

He surprised her and answered, "I'll tell you what—if you

answer your own question, then I will."

Hmmm. What the heck, she thought. "Well, I guess you could say I never had any real interest in anyone until after my mission. I met two different guys at the Y and at different times felt that I might be able to develop a relationship with either one, but it didn't pan out. No one's ever rung my bell."

"That's it? No heartbreak romances? No one died on you? You just never found anyone you liked?"

"Hey, have you been around the math department at BYU or Yale?"

Carver smiled. She couldn't remember the last time she had seen him smile. "That bad?"

"Worse," she responded. "I mean, have you ever seen a guy with the Pythagorean Theorem tattooed around his arm?"

He laughed again. She liked his laugh. It wasn't loud and obnoxious. It was kind of soft and inviting.

Neither of them said anything for a minute as they kept walking. Finally, she stopped and looked him straight in the eye. "Well, I'm waiting."

He sat down on a log and motioned her to sit down next to him. "Not much to tell. It's the old story of boy meets girl, boy falls for girl. Girl tells boy he is the beginning and the end and will wait until the end of time. The only problem is girl forgets and marries the boy's best friend."

"How long ago?"

"While I was on my mission," he said.

"That's a long time ago. You should have recovered from that fall by now—or were you permanently disabled?"

"Oh, I finally came to realize I could never have married her. The problem is, I just haven't found a girl that understands the definition of forever. But then I guess no one's ever really rung my bell either." He rubbed his hand along his jaw. "Sometimes I wonder if it wasn't just that my pride got hurt and I was afraid to try again."

"Chicken, huh?"

"Maybe. And how about you?"

"Definitely not," she smiled.

Rylan, Cass, and Carver sat around the table discussing the upcoming field trip to Rock Creek, although Cass thought it was more like a briefing for a small covert mission than a discussion. Rylan expressed his disfavor of having to sit home while Cass and Carver went to try to find what was buried near the giant cedar at the old Rock Creek cemetery. Cass finally felt needed, even if all she had to do was drive the getaway car. She didn't even complain that Carver was the only one who had any input on the plan.

Carver committed Rylan and Cass to absolute secrecy, prohibiting any phone conversations about the excursion or anything to do with the latest cipher. As a further security precaution, he installed equipment that would jam any listening device near the Edison home. He had also scanned the home for bugs. It was clean.

Carver then briefed them in detail on how the operation would be conducted. "I was able to obtain some recent satellite imagery of the area. It appears the area is all but forgotten, except for the Utes and some archaeological thieves. The Utes, however, maintain a decent protective ring around the cemetery. Recently, it seems there have been some uninvited folks helping themselves to artifacts in the area. I think they were really looking for clues to the location of the Mine. The Park Service has a ranger permanently stationed nearby, but the Utes are much more vigilant and stop anyone that tries to come close to the reservation, and particularly the cemetery."

Carver continued, "I've also learned that the Ute Tribal Council is on high alert, which might also explain the tight security at the cemetery."

Rylan spread out several topographical maps and began indicating points of interest and concern. "Right here is the junction of the Duchesne River and Rock Creek. Just above the junction is this small vista, and this is a bench which overlooks the vista. Back here is the old cemetery, and here is the area where the Utes once raced their horses."

Rylan scribbled some notes on a sheet of paper. "That's the very spot where they found Caleb Rhoades's old pack saddle in 1992, so if you can find the old mine tunnel, you should be able to locate the giant cedar and then find whatever is buried close to it."

Carver replied, "I think the mine tunnel is in this area." He pointed at a place on the map, then grabbed an aerial photograph of Rock Creek. "If you look right here, you can see a grove of cedars, but I don't see anything that would be considered giant. However, it's hard to tell from this viewpoint."

Rylan pulled out another book and found the page he wanted. "Carver, there's supposed to be a trail on the side of the canyon opposite the cemetery leading to Sadie's Flat. About halfway up the trail, there's a big round rock with a deep V groove cut in the top. It's called a sighting rock. It's used like a rifle sight. If you look through the notch, it should show you where the cave opening is, which could be very helpful since I understand the Utes have covered up and hidden the old cave entrance."

"That's great recon work, Rylan. I have a couple of things I need to check on. I'll be back in a while. Do you think you can keep your daughter close by until I come back?"

Carver returned about two hours later and gathered the three-some together. "Okay, here's my plan," he said. "I'll have Cass drop me off right here on Route 35 at about 8:20 PM. That should give me enough time to get to the sighting rock before dark. Once I locate the entrance to the tunnel, I'll hike over to it in the dark. I should be able to locate the giant cedar tree, if it's still there. I'll dig around and hopefully be out of there before daylight.

"Cass, I've got two satellite phones. I'm going to give you one. I should be able to finish that night. If I don't call you by 6:00

AM you'll have to wait around Roosevelt for another day. If you don't hear from me by the next morning, you'd better call the Forest Service and cops to come looking for me."

Carver looked at her, his eyebrow raised. "While you're in Roosevelt, Cass, you need to make yourself as inconspicuous as possible. Don't draw any attention to yourself. Take some old baggy clothes and find a John Deere baseball hat. You've got to become one of the local townspeople, not a PhD candidate at Yale. You've got to talk like them, walk like them, be one of them. It will be best to stay out of sight, if possible, because I'm afraid you can't hide the fact that you're a beautiful math wizard who doesn't belong in Roosevelt."

"Was that a compliment?"

Carver ignored her. Rylan decided it was his turn.

"I want both of you to be careful, okay? There have been some strange things happening in the Rock Creek area. Some are scary and some are just intriguing. For example, in 1969, two fishermen found a hole near the waterline of the creek. They were able to squeeze through the hole and inside they found an elaborate water trap. They swam under it and found five different chambers, or rooms. In one room they found eighty gold bars, each heavier than a man could lift. Later, they went back to try to remove a few. They had some pretty harrowing experiences but were able to escape with a couple. Apparently they were worth enough to keep the men in chips for the rest of their lives.

"However, not everyone was as lucky as those two fishermen. Seems that more than one person has lost his life looking for gold in the area. White people are not invited nor welcome at all in the Rock Creek area."

That evening Carver met Cass at a movie theater in Heber. Step one of the plan. She drove her own car and did not try to lose anyone that might have been following her. At 6:30 she and Carver silently slipped out the side exit door of the theater. He had a truck waiting that Cass had never seen. It was beat-up and vintage, but Carver assured her that it was in top mechanical condition. He told Cass to drive while he climbed in the backseat.

They drove out of Heber, heading towards Strawberry Reservoir. One mile out of town, Carver asked her to pull over and stop. They sat there for ten minutes waiting and watching. It didn't appear anyone was tailing them.

"I think it's okay. No one seems to be following us," said Carver.

"Where did you find this truck?" Cass asked. "It looks like it belongs in the junkyard, but it does respond when I push on the gas pedal."

"Hey, no one in Roosevelt will even notice. It looks like it came off any farm in the area," said Carver.

They drove in silence until they passed Strawberry Reservoir and on to Fruitland on Highway 40. Just past Fruitland they took route 208 towards Tabiona, turning east on Route 35. Carver continued to check to see if they were being followed, but it seemed they were in the clear. He had changed into a night combat uniform. He had his backpack loaded with gear along with his sniper rifle, which was broken down and strapped to the side of the pack.

Rylan didn't like being left behind and had trouble finding things to keep him occupied. While he was channel surfing, someone knocked at the door. He stuck his gun under his shirt, peered through the peephole and looked straight into the face of Reber Kolb. He opened the door and said, "Cass isn't available right now."

"I didn't come to see Cassandra, I came to speak to you, Mr. Edison," he said. "Do you mind if I come in?"

"Why?"

"It's a long story. Can we sit down?"

Rylan motioned Reber toward the chairs on the porch. "You have my attention," he said.

Reber blew out his breath and said, "Mr. Edison, I work for the Ute Tribe. I'm in charge of security. During the last year we've had some very serious problems on the reservation. Someone with a lot of money has been tossing his weight around. This guy and his thugs are professionals who are very serious about what they are doing."

"What does that have to do with me?" asked Rylan.

"Well, it seems that you have become involved in the hunt for the Rhoades Mine, which is what the other guys are after. We don't know the extent of your search or how it will impact the reservation. What we don't want is a lot of people wandering the hills, looking for the mine. It has been lost for a long time and we would like it to remain that way. More importantly, I don't want to see Cass placed in any position where she can be harmed."

"What makes you think I'm searching for lost gold?" Reber knew more than he should have. Rylan wondered just how much he knew and more importantly, how he knew.

"Let's put it this way. I know you found a coded message purportedly written by Thomas Rhoades that you hope will lead you to the mine."

"How do you know that?"

"Mr. Edison, let's talk, man-to-man. I'm not going to lie to you and I don't expect you to lie to me. I know you don't have any reason to trust me, but believe me, I'm one of the good guys."

"I always put my hand over my wallet when someone asks me to trust them," replied Rylan.

Reber didn't comment. "I have another reason for coming here to talk to you," he said. "You see, I've had some pretty strong feelings for your daughter ever since she was a missionary on the reservation. I want to date her and see if anything develops, but right now, she doesn't know if she can trust me."

He continued without letting Rylan say anything. "Mr. Edison, can you tell me why you are looking for the Rhoades gold?"

"Reber, all of my life I've been able to tell if someone was lying.

I believe you, but I still have some concerns. As for courting my daughter, well, that's up to her." Rylan had no idea how Cass felt about Reber, and couldn't have given the young man a hint if he'd wanted to. "The Rhoades Mine—you ask an interesting question. Let me try to answer it as honestly and as best I can.

"I've lived in this area for as long as I can remember. I've always heard stories of the lost mine. The story and the legend have always intrigued me, particularly Chief Wakara. He is a man of which legends are made. He wasn't so impressed with the wealth of the mine and what he could buy with the gold, but with his obligation to protect it. There aren't many people who would let billions of dollars of gold sit in a cave and not take any to make their lives more comfortable."

Reber asked, "So, do you actually believe such a place existed?"

"Certainly, I believe it. I also believe there are things of more value in that mine than some gold bullion bars."

"And that would be?"

"Golden plates and artifacts."

"And why would they be important to you, Mr. Edison?"

"Well, Reber, my daughter taught you about the Book of Mormon while she was on her mission. The Mormons believe the Book of Mormon was translated by Joseph Smith from golden plates which were records of the ancient people that lived on this continent, some of whom are your ancestors. Now think about it. Suppose there are some golden plates in that mine, created by your ancestors as a record of their time on this earth. What do you think that would say about the Book of Mormon?"

"Are you telling me you don't care about all the gold and money you could take from such a mine, Mr. Edison?"

"Why do I need more money? I've got all I need right here."

"That seems a bit altruistic, doesn't it?"

Rylan was perturbed at his audacity, but at least he wasn't sugar-coating everything he said now. "Imagine having the ability to prove that the whole legend surrounding the Carre-Shin-Ob is true. Imagine being able to confirm the mythical legend of Thomas

Rhoades, Chief Wakara, and sacred gold."

"So where does that get you, Mr. Edison?" asked Reber.

"How about calling me Rylan."

"Let me tell you a story, Rylan, because it has bothered me for a long time. Wakara and Brigham Young must have had a pretty close relationship because Brigham adopted Wakara as his son. But then in 1864, President Lincoln asked Brigham Young about establishing the Uinta Valley as a reservation for the Utah Indians. President Young told President Lincoln, and I quote, 'that the land was so utterly useless that its only purpose was to hold the other parts of the world together.' In other words, it was perfect for an Indian Reservation.

"Brigham Young spoke negatively about my land and my people. But he only said what he thought after Wakara had allowed Thomas Rhoades and his son Caleb to take enough gold out of the mine to rescue the fledgling church from financial ruin. I guess my question is, did Brigham Young adopt Wakara so he could get the gold and then abandon him and his people as soon as he didn't need them?"

Before Rylan could respond, Reber added, "That's one reason I never joined when Cass was teaching me. I didn't like Brigham Young."

Rylan laughed. "You need to understand Brigham a little better. He said a lot of things that didn't sound right at the time. For instance, when he told President Lincoln about the Uinta Mountains being worthless, don't you think that sealed the deal and insured the Utes would get that land?"

"For sure!"

"Well, maybe that's why he said it."

"Are you saying he wanted us to have that land and responded accordingly?"

"Well, I'm not saying that's the reason he made the statement, but it could have been. You know he wasn't a great friend of the federal government."

Rylan and Reber discussed religion and the gold for two more hours. Finally Reber said, "That brings me to the real reason why I need to speak to you. Right now, no one, Indian or white, knows the exact location of the Rhoades Mine. Oh, there are a lot of people who think they know, but they don't.

"Maybe we can blame that on Brigham Young, too. When he dedicated the Manti temple, he prayed," Reber drug out a piece of paper from his back pocket and read,

> We ask thee, in the name of Jesus Christ thy son, that thou wilt hide up the treasures of the earth, that no more may be found in this section of the country. Wilt thou, O Father, rule and overrule in this? But we say not our will but thy will be done.[1]

"So maybe the Lord heard Brigham's prayer," Reber continued, "Maybe that's one of the reasons no one has ever been able to find the mine. The secret wasn't passed down from Wakara to any younger brave."

He looked at Rylan, his eyes growing intense. "I think you might have some information that's going to change everything. Maybe, just maybe, it's time for the mine to be found. Maybe it's time for the treasures to no longer be hidden."

"What are you asking me?" Rylan wondered.

"I just don't want you to inadvertently lead a bunch of the thugs to the mine. There would be a lot of bloodshed."

Chapter Nine

"Take this cell phone, but don't call me under any circumstance; I'll call you. You know the rules. We're almost there. See up ahead, where the road makes a curve to the left and there are some trees on the right side? When you take the curve, hug the right shoulder and slow down. I'm going to jump. I'll meet you at the same place when I'm done, after I call."

"Carver," she said. She paused, pinching her fingers against the bridge of her nose. "Be careful, okay?"

Cass slowed enough for Carver to hop out, hit the ground, and disappear in the trees in a matter of seconds. Cass continued on down the road, slightly increasing her speed. She drove on for about two miles, blinking the tears out of her eyes enough to be able to see the road. Then she pulled over and stopped. She was a mess, an emotional basket case. She didn't like him going into danger by himself and she couldn't do a thing but sit and wait. Finally she pulled out and started down the road again.

Carver had the map of the area in his head and knew exactly where he was and where he needed to go. He figured he had a good three-mile hike to reach his destination. The sun was just dropping below the mountains, so he reckoned he had about an hour before dark. He would be traveling as the crow flies, which meant he wouldn't have a trail. If he hustled, he figured he could make his destination before dark.

Before he left the trees, he assembled his rifle, affixed the sound suppressor, and slung it over his shoulder. Then he checked his pistol, knife, and backpack. He was carrying some high-tech equipment, including binoculars, which he used to scan the area in the direction he would be going. As he scrutinized the area, nothing of interest caught his attention, so he set his course and headed out. His night combat suit blended in with his surroundings, making him almost invisible.

He reached his destination in just under an hour. He had stopped several times to survey the area for lookouts or guards. Nothing he saw looked suspicious. He slowed his speed and took extra stealth precautions as he approached Rock Creek. He wanted to be invisible to anyone watching, but more importantly, he wanted to know the location of any observer.

It didn't take him long to find the trail on the side of the canyon opposite of the cemetery. Dark was closing in fast as he started up the trail. He picked up his pace to ensure that he reached the sighting rock before dark. His watchful surveillance continued as he ascended the trail. It wasn't long until he located the rock.

He froze when he heard the sound of a vehicle across the canyon. The sound came from a park ranger who was leaving the area for the night. As soon as the vehicle cleared the area, Carver used the sighting rock to try to identify the critical landmarks.

Something was wrong. The topography wasn't right. The rock was either pointing him in the wrong direction or his reconnaissance was inaccurate.

At that minute, he heard two Ute Indians talking quietly to each other, and hid behind the sighting rock. They were near the cemetery. As they finished speaking, they split and went in opposite directions. Carver watched both of them, noticing that they each carried a portable radio. Each guard reached elevated observation positions, which gave them perfect vantage points of the entire area surrounding the cemetery. Each also carried a rifle and pistol.

Carver again checked the sighting rock. He carefully examined the rock from top to bottom and noticed that the soil supporting it had been disturbed. The rock was huge, but it was obvious it had somehow been intentionally rotated. Carver couldn't tell how far it had been moved and gave up using it.

He carefully studied the area behind the cemetery where he figured the tunnel should be. He noticed a pile of stones that were colored differently from the surrounding stone, and concluded that they had been brought in to fill the outlet of the old tunnel. He also made a mental note to carefully avoid the areas the sighting rock pointed out, as those areas would most likely be booby-trapped to catch an unsuspecting treasure seeker.

As he scanned the tree line near the tunnel outlet, he found several large cedars, but nothing that would be classified as giant. He decided he would have wait until he got up close to search the area for a large stump or the remains of an extra large tree.

He hadn't counted on dealing with the two guards, who had excellent vantage points to see all of the area surrounding the cemetery. He wasn't afraid of a shoot-out, but didn't want to face the cavalry that would be sure to come to the rescue if they were summoned.

He slipped down the trail and across the valley, almost silently. His night vision equipment assisted him as he kept his attention focused on the guards. He spent over two hours searching the ground around the trees and had no luck finding any evidence indicating the location of where a large tree had once grown.

He noticed that the closest guard was dozing, and ventured away from the trees into the clearing. About one hundred yards from where he thought the tunnel opened, and very close to the cemetery, he found the stump he'd been looking for.

Carver turned to look at the dozing guard. He was now awake and looking directly towards Carver's location. Carver immediately flattened himself on the ground next to the old stump and didn't move for several minutes. Then he adjusted his night vision equipment, focusing on the closest guard, who studied the area around the cemetery. Something had drawn his attention, although Carver didn't think he'd been spotted. He listened as the guard spoke into his radio, then started moving towards Carver's position. Carver situated himself between two old gravestones, able to defend himself, if discovered.

The second guard remained in position but was on alert. The first walked around the area where Carver had been. Carver was glad he'd been able to wipe away all footprints and signs that he'd been there. He slowed his breathing as the guard walked within twenty feet of where he lay. He heard the crackle of a radio as the guard stopped and looked directly where Carver hid. Carver's rifle was aimed and ready to fire.

Cass pulled off the highway in an isolated location and changed into her "Roosevelt" clothing. Looking in a mirror, she was pleased—not even her best friend would be able to recognize her. She thought she had her emotions under control as she climbed back into the beat-up truck and drove through town, surveying the available motels. On her return trip, she stopped at what looked like the cheapest. The desk clerk hardly paid her any attention except to ask for thirty-five dollars for the night, which she paid with cash, no identification required.

Keeping herself occupied for the next twelve hours was going to be a problem. She knew she was not going to be able to sleep—her brain was on full worry mode and she didn't know how to shut it off. She didn't like the thought of Carver out there all by himself. She hoped she could distract herself by studying two very complicated mathematical papers she intended to use to support her thesis. If she could get into either of them, she would be lost to the world.

She was restless, unable to sit and study anything. She was worried about her father, but Carver had promised that his mysterious friend Lassiter would be keeping an eye on the homestead, so she tried to simply trust him. But she wanted to know where Carver was, and what he was doing. She was up and down, walking circles in the room at three in the morning. *You would think* she thought to herself, *that after eighteen years of school, I would have learned to control my mind.*

She tried to sleep, but that was fruitless. She tried TV and watched a rerun of *Scrubs* and then the news, hoping her body would convince her brain she needed sleep. She set her alarm for 6:00 AM and finally was able to drift off.

She was already awake at six. She had been lying there for half an hour, waiting for the alarm to go off or the phone to ring. The alarm sounded, but the phone remained silent. She would have preferred it the other way around.

She got up and changed into her traveling clothes, tried TV again, tried reading one of her math papers again, and finally resorted to bodily punishment, push-ups and sit-ups. She was getting hungry and the clock was doing a snail crawl. Carver must have run into some trouble. She wasn't sure she could take another night in this hotel.

Panic gripped her like an iron claw. What could have gone wrong? He should have called her by now. The delay only meant he had encountered a problem. She wanted to do something, but was afraid if she did, it would just make things worse. She tried to calm herself. She said a silent prayer and steeled her nerves. He was okay; he had to be.

At 10:00 AM she decided she might just have to be here for another day, and she needed to get some food. She chose McDonald's because it was quick and matched her present station in life. She used the drive-through, got her food, and hurried back to her room.

When she walked in, she froze. Her papers were scattered everywhere, drawers all half open, and the bed torn apart. She had only been gone twenty minutes, max. Someone had located her and was now watching her. She knew she had to do something. If they were watching her, then they could follow her when Carver called. She didn't want to sit still and do nothing, but she wasn't sure what she could do.

Then she had an idea.

Carver had not been able to move. The guard had raised his rifle. Apparently he thought he had seen something and was using the telescopic sight to inspect the area. Carver put the guard in his crosshairs, preparing for the worst. At the last moment the radio crackled again. The guard lowered his gun and continued on his round, continuing to circle the cemetery until dawn.

Carver had used his knife to dig his own shallow grave. He thought it was appropriate for his location. He then slipped in the hole and covered himself with dirt, making a little mound over him. He left his head exposed until it became light, then he laid a wooden carving from the adjacent burial plot over his head, hoping it would look like it had just been blown over.

All day he lay in his makeshift grave without moving. He had been taught different forms of self-hypnosis methods. They all required total relaxation, otherwise it would not have been possible to remain perfectly still without muscle cramping and boredom getting the best of him. And yet he could not allow himself to slip into a state so deep that he wasn't aware of his surroundings. It was a delicate balance that required total and absolute concentration. Occasionally his mind drifted to thoughts of Cass, which he could not let occur if he wanted to retain his self-induced trance.

He occasionally heard people talking and a few vehicles driving by, but no one actually ventured into the cemetery. Then, nothing. He remembered that the two guards hadn't shown up until past dusk the day before, and he hadn't heard a sound in more than an hour. He figured he would have a couple of hours to do his exploration before the night guards showed up.

He crawled out of his grave and cleaned the area, making sure the night shift hadn't returned. Finding no one, he quickly went to the old stump and started digging. It took about an hour and he had excavated completely around the tree before he hit something solid.

Ten minutes later he uncovered an old pair of saddle bags,

wrapped in several blankets and covered by animal skins. He tried to lift them from the hole but the leather broke against the weight. He decided he would have to transfer whatever was in the saddle bags to his backpack.

He opened the bags and found each stuffed with gold coins, which nearly filled his backpack. He also discovered a small wooden box, which he placed on top of the coins. Last, he found a satchel similar to what they had found before, and he guessed it contained more documents. He placed it in an inside pocket of his night gear. He figured he could dump the gold if he had to, but the documents would be more important. Then he moved the wooden box to a leg pocket. It was probably as important as the documents.

He immediately began to fill in the cavity with dirt. He had almost finished when he heard the night guards approaching. He wanted to finish his work but didn't have time. He slipped into the trees, hoping they would not discover the shallow depression by the old stump.

He was not so lucky. The guards spotted it immediately. One spoke into his radio while the other went closer to investigate. Carver had already begun his exodus. He moved through the trees and up the hill as quickly and quietly as he could. He needed to go southeast but he headed directly northeast. He wanted anyone searching for him to go the wrong way.

Carver heard three or four vehicles approaching from two directions. If they determined he'd been there recently, they would seal off the roads, making it impossible for Cass to pick him up.

From his vantage point, he heard them talking—they thought he was still in the area. He needed to cause a distraction. On a hunch, he threw a couple of rocks into the area he had viewed through the sighting rock. A couple of explosions went off that sounded like grenades. He had his distraction.

He figured he shouldn't go back to Route 35. It was too isolated and traffic was too easily checked. He headed for Highway 40 instead. If he drew a straight line southeast through the boonies, he estimated he would intersect with Highway 40 about ten miles east of Duchesne, and it would take him about nine hours to get there, if he hustled. He used his wrist GPS to give him directions and set off at a jog. His pack must have weighed at least eighty pounds, because it was heavier than a fully-loaded combat pack. He would abandon it if the going got hard, hiding it if necessary. His rifle was excess baggage and he buried it in a sandy ravine.

He would call Cass at about five in the morning and give her a location and time for the pickup. On he went, alternating between jogging and walking. He noticed headlights of vehicles obviously searching for him, all traveling off-road in what looked like a well-orchestrated search pattern. A number of vehicles drove up towards Rock Creek Road and returned to Highway 35. He knew if they had good trackers, they would find his trail at first light. Following him tonight would be impossible—it was simply too dark.

Then he heard a couple of rifle shots and froze.

Cass knew she had to lose the truck and find some other mode of transportation, and that was a problem. She wasn't a car thief by trade. She bought some time by going into the hotel office and paying for an additional day. She looked around the motel grounds without trying to be too conspicuous but didn't see anyone who looked out of place.

She waited in her room until dusk, gun in hand. Then she placed a phone call.

"Reber, is that you?"

"Yes. Is this Cass?"

"Reber, I need a favor. No questions asked," she said.

"Name it."

"I need a car I can use for a couple of days."

"That's it?" he said. "Where are you? I'll bring it to you."

"No. I want you to leave it in front of the market in Duchesne at six in the morning. Leave the keys in the ignition. I'll call you about returning it in a day or two."

"This sounds very mysterious."

"No questions, remember?" she asked. "What kind of car will you leave?"

"It will be a brown Ford pickup. The keys will be under the floor mat."

"I have one other favor."

"What's that?"

"At 6:05 in the morning, I am going to leave a green pickup truck in front of the café in Duchesne. The keys will be in the ignition. Can you have someone in the cafe before 6:00 AM and tell him to leave precisely at 6:10 AM, get in my truck and drive west, then keep it for me?"

"No problem," he said.

"Reeb, I don't want anyone following me when I leave. I mean it—not you or anyone else. Do I have your promise?"

"Scout's honor," he replied.

She hung up, instinctively feeling she'd done the right thing, although the lingering question remained in the back of her mind—just who was Reber Kolb?

The rifle shots came from the area around Rock Creek. They were not directed towards Carver as far as he could tell. He needed to put as much distance as he could between himself and his pursuers—come light, they would know which way he was heading.

He decided to throw in a little misdirection. He turned due north to make any pursuers think he was heading towards Talmage. This detour would cost him valuable time, but might save him in the morning. He headed north for about a half mile, making sure his tracks were visible until he found a rock formation that ran south. He jogged on the rocks for about a quarter of a mile, stopped, set his GPS back to his original destination, and headed out.

At 5:00 AM it was just getting light. Carver placed his call to Cass. Her phone rang two times before she picked up.

"Carver, is that you?"

"Yes."

"Are you all right?"

"I will be when I see your smiling face," he said.

"I've had some problems," she replied. "But I think I've solved them."

"Are you okay?" he asked.

"Yeah, I'm fine. A little scared right now, but I'm okay. I'm on my way to Duchesne to pick up another car."

"What?"

"Carver, I don't have time right now. What time and where do you want me to pick you up?"

"I have a new location," he said.

"Time and place."

"Ten miles east of Duchesne on Highway 40, at 6:00 AM. Can you be there?"

"Make it 6:10, but I'll be driving a brown pickup truck and coming from the west."

"You didn't like the one I left for you?"

"I'll explain everything when I pick you up. Did you find what you were looking for?"

"Yes, but I have some people in hot pursuit."

"Will you be okay until 6:10?"

"Look for something on the side of the highway when you get ten miles east of Duchesne. I'll be there."

Cass watched the cars behind her closely. She didn't think anyone had followed her, but then, what did she know? She was new to this cloak-and-dagger stuff. She pulled up in front of the café in Duchesne, went inside, and immediately left by the back door. She was so nervous she could barely walk. Her heart pounded and she was sure her face was stark white. She took a back alley north until she found Reber's truck. A sigh of relief swept over her and she said a silent prayer. She slipped inside, pushed her hair under her hat, and pulled it down, hoping to look like a farmer. She started the truck and headed east on Highway 40, constantly checking her rearview mirror. Her pulse rate was still substantially above normal. She wasn't cut out for this stuff.

Again, it didn't appear anyone was following. She hoped the switch would have anyone following her going in the wrong direction. As the miles rolled by, her breathing returned to normal; well, normal if she had just completed a marathon. She knew now why she had chosen math. Suspense was trying to find a new prime number, and no one would be shooting at you if you did.

As she neared the nine-mile mark, her cell phone rang. "How close are you?" Carver asked.

"Nine miles east of Duchesne. Is there a problem?" She gripped the steering wheel harder and pressed on the gas. She was so close.

"Kind of," he responded. "That someone who was on my trail is closing fast."

"I'll be there in one minute." An eternity, she thought.

"Okay, just past the ten mile point you'll see a culvert running under the road. Slow down as you approach it. Make it look like you're throwing something out the window. I'll slip in the bed of the truck. As soon as I land, take off and don't stop for anything until you reach Myton. At that point, I'll get in the cab and we'll go back to Roosevelt."

"Okay." She wiped her eyes. This wasn't the time to cry.

Cass didn't see anyone, including Carver, as she approached the culvert. She slowed, opened her window and dumped the rest of her soda out. At that moment, she felt something land in the back of the truck. She glanced back and saw Carver, still in his night combat outfit, lying in the bed. She was never so glad to see anyone in her life. He looked good, even dressed as a terrorist. Her heart slowed to an accelerated-above-normal pace, but at least it was still beating. She looked around and saw a cloud of dust in the field heading their way. She decided it was time to go and she pushed the gas pedal to the floor.

She slowed as they approached the outskirts of Myton. Carver opened the door and climbed in the cab before she had a chance to stop. "Flip a U and start heading back to Roosevelt," he said.

"Well, it's nice to see you too," she said. She cast him a half-hearted smile. She felt the steering wheel for the imprints she was sure she had pressed into the plastic.

"Sorry."

He looked like he had just finished the Iron Man Triathlon—basically dead. She regretted being so quick with her tongue. "Are you okay?" she asked in a more subdued tone.

"Yeah, I'm fine, just a little tired, but nothing three days of sleep won't fix." He reached over and put his hand on her arm and gave her a squeeze. "Thanks, Cass. I could never have done this without you." He stifled a yawn. "Just before we get into Roosevelt, you'll see a yellow abandoned house on the right. You'll recognize it by the half-fallen brick chimney. Pull into the driveway on the far side of the house and go directly into the garage. Don't worry about opening or closing the door. It works automatically. As soon as I change my clothes and clean up a little, we'll leave the truck and take the car in the garage."

"But the truck belongs to Reber," Cass said. "And . . . whose house are we invading? And . . . how do you know there's a car there?" She had more questions she wanted to ask, depending on his answers.

"Don't worry about the car. I'll make sure it gets delivered to Reber tomorrow." Irritatingly, he didn't answer her other questions.

She saw the house and pulled into the driveway, surprised when the garage door popped up. She parked alongside another car.

"Let's make it quick," he said. "You okay?"

"I'm confused," she replied. "I think you've got a lot of explaining to do."

"You're right. Just wait until we're back on the road and then I'll tell you everything. Okay? Listen, Cass, you've got to trust me. And do you want to explain to me how you came up with the idea to change cars with Reber? It was beautiful and probably saved us. All this time I thought you were a space-case mathematician when you were actually a closet CIA agent."

The inside of the house looked anything but abandoned. It was clean and had stores of all of the basic survival implements. She surveyed the house before Carver told her there was a change of clothes for her in one of the bedrooms. She found a jogging suit and quickly changed—it wasn't her size but she rolled up the sleeves and it worked. You couldn't have everything.

Carver stripped out of his combat suit and took a much-needed shower while Cass prowled around the rest of the house.

She was surprised to find that the house was loaded with high-tech equipment: computers and the works. There was no doubt about it—this was a safe house, possibly for the FBI. She was curious but held her tongue until they were in the car headed back towards home. She was going to hold him to his promise.

"Okay, Mr. Nash, I think it's time we have our little talk." She turned to face him while he drove. He glanced at her, but kept his eyes on the road without responding.

"Let me review a few facts. You just happen to move next to my father at the time all of this trouble began. You discover a box full of gold and a letter from Thomas Rhoades. You keep getting phone calls from someone that seems to know more of what's going on than we do. Mysterious people pick up intruders you've immobilized, like they are on your beck and call. Then you just happen to have an old truck available for your use parked at the rear of the theater. We've just left a house that looks like a dump but is, in fact, a high-tech hideaway of some type, and oh, by the way, there just happens to be another car you can use. What's going on, Carver? Who are you?"

"You can't say a word to anyone, even your father. Not yet."

"My dad? You don't want me to say anything to my dad?"

"Not now. If you can't agree, I can't tell you anything."

She bit her lip, wondering what he was going to tell her that she couldn't tell her father.

"Okay, you win. And I want you to know that I don't even have my fingers crossed," she said with a smile.

"The day after I discovered the Rhoades box on my property, I was contacted by someone from Homeland Security. They have an ongoing investigation regarding an international crime organization working in the area, which seems to have an interest in the Mine. Homeland Security got involved because they were invited to do so by the Ute Tribe, and Homeland Security, in turn, contacted the FBI for assistance. But some members of the tribal council don't want outsiders or the FBI involved. They think they can handle the problem by themselves."

"So, why did they contact you?"

"They knew your father and I found the box, although they had no idea what was in it. All they knew was that the thugs were interested in it, and they persuaded me to tag along to offer some protection for your father and to aid in their investigation."

"And they knew to call you . . . how?"

"I served in the Army with some people that now work for the Bureau. They know me."

"So basically, you were in the right place at the right time and it all fell together?"

"I guess you could say that."

It all seemed conveniently coincidental to Cass, but she wasn't about to squawk. Her father was in danger, Carver was there to protect him, and that was all that mattered.

"Do they have any idea who the turncoat Ute is?"

"Are you asking me if they suspect Reber Kolb?" he asked.

"Yeah, I guess I am," she replied.

"They don't know."

"So are you going to tell me why you had me sitting on pins and needles for an extra day? I mean, you really had me worried when you didn't call me after the first night."

"Not much to tell," replied Carver.

"I find that hard to believe."

"Why don't we wait until we get home, and I'll only have to tell the story one time?"

Rylan threw his arms around Cass when they arrived home. Carver lugged his backpack into the house and poured the contents on the table. There were hundreds of Mormon gold pieces minted between 1850 and 1860, in perfect condition.

Rylan picked up a few. There were $20, $10, $5 and $2 ½ pieces. "When you told me on the phone about the gold coins, I looked up their value on the Internet. For instance, there are only between thirty and seventy-five of these $5 gold pieces known to be in existence. This $5 gold piece is worth between $75,000 and $100,000. Do you realize you have a fortune in gold coins on this table?"

Carver blinked at the value of the gold coins, and yet he wasn't tempted. These coins belonged to someone else.

Rylan continued, "Now, I figure a conservative estimate of the gold we found on your land was almost 1.3 million dollars, with approximately that much in the second find. But this sack of coins, if sold for their numismatic value to dealers, could be worth maybe $10,000,000. I think we should get these coins into a safe deposit box, now!"

Cass picked up the wooden box. She opened it and found a second cipher wheel. She was sure that it would fit perfectly with the gears of the first. She looked around and couldn't see any documents. If there wasn't a cipher, then why go to the bother of having wheels?

"Is this everything you found?" asked Cass.

Carver pulled out the pouch and handed it to Cass. "Is this what you were looking for?" he asked.

Chapter Ten

Cass already had the gears of the cipher wheels engaged and was adjusting them in preparation for their use in decoding the cipher when Rylan spoke up. "Tell me how these things work."

Cass placed the rings down in front of Rylan. "Notice," she said, "that the letters of the alphabet on the outer ring are randomly dispersed around the ring, while those on the inner ring are in alphabetical order. You decode a message using the cipher rings by aligning *A* of the inner ring with the key letter or first letter in the key phrase on the outer ring, similar to the Vigenere coding techniques. The first letter of the cipher text is found by locating the first letter of the plain text on the inner ring. The first letter of the cipher text is then the corresponding letter on the outer ring." She held it up, and Rylan nodded.

"I hope the pattern continues and a clue to the key letter or phrase will be somewhere in the documents contained in this packet." She nodded toward the packet Carver carried back from Rock Creek.

Carver spoke up, making one of his rare contributions to the discussion. "I remember that cipher wheels were used in the Civil

War by the Confederacy as a means to pass encrypted messages. They used key phrases known only to them, such as 'complete victory' or 'come retribution.' So the phrase we're looking for could be a well-known word or phrase attributed to Thomas Rhoades, Wakara, or even Brigham Young."

Cass handed the documents to Rylan, who carefully unfolded them and immediately made copies to use. The first document was a letter written by Thomas Rhoades:

Towats is the guardian of the treasure you seek. He is not to be lightly regarded. I know of his power. Disbelievers have paid the consequences. Proceed with this quest only if you are prepared to accept his direction.

Your journey to this point has most likely been arduous and you are to be congratulated for your ingenuity and perseverance.

Just prior to my death, I drew a map and left it with my wife. Only she knew the map was prepared for the purpose to deceive and misdirect those who had been attempting to wrongfully discover the location of the sacred mine.

I have, in fact, prepared two maps that together provide the location of the sacred mine. This I did with the full knowledge of President Young and Wakara. If you continue on this quest you will find two maps. Directions for their use have been left with the last map.

The gold coins you discovered with this note belong to me personally. They belong to the finder. Use them as you deem just and proper. They did not come from the sacred mine but from other sources. The gold bars you discovered in the first two caches are Spanish gold that also belonged to me and is not part of the gold of the sacred mine. That gold now belongs to you.

Everything you have heard of the treasure located in the sacred mine can in no way describe its actual magnitude and beauty.

Thomas Rhoades

"Very interesting," said Rylan. "The old switcheroo. Both Thomas and Caleb reportedly left maps of the Sacred Mine. Most people thought they had breached their promise of secrecy by leaving the maps, but as it turns out, Thomas and Caleb were both true to their word. The maps they left were bogus, made to throw would-be treasure hunters off the path. It's no wonder no one was ever able to find the mine using those death maps."

Cass surmised, "So, for us to locate the mine, we have to find both maps, which means we still have some additional caches to locate, unless you have two maps in that packet, Dad."

Rylan shook his head.

Carver glanced over at his friends and said, "So, that brings us to the gold."

"What do you want to do with it?" asked Cass. "It probably belongs to you."

"We need to get the gold to a safe location. More importantly, we can't breathe a word of its existence. I'll take care of transporting it in the morning, if everyone agrees."

Rylan agreed with Carver, but was anxious to see what else was in the pouch. He opened the next document and showed it to Cass and Carver. It was a cipher text:

If you have found this box you successfully evaded the guardians of this area. The box was safe for all of these years because it was hidden on sacred Indian ground. Hopefully no one discovered you, for if they did, the blood oath will need to be exacted.

b p m z k x d h d j o x s o m p e b
b o e d r x i z p t w f i q o d u p g t y b s
b h l x k k
w q j a I z I x q e d a l y x a r p

If you are able to decode this cipher you will be close to the gold of the Carre-Shin-Ob.

Cass said, "That is definitely a text created with these cipher wheels. This cipher is going to have to be cracked by the old trial and error method, using the cipher wheels. I suggest we make a list of key letters and phrases. I can then start running them through the cipher rings."

Rylan was still lost in his own world, unfolding the last document. "This appears to be a statement from Isaac Morley, the best friend of Chief Wakara. He introduced Wakara to Brigham Young and was reportedly the first white person to see the Carre-Shin-Ob. In fact, at one point, Brigham Young was suspicious of Morley and he supposedly said 'that Brother Morley cared more for the Indians than his own Mormon affairs.'" Rylan read:

Isaac Morley wrote to Brigham Young on March 23, 1850:

Thinking this to be a matter of the utmost urgency and for your eyes only, I remit this letter among those sealed as matters of intelligence concerning the Natives of this place. [Chief] Walker has this day come to see me, bringing with him a pouch of what appears to be the purest gold, in the form of nuggets uniformly the size of the nail of the thumb or larger. He reports these to come from an ancient mine somewhere high in the mountains to the east of this place, and has offered to take me there, and to give me the gold on the basis of our friendship. He tells a marvelous story of a vision, in which the spirit of Towats appeared to him, making him the keeper of the money-rock, as he calls it, until the Mormons came, at which time he was told to give it to them.

I firmly believe in the truth of Walker's statement that such a mine does exist somewhere in the mountains, and I am willing to go with him there to verify it, if you see it in your wisdom for me to do so.[1]

Carver asked, "Why do you think Thomas Rhoades would include this tidbit of information with the other documents we found at Rock Creek? I mean, what does it have to do with our search or quest? And why include a document from Isaac Morley?"

"Good question," Cass said.

"I bet this paper has something to do with the key letter or phrase," offered Rylan.

Carver spoke again. "Maybe not. Maybe he was simply trying to give us testimony from another party who had actually been to the mine. You know, two witnesses."

Cass couldn't believe the change in Carver. He'd gone from silent cynic to helpful partner in the quest, seemingly overnight. She reluctantly pulled her attention back to the cipher, trying to ignore the warm eyes Carver turned on her.

"Does anyone have any hot ideas for keywords or phrases?"

Rylan said, "Let's look in the documents."

The trio agreed. Each took a copy of the documents from Rylan and sat down to study them. Cass was interrupted when her cell phone started ringing. She looked at the caller ID and walked into the other room to answer.

"I don't know how to thank you. I'm afraid I might not be speaking to you right now, if you hadn't arranged to have that car there when you did."

"You can thank me by coming out to my house to dinner. My mother has been bugging me to invite you. If you come, I'll even go to church with you."

Cass had met Reber's mother one time before, and she'd seemed nice enough. She had been educated and demanded that Reber go to college and return to help their people. Cass had been impressed with her commitment to her heritage, while wanting to make life better for her and her people.

His promise to go to church definitely interested her. She'd wanted to see him be baptized for years and had all but given up hope that he ever would.

"I'll call you back in a minute," she said, pressing "end." She'd better run the idea past Carver and her father.

They both agreed she could go. Cass studied Carver's eyes for an extra minute, wondering what was going on behind them. He'd been investigating Reber, she knew that, and while he wouldn't tell her what he'd discovered, she knew she could trust him not to lead her into danger.

"It's all right, Cass," he told her, and she dialed her phone.

"Okay," she said. "Time and place."

Sunday morning, Cass drove into the church parking lot in Roosevelt, parked the car, and headed for the door. Lassiter was watching from . . . somewhere. She didn't know where, but Carver had arranged it all and she trusted him. Reber stood by the church door, holding it open for her.

She didn't know what to think of his apparent sudden interest in the Church. She wondered if he was only coming because of her, or if he really wanted to attend. He took her hand and led her toward the chapel. Surprised, she didn't pull her hand away.

A nice-looking gentleman stopped them as they approached the door. Reber said, "Bishop, I'd like you to meet Sister Edison. She served her mission here, but that was several years ago."

Cass wondered how Reber knew this guy was the bishop, but then, Roosevelt was a small town. She noted that the bishop didn't act surprised to see Reber.

"Well, Sister Edison, I'm certainly glad to meet you. I assume you'll be going to the Gospel Doctrine class. Will you tell me what you think of Reber's lesson? Some of our members have been questioning his sources." He smiled as he slapped Reber on the shoulder. You could have knocked Cass over with a feather. She turned and looked at Reber. He had a sheepish grin and shrugged his shoulders as if to say, I guess *I should have told you before.*

"What . . ."

"Well, I have to confess. I told you I was listening when you were teaching me, but you thought I was just chasing you. Soon after you left, I let them dunk me. I've been teaching the Gospel Doctrine class ever since I came back from college."

She slugged him in the arm, then threw her arms around him for a hug. "You're a jerk, but I'm so happy for you."

"If that's all it took to get a hug from you, I would have let them baptize me a long time ago."

The bishop looked at Cass. "He's been needing a good woman to take care of him for a long time."

Cass let go of Reber like a hot potato. She was happy for him, but . . .

She listened as he gave a lesson about Captain Moroni. He was good—he knew his stuff, and that surprised her. Everything seemed to surprise her these days. Plus, he looked pretty good in a suit and tie.

"Cassandra Edison is at church with Reber Kolb right now," Pedro reported.

Vincent Vargas leaned forward and rested his elbows on his richly polished desk. "Is Nash with her?"

"Nash is nowhere in sight. Do you want us to take her?"

Vargas pondered a moment, then shook his head. "No," he said. "Nash may not be visible, but he is watching, somehow. I'm not yet ready to deal with the problem of Mr. Nash. Wait for my order."

Pedro bobbed his head and stepped out of the room.

"The problem of Mr. Nash." Vargas repeated his own words to himself. "A problem, indeed."

"Okay, Lassiter, what else have you found out about Reber Kolb?" Carver pressed his ear more firmly to his cell phone. They'd learned enough to trust that Cass would be safe with Reber, but that's all they knew. He wanted more information—all he could get.

"Reber is the one who suggested that the interrogations be conducted on Ute land. The guys you bagged for us were the first taken there. You know, it's a sovereign nation—no hassle with federal rules and regulations. Besides, they can hold them without anyone knowing anything. Other than that, we've heard nothing but good things about Kolb since he returned from college. I think he's going to be a real asset to the Ute Tribe."

"Are you getting any closer to finding the traitor?"

"The three sleaze balls you've turned over to us a while ago don't know anything. That, or they are better at lying than anyone I've ever interrogated. They're just hired guns, but all have records and outstanding charges long enough to keep them locked up for the rest of their lives."

"What about those new guns? Have you been able to get your hands on any of them yet?"

"I'll let you know when I do. Keep on your toes—these boys play for keeps. I've got to run. You've got my number and, Carver . . . thanks for your help. I know you wanted to stay away from this kind of stuff."

Before Carver broke the connection, Captain Lassiter asked him one more question. "Hey, you're not falling for that Edison girl, are you, Carver? I mean, not that she's not something to fall for, but I've never seen you act like this around a woman. Does she know the truth about you yet?"

"I'll talk to you later, Lassiter." Carver hit the end call button. What was he feeling? He knew Cass was something special. He knew she had already taken possession of a portion of his heart, but he wasn't sure he was ready.

Cass was supposed to be home by now. Lassiter was still on the case, but Carver wouldn't be able to relax until she was back home where he could see her for himself.

"Let's think up some keywords for this cipher," Rylan suggested.

Carver sighed, ran his hands through his hair, and tried to refocus his attention. "Well, some common words or phrases could be: Zion people, Danites, Kamas Valley, Yambow (which is another name for the Kamas Valley), Thomas Rhoades, Wakara, Towats, Carre-Shin-Ob, Holiness to the Lord, or Lion of the Lord. Let's go from there."

Rylan wrote Carver's suggestions and added, "Now, if we look at the document and try to focus, let's see what we can come up with. Morley's letter uses a few distinct words: Spirit of Towats, keeper of the money rock, Walker, ancient mine, or even Isaac Morley. Historically, people writing ciphers have used their name as the keyword."

Carver studied the Rock Creek letter. "There aren't very many distinctive words that jump off the page in this letter, but you could consider: guardian of the treasure, false map, sacred mine, deceived and misdirected, gold coins, Spanish gold, and maybe even magnitude and beauty. That's about it."

He kept looking at his watch. It was aggravating to have to sit and wait. Rylan started laughing.

"What?" said Carver.

"Look at you. If I didn't know better, I'd say you're a little upset that Cass went to see Reber, and not just because you're not there to protect her."

"I'm not happy about it, but the reasons aren't important." Carver wanted to find a way out of this conversation. He knew if he asked the right question, the professor would be distracted. "Tell me, Rylan, why do you think Brigham Young never told anyone of the gold or of his relationship with Wakara?"

Rylan started digging through a bunch of papers. "There's been a lot of speculation on that question. Most people think that if word had gotten out that Utah had these hidden treasures, it would have caused a gold rush bigger than that of the California hysteria. Brigham often preached excommunication for prospecting, but he couldn't do that with one hand and send Thomas Rhoades out to get the gold with the other. Plus, he promised Wakara he would not disclose the mine's existence or its location."

"Do you think the angel Moroni is covered with Rhoades gold?" Carver was pleased that his little diversion tactic was working, but surprised himself to realize that he was curious to know the answers to these questions. He might turn into a history buff yet.

Rylan started digging through some more papers. "Here it is. Listen to this. Kerry Boren was a noted historian. At one point he obtained a job overseeing the Church archives in the vault in Big Cottonwood Canyon. He stated that he had seen documents proving that gold was taken by Brigham Young's associates, as they were probably instructed to do by the Lord, from the Lost Rhoades Mine. He wrote:

> 'There are several document boxes, marked TOA#5 and TOA#6, that hold a number of sheets with copper and gold leaf designs. Contained with the gold leaf is a sheet of paper with the Church letterhead on it, which reads as follows, 'copper and gold leaf strips used in the original design of angel Moroni. Copper obtained from Dyer smelter. Gold from Caleb B. Rhoades storage tithe. Moroni plate from same source over copper and brass framework. Samples for storage. Likeness were placed in time capsule, foundation stone of Eagle Gate. I attest to the authenticity of my craftsmanship.
> Truman O. Angell[2]

Angell was the architect who supervised much of the construction of the Salt Lake Temple."

Carver was struck by a thought. "Rylan, everything in the Rock Creek cache referred to the gold from the Lost Rhoades mine. Maybe we should limit our search to any phrase using the word *gold*."

Rylan was quiet for a minute, thinking. "You're right, Carver. You just might be on the right track."

Just then they heard a car drive up. Carver was at the window and saw that it was Cass. He tried to get control of his emotions. He intended to act normal.

She knocked three times and then used her key to open the door. Carver stood, and stared at her, his emotions running high.

"What? Did my mascara run? Is my hair a mess? What are you looking at?"

Rylan looked from one to the other, knowing they needed to work some things out, but realizing they should do it later, after the high-tension moment had passed. "Cass, come and sit down. Carver has an idea that may help us with the keyword or phrase."

"Can't this wait until tomorrow?" she said, groaning.

"It can, as far as I am concerned," said Carver as he walked out the door.

"What's his problem?" she asked.

"If you don't know, I'm not going to explain it to you," replied Rylan.

Without taking a breath, he continued, "Carver suggested that everything in the Rock Creek Cache was related to gold and that maybe the keyword is tied to gold. First thing tomorrow, I'll have a list ready for you to run through your little cipher machine."

"Carver's more confusing than any cipher we've looked at," Cass said, heading for her bedroom to change her clothes.

Gold coins, gold bars, Spanish gold, gold, gold of the Carre-shin-Ob, and purest gold were all listed for Cass to try, and in that order. She worked for a couple of hours and informed Rylan that nothing worked." Okay, try these," he said, "Guardian of the treasure, nuggets, and money rock." About twenty minutes later Rylan heard, "Bingo."

"What?" he asked.

"It's money rock. Listen to this."

Hidden in plain site

Hawkins knew but didn't know he knew Rhoades to Timpanogo.

"This has to be it. It decodes into words but it sounds like a bunch of double-talk to me. You've got this Hawkins guy who knows but doesn't know he knows. It's hidden in plain 'site' but no one's ever seen it or recognized it when they saw it. Is *site* misspelled, or is it referring to a place? And then maybe the last line is a play on words, meaning the road to Timpanogos."

"Let me play with it for a while. You go out and see if you can find Carver."

"Why do I need to go find him? Can't you just call him on the phone?"

Rylan turned an exaggeratedly patient look toward his daughter. "Cass, can't you tell Carver likes you?"

"Did he say something to you?"

"He didn't have to."

Cass wandered over to Carver's homestead, glancing around to see if she could spot the "eye in the sky" she knew was there. Of course, she didn't see anything—that was the point.

"We decoded the cipher," she said when she saw Carver, skipping an ordinary greeting. With her father's revelation, she didn't know if she trusted herself to say more. Carver didn't seem to mind, and followed her back to the house, neither one of them speaking.

The three brainstormed about the cipher text for at least an hour. The last of the sun's rays filtered through the trees while a light breeze rustled the pines. "It's like looking for a needle in a haystack," said Rylan.

Cass's phone rang, but she looked at caller ID and didn't answer. Carver was sure it had been Reber calling. The fact that she didn't answer was somewhat encouraging, but the fact that Reber was calling her every day really bugged him. Rylan wasn't distracted by the interruption. He was like a bloodhound tracking someone. " 'Rhoades to Timpanogo' implies that one is giving or going somewhere. Since Rhoades wrote it, I'm going to assume he was not using his name as a play on words. I have no idea who or what Timpanogo is, but it appears to be a person. So that means that we have one person going to, or giving another person, something." Cass studied the document. "Plain site must mean something written that everyone can see, but not recognize what they are seeing. Maybe it's a sign or some kind of public document." Carver looked at Cass for a long time and then ventured, "Maybe we should do a search on the names Hawkins and Timpanogo. Limit the search to someone living between 1850 and 1870. Someone that was prominent or well known. Hawkins is not a very common name. Even so, we probably won't get a lot of hits during that time period. Timpanogo is probably an Indian name, so we can limit the search to Ute tribe records."

They were mulling over each other's thoughts when Carver's phone rang. He glanced at the caller ID, rose, and walked to the door. "Lock this and go to high alert. Both of you get a weapon and stay away from the windows." Carver listened as Captain Lassiter gave him the setup. "We have the satellite on you right now. There are three guys at your house, one inside and two outside providing cover."

Lassiter gave Carver the approximate locations. The two outside guys had situated themselves so they could catch anyone approaching the cabin in a crossfire. Carver decided he would have to take them out one at a time, silently. If one was able to sound the alarm, he would have to deal with all three at the same time. In that case, he might not have anyone left to question.

The night vision equipment helped him, but he assumed they would have the same. As he approached the first man, he stooped and picked up a stone, throwing it to the left. The man turned to focus his attention on the sound, and Carver hit him over the head, instantly knocking him out. Within seconds, the man was bound hand, foot, and mouth with duct tape and left lying on the ground.

Carver took the man's radio and was about to push the call button when he heard someone say, "Clear one," followed immediately by "Clear two." He spoke crisply. "Clear three." The radio again went silent, and he moved towards the second man. As he got close, he pushed the send button and spoke in quiet, broken words, "He's coming my . . ." and then made a garbled noise. Number two started moving towards the downed man. Carver grabbed him around the neck as the man passed the tree behind which he was hiding.

This man didn't go down easy, but fought for a good minute before Carver brought him down. He secured this guy in much the same manner as he had the first. Both of them carried silenced guns, which he took and pocketed. Neither man had any identification, although one had a set of car keys in his pocket.

As Carver approached his house, he reached beneath the front porch and threw a switch. Immediately, speakers he had installed in the attic began playing the loud and uninterrupted sound of barking dogs hot on the trail. He heard the third man try to speak into the radio, but his voice could not be heard above the barking. As he bolted through the front door, Carver took him head on like a linebacker filling a hole. After a brief tussle, Carver taped his hands behind his back then went to work on the man's feet. Carver asked one question: "Who sent you?" The man didn't say a word. "If you don't start talking within five seconds, I'm going to throw you back in the house with those dogs." The sound of scraping filled the air, as if dogs were trying to get through the door.

The man spoke urgently. "I don't know. I got a phone call to hire two guys and search this house. I don't know who it was, or who owns this house. There was a pouch containing $10,000 in cash on my front porch, with a map here. I was told I would get more if I found anything of interest."

"I want the phone number of the man who called you."

"It's on my cell phone, in the car back at the road."

With that, Carver taped the man's mouth shut, pulled out his own cell phone, and spoke into it. He then moved the three guys to a convenient location for their pickup and removal.

"It's too bad you guys couldn't stay for dinner," he said to his muted friends.

Vincent Vargas pulled on his suit coat and grabbed his brief-case, anger oozing out of every pore. "Why is it so impossible to find good help?" he muttered. He stepped out the door and slammed it.

I'll go take care of it, myself."

Chapter Eleven

Cass jogged up as Carver was speaking on his cell phone. She didn't recognize the language he was using, just the word *Lassiter.* She looked around, wondering what had happened. The three men on the ground didn't exactly look like the skinny guys at the beach. She hadn't heard any shots, and Carver didn't look the worse for wear, but she could tell he'd had a workout.

"Who are your friends?" she asked, gesturing toward the trio on the ground.

"I thought I told you to batten down the hatches and stay put, yet here you are running alone to my house. You don't listen very well."

"You didn't answer my question," she said. "Who are these guys?"

"No one you know or want to know," he replied.

She accepted his brief response, figuring she wouldn't get a lot more out of him. She asked a new question. "What language were you speaking?"

"Navajo. I learned it on my mission in Arizona. I was speaking to my mission trainer, Bill Lassiter. He also speaks Navajo."

Somehow his surprises never really surprised her. "So what happens to them now?" She motioned toward the three captives.

"Someone will be by to pick them up in a few minutes. Bill will squeeze every drop of information out of them that they possess."

Carver motioned to her to walk with him. "Let's put a little distance between us. I want to make sure they can't hear us."

"Do you want to tell me about what happened?" she asked.

"What do you mean?"

"In the war," she responded.

She watched him go silent, not that he was a regular talking machine. She could almost see him flinch at the thought, and she was sure he didn't flinch easily.

"I wish I knew what was going on behind those baby blues," she said. She knew she wasn't going to get an answer.

She continued, "Okay, so now's maybe not the time for war stories, but at least you can tell me more about Bill, or Lassiter if that's what you call him."

She could see his demeanor change. "Like I said, Bill was the trainer on my mission. I didn't have many friends before that."

Carver looked like he was on the witness stand. Stiff, eyes forward, unblinking, and not wanting to answer the question. She waited for him to continue. "I guess you could say I was a loner. It didn't take long for Elder Lassiter to become my best friend. He was a no-nonsense type of guy and worked his guts out. We had a great experience together. It was a sad day when he got reassigned to a new companion. I kind of lost track of him for a year or two after he went home."

They took a seat on two rocks set side by side, and Carver continued his story.

"When I signed up for the Army, I was immediately assigned to the Rangers. When I reported to my commanding officer, I found out why I was accepted into the Rangers so easily. Captain Lassiter sat behind the desk, smiling. He became my trainer a second time, now in counter espionage. We often had the chance to use our language skills in the field. No one ever knew what we were talking about, not even our own guys. It really was like the code talkers in

World War II. Eventually our unit was sent overseas."

He went silent. She didn't want to press him too hard, but she wanted to hear more. "And this Captain Lassiter is the same guy you keep talking to on the phone, the same one who recruited you to protect my father?"

"The same one. I wouldn't have done it for anyone but him," he said.

"Do you want to tell me anything else?"

"No . . . I think you know everything now."

Cass sincerely doubted it.

A van drove up. Two burly guys climbed out without saying a word and stowed the three thugs in the back of the van. One looked at Carver and nodded. Then they were gone.

Cass shook her head. She reached over, took Carver's hand and said, "Walk me back to the house. Okay?"

Cass drove Rylan to Heber to see the doctor. He was supposed to get his cast off, if he had been a good boy. Cass knew for a fact he had not been a good boy, but wanted to know what the doctor thought.

She walked her father into the doctor's office and promised to return in one hour. She had some shopping to finish. As she left the office, she turned left and almost tripped over some long legs extending from a bench into the walkway.

"Fancy meeting you here," said Reber.

Cass jumped back. "You scared me. Why are you always sneaking up on me?"

"Hey, it's the only way I ever get to see you," he replied, his face alight with a captivating smile.

She sat down on the bench next to him. He reached over and took her hand, tracing a line on her palm. "This line means you are going to live a long time. This one over here means you are going to have a lot of children, six to be exact, and this one indicates that you are going to meet a tall, good-looking guy named Reber."

"Really? You can see all that just looking at the wrinkles in my hand? If so, I don't want you to ever start examining the wrinkles on my face."

He looked her straight in the eye and said, "Sister Edison, I think I've been in love with you since the first time you knocked on my door."

Cass didn't know what to say. His confession didn't really surprise her but it made her squirm. She didn't know how to respond because she . . . well, Carver and . . . she wiped her hand across her forehead. It was damp. She remained silent, not daring to look at him.

Finally he continued. "I'm sorry. I didn't mean to . . . but I just want you to know. I hope sometime in the future you'll feel the same, but I don't want to push you. Take all the time you need. I just want the chance to show you how much fun we can have, living in a teepee up on the mountain with six kids."

She had to smile, but couldn't think of anything to say. She didn't want to hurt him, but how could she give him any hope for a relationship?

He broke the silence. "There's another thing I need to talk to you about. I told you the other day that I was working with federal authorities, trying to catch the slimeballs that are wreaking havoc on the reservation. Don't take this wrong, but I'm thinking the name of your friend, Mr. Nash, comes up far too frequently."

Cass jumped to her feet, turned to face him. She pointed her finger and said, "Reber, this has gone far enough. Mr. Nash doesn't have anything to do with your problems."

"Hold on, Cass. I wasn't suggesting Mr. Nash was responsible for the problems we are having on the reservation. However, he seems to be in the middle of your problems in Marion."

Cass was shaking, she was so upset. What was Reber suggesting?

Reber asked, "Do you know anything about his life before he came to live on his grandfather's property? How about his military involvement? Do you really know anything about him?"

"Reber, you're barking up the wrong tree," Cass said, preparing to walk away. "Carver is on our side, I'm sure of it."

"Okay, but just keep a good lookout. I don't trust the guy."

Reber stood and took her face in both of his hands, gently kissing her. She didn't resist. She wasn't knocked off her chair, though; she could still breathe and she didn't see any stars, but then, it was still daytime. On the other hand, she didn't feel like throwing up, either. Maybe that was a good sign.

Reber smiled at her and said, "Got to run. I'll catch you again when you least expect it. By the way, my mother loved you, Cass."

"How does your leg feel?" Carver asked. Rylan had returned from the doctor's office with the cast off.

"No problem. The doc said I was as good as new—or old, in my case. He told me not to jump off any houses or use any trampolines for a while, but other than that, he said I was good to go."

"I didn't hear him say anything like that. I heard him tell you to take it easy, and that old bones don't heal as well as they did when you were younger," added Cass.

"Did you run your name search?" Rylan asked. She knew he wanted to get off the topic of his leg.

She responded, "A name search between the years of 1850–1870 didn't give me much to work with. The only names that came up were prominent people who had their names in a newspaper or some kind of public document. For instance, this guy named Leo Hawkins popped up. He was the Salt Lake County Recorder between 1857 and 1859."

"What did you say?" asked Carver.

"Hawkins was the County Recorder, why?"

"Read the cipher again," said Rylan.

Cass read the message. Rylan replied, "Hawkins knew but didn't know he knew. If Hawkins recorded a deed, he would technically know about the deed, but he wouldn't necessarily know the contents of the document being recorded. Most of the time when you are speaking you would just describe the conveyance or deed as 'Rhoades to Timpango' even though the deed would use the complete legal description and some other legalese. So I'll bet we are looking for a deed from Rhoades to Timpanogo recorded between 1850 and 1870.

"Moreover, hidden in plain site is another giveaway. When you record a deed, it's a matter of public knowledge. Anyone can look at it."

Carver said, "I don't think they had a county recorder that early. I mean, the Saints didn't even get to the valley until 1847."

"Not so," said Cass. "The document I pulled up is the history of the Salt Lake County Recorder. The first recorder was a guy named Bullock who served between 1852–1856. Leo Hawkins was the second recorder and he served until 1859."

Rylan was up and pacing again, despite the doctor's warning to take it easy. "The recording books at the county recorder's office are all bound and kept in chronological order. We'll just have to search the two years while Hawkins was the recorder for a deed from Rhoades to Timpanogo."

Cass said, "Of course, it may also be a dead end."

"No way," said Rylan. "This is it, for sure. Mark my word. It all fits."

Carver drove up early the next morning in his Land Rover. He had another pistol in a holster and an automatic weapon on the floor beside him. There was a pistol under the passenger front seat and one under the back seat as well. A big metal box sat between the two front seats. Cass climbed in the back and Rylan sat down in the front. Carver explained about the guns, and told them to familiarize themselves with the guns' locations.

Carver wore his usual Levis, cowboy boots and plaid shirt. Rylan dressed a little more formally in slacks and golf shirt. Cass looked better than both of them—at least, Carver thought so—dressed in standard Levis and a T-shirt.

Rylan spoke first. "I guess we're going to the bank first, to deposit the contents of this box. Right?"

"That would be best," said Carver.

"Do you mind if I stop by my old office for a minute before we go to the recorder's office? I would like to introduce my daughter to a few of the guys."

"Dad, I told you I'm not interested."

"Just kidding," teased Rylan. "I need to see someone about a problem I'm working on." Cass didn't know whether to strangle him or . . . strangle him.

"When we get to the bank, I want you, Rylan, to go in and rent a safe deposit box. I'll wait in the car until you're finished. I'll come directly to the room used for viewing the safe deposit boxes. I can sign as a co-owner when I come in," said Carver.

After stopping at the bank, visiting Rylan's old law office, and letting Cass run into the store, they headed to the county recorder's office.

The attendant at the desk pointed them to a room where the early recording books were kept. There was a Xerox machine in the room they could use for a quarter per copy.

Cass pulled out the 1856 book. "Look at the handwriting. It's incredible. The recorder must have taken a calligraphy class."

Rylan suggested she find the deed they were looking for, and she could come back on her own time to look at the penmanship of the recorder. Cass quickly found it. After she read it, she said, "The words on the deed certainly don't seem to describe the property shown in the drawing."

Rylan took the book and said, "Rhoades was one sharp cookie. Imagine—one of the maps to the Lost Rhoades Mine has been right here in front of our eyes all the time."

QUIT-CLAIM DEED

Thomas Rhoades.. **Grantor,**
of Salt Lake County, State of Utah hereby *quit-claims* to
    Timpanogo.. **Grantee,**
of Utah County, State of Utah
for the sum of Ten and No/100 ($10.00) .... Dollars,
the following described tract of land in Salt Lake County, State of Utah:

Commencing 96.8 rods North and 155 rods West from the Southeast corner of Section 11, Township 1 South, Range 1 West, Salt Lake Meridian, West 105.495 feet; thence South 98 feet; thence West 60 feet; thence South 34 feet; thence East 10.03 rods; thence North 8 rods to the point of beginning; thence South 98 feet; thence East 60 feet; thence North 10.03 rods; then West 8 rods to the point of beginning; together with all mineral rights water rights subject to an easement **for ingress and egress lying along the Westerly 10 feet of the Northernly section and the Easterly 10 feet of the Southernly** section.
As per the map shown below:

WITNESS, the hand of said grantors this 1ˢᵗ day of June, 1855.

Thomas Rhoades

STATE OF UTAH   )
                :ss
County of Salt Lake   )
    On this the 1ˢᵗ day of June, 1855, personally appeared before me Thomas Rhoades the signer of the within instrument, who duly acknowledged to me he executed the same.

NOTARY PUBLIC residing at

Assigned to B. Young on the 2ⁿᵈ day of June 1855

He took the book and made two copies on the machine, then Carver moved to return it to its shelf. Pretending to trip, he dropped the book, which came open to the deed since he had his finger there. He used a razor-sharp knife to slice the page from the book with such a clean cut, it wouldn't be noticeable that a page was missing unless someone were counting page numbers. He slipped the page into a file he carried.

"Was that necessary?" asked Cass in whispered tones.

"Depends whether you want someone else to find what we found," replied Carver.

Rylan studied the deed the entire ride back. He didn't have much to say, because he was preoccupied with the map.

When they got home, Cass asked, "So, is there a cipher on the deed? Where are we going next?"

Rylan came out of his trance. "The only thing here is a map. We need two pieces to the puzzle and we only have one. Where is the second piece? We must have missed something in the message that would point us to the second piece—otherwise, we just hit a dead end."

Cass asked again, "So, where do we look for the second map?"

Rylan went back to the deed. "I don't know," he said. "I've read and reread it, and it's just a property description, signature line, notary, and a map. There's nothing out of the ordinary."

Carver said, "Let me look at the deed. Maybe new eyes can see something."

Carver studied it for some time, not saying a word. Finally, he pointed to the bottom line and asked, "This looks out of place. What is it?"

Rylan took the deed back and looked at it again. "You're right— it doesn't make any sense to put an assignment on the bottom of a deed. Why didn't I see it?"

"Maybe you thought it was just part of the notary acknowledgment," said Carver.

"What does it mean, anyway?"

"It must be a reference to another recorded instrument, an assignment from Timpanogo to Brigham Young the day after this deed was recorded, June 2, 1856. We've got to go back, right now!" said Rylan.

"Not today," said Cass. "It will close before we ever get there."

"I've got to check our perimeter defense and cameras to see if anyone visited us while we were gone. After I check out your house and talk to Lassiter, you guys go inside and stay there for the night. I've got some things to do."

"I'll go by myself in the morning," said Rylan.

"No, Rylan, you won't. No one is going to do anything by themselves until we get through this, and that includes you, Ms. Edison." He gave her a look that said, *and I mean it this time.*

That night Cass got a call from Reber. They talked about nothing, and everything, for around twenty minutes. He didn't directly try to pry, but she just had the nagging feeling she was not the sole motivation for his phone call, and he wanted information on their search. She decided it was time she tried to find out some information herself. It didn't work. He was an expert at dogging questions, and worse, he liked to drop a few bombs along her way.

"Cass, what's new at the county recorder's office?" She was shocked. How did he know they had been there? Carver had made sure they weren't followed, and yet Reber knew. Maybe he just wanted her to know that he knew.

She wasn't good at telling lies, but she didn't feel like giving him any information, not yet. She figured he was trying to solve the problems they were having on the reservation, but she wasn't sure their paths were going in the same direction.

"Dad just wanted to see if the deed for Carver's land got recorded. Why do you ask?"

"It's not very often three important people drive all the way to the Salt Lake Recorder's Office, especially when Mr. Nash's land is in Summit County."

He had caught her and wanted her to know that she had been caught. "Well, my dad had to see some of his old partners about a case he's working on. They have an internet connection to the Summit County Recorder's office at his old office and then he took some of his work to record in Salt Lake. Carver was kind enough to drive us in his car." It didn't sound real convincing, but then it really wasn't any of Reber's business anyway.

"Cass, you know I really can't lend my help if I don't know what's going on."

He was deliberately pushing her into a corner. She bristled, her normal reaction. "Reber, for now I have to leave it like it is. I'll talk to you later." She hung up the phone, relieved to be through with the conversation.

Early the next morning, they all headed to Salt Lake again. Cass decided to liven up the conversation. "I got a call from Reber last night. He wanted to know what we were doing at the recorder's office in Salt Lake."

Rylan asked, "How did he know?"

"That's what I want to know. Carver, has anyone been following us?"

"Not that I've been able to spot," he replied, his voice calm, although he tensed.

Cass added, "I told him we went to check the recording of the forest service deed on Carver's property. He wanted to know why we would go to the Salt Lake Recorder's office when Carver's property is here in Summit County."

"What did you tell him?"

"I made up something about going to your office and recording something you picked up there and using the internet at your office. He knew I wasn't telling him the whole truth."

Cass watched as Carver stopped on the side of the freeway a number of times. When he got to Salt Lake, he pulled into a parking lot and had them all get in another car parked nearby. He opened the trunk and put on a jacket, along with an old geezer hat. He put on a set of dark glasses, and had Cass and Rylan hide below the window level as they drove out of the parking structure and had them stay down for a few blocks. When they got close to the county recorder's office, he stopped and parked in an older residential area, telling them to stay in the car. He would go get the document by himself.

It took him about twenty minutes. He came back with another page out of the recorder's book and handed it to Rylan.

"Well, it's a pretty simple document," said Rylan. "However, it looks like there's a cipher at the bottom. We'll let you deal with it, Cass."

Assignment

I, Timpanogo, assign my entire right and interest in and to the property conveyed to me by T. Rhoades on the 1ˢᵗ of June, 1855, to B. Young.

Witness, the hand of said grantors this 2ⁿᵈ day of June, 1855.

<u>X</u>

Timpanogo

State of Utah)

.ss

County of Salt Lake)

On this 2ⁿᵈ day of June, 1855, personally appeared before me Timpanogo, the signer of the with within instrument, who duly acknowledged me he executed the same.

Notary Public
State of Utah

Notary Public

mfwpidrkagrpjqolcnxddeayfo

He handed her the page. She looked at it and said, "Well, we're back to square one. We still need to find the keyword or phrase. However, I suspect it will be in this document, or in the deed."

Later that day and back at the Edison's home, Cass played with the cipher wheels for some time, trying different words without any luck. Carver received a call and walked into the other room to take it, but Cass eavesdropped. He spoke what she assumed to be Navajo again—she didn't understand one word.

When he came back, she asked, "Was that your code-talking buddy on the phone?"

"That was Lassiter," he said.

"Are we under threat of nuclear attack?"

"Not at the minute," he said. "However, someone went to the county recorder's office today just after we were there, and looked through the old books."

"Well, they didn't find anything, did they? By the way, I take it back," she said.

"What?"

"I thought you were a jerk when you cut the pages out of those books, but now it seems like it was a good idea." Cass spun the wheels on the cipher wheel. She wasn't looking in his direction.

She nonchalantly added almost as an afterthought, "Was your friend able to identify the guy who went into the recorder's office?"

They didn't have an answer yet, and Cass went back to work. About an hour later she said, "The decoded message is 'The house of the Lion of the Lord.' "

Rylan was on his feet, looking over Cass's shoulder. "Well, we know the 'Lion of the Lord' was Brigham Young. His house was the 'Lion House.' "

Carver said, "Looks like we're taking a trip to the Lion House."

Chapter Twelve

After concluding a tour of the Lion House and looking around surreptitiously, Rylan, Cass, and Carver left, confused by what they had not seen. They felt they had been very observant and yet hadn't seen anything that appeared to be an encoded message. They wanted to talk over lunch and try to regroup.

Rylan picked up a menu as Cass slid into the booth next to Carver. She sat as close to him as possible, wanting to see what he would do when cornered. That, and she knew she was beginning to like the big lug.

Carver squirmed a little but didn't say anything. She liked sitting close to him.

After ordering, Rylan said, "It's got to be the Lion House. Nothing else makes any sense. What do you think, Cass?"

"I think it has to be the Lion House. I thought the cipher would stick out like a sore thumb, but I didn't see anything resembling an encoded message."

"If it's at the Lion House, it has to be something people have been looking at for a hundred years without realizing it," Carver said. "It's not going to be a flashing neon sign. It'll be something that looks like it belongs."

Rylan added, "You're right. I'll bet it's a written document, but then it could be a pictograph in the carpet or even part of a wall decoration."

Carver tried to slide closer to the wall but Cass wouldn't let him escape. She silently laughed as she smiled.

"What?" asked Rylan.

"Nothing." Cass threw Carver a sly grin.

After eating almost his entire sandwich, Rylan said to Cass, "When we return to the Lion House, I want you to photograph everything. If we don't recognize the cipher while we're there, we can study the photos when we have more time. If we can't find it, we'll have to rethink the last message."

Carver added, "We have to be careful not to be so conspicuous that we raise suspicion. We don't want someone asking a bunch of questions, or thinking we're casing the place and call the police."

"I think we should go separately and not be influenced by what someone else thinks or sees," Cass said. "Sometimes things jump out at you when you're not influenced by someone else."

They each spent two more hours walking the grounds and going through the Lion House on their own. None of them saw anything that looked like it could contain a cipher. Cass wondered again if they had misinterpreted the last message. Cass photographed everything, but then she caught herself and wondered if the document containing the cipher had been removed or replaced. Maybe it was stored in the attic or somewhere else. If that were the case, they could be facing a dead end. Maybe they could try to find out if there were any documents that had been previously displayed, then removed. She would try the Internet when they got home and maybe call the Church's historical society.

Cass needed to talk to Rylan—this plan wasn't working, and something was wrong. She went looking for him and bumped into

Carver as she turned the corner.

"Have you seen my dad?" she asked.

"He told me he was going to check out the backyard."

"I need to talk to both of you. Let's go find him."

They walked toward the rear of the building. As they turned the corner, they heard a car pulling away fast. Neither got a glimpse of the vehicle. Carver bent down and picked up a cotton cloth lying on the ground. He smelled it. "Chloroform."

He grabbed Cass's hand and ran toward the street on the side of the house. The car was long gone.

"Do you think someone kidnapped my dad?" she asked, beginning to lose control of her emotions.

"Let's search the house one more time before we jump to any conclusions."

They decided to divide forces—she took the upper floor and he the main. They hurried through the house and grounds. Rylan was not anywhere to be found. "Let's go," Carver said as he pulled Cass toward the car.

Cass knew someone had taken her father. Once in the car, it hit her, and she couldn't control her emotions any longer. Carver reached over and put his arms around her. He didn't say anything, but just held her. When she stopped sobbing, Carver let her go and pulled out his cell phone to call Lassiter. "Who took him?" she asked, trying to mask her anger.

"We should know more by the time we get home. I don't believe whoever took him will do anything until they learn all we know about the location of the mine. Since Rylan doesn't know where it is, they may consider using him as an incentive to force us to tell them everything we discover."

She couldn't take her eyes off him. She could see the muscles in his forearms flexing, his jaw muscles twitching, and his temple pounding. She couldn't remember seeing him quite so tense—or was it focused?

"These people just raised the stakes to the next level," he said. That was all—nothing else was said by either of them the remainder of the ride home.

She knew one thing—she wouldn't want Carver coming after her in his present state of mind. She meanwhile continued to ride the emotional roller coaster. She loved her father. He was all she had. She should have stopped this crazy quest, like Carver had suggested. All the gold in the world wasn't worth this.

Carver drove straight to her house. He told her to follow in his footsteps and stay right behind him. When he finally told her the house was safe, she checked the phone and computer to see if there was a message or some kind of ransom demand. There was nothing.

Not fifteen minutes later, Lassiter showed up with two of his men. Finally she got to meet the other code talker, the voice on the phone, Carver's friend. He was a bruiser, a large man, obviously able to take care of himself. But he seemed nice. If she played her cards right she just might be able to get some information from him about Carver.

He asked Carver to brief them on the operational security for the area, and then said to Carver, "Let's go outside to finish this."

"Umm . . . either you let me go with you or you stay right here so I can hear just what is going on," Cass said. "I'm sorry, Mr. Lassiter, but I think I've been in the dark long enough."

Lassiter was taken by surprise and froze in his tracks. Carver smiled and then said, "Cass, I promise you as soon as we're finished I'll come back in here and answer any question you have. Just give me a minute with Lassiter. Okay?"

About a half hour later, Carver returned to the house carrying a backpack. Lassiter trailed him. As they entered, Carver ignored Cass and said to Lassiter, "Let me have everything you have on him."

"Who?" asked Cass.

"We don't think he's associated with the mob. We think he's an international thief based out of Cypress. He's into discovering, stealing, or whatever it takes to obtain lost treasures and ancient artifacts. He doesn't care whose feet he steps on, and he has a lot of money behind him. He's ruthless. He never gets his hands dirty and hires cheap thugs to do his work for him. There are a number of countries that would like to get their hands on him. I'll get you the complete file on him as soon as possible."

Cass raised her voice, "Him? Who?"

Carver finally looked at Cass, held her gaze, then turned to Lassiter. "I don't know when I'll be back. Can I count on you to take care of her?"

"You've got my word, buddy."

Carver didn't even look at her, but turned and walked out the door. Cass felt like she had been abandoned by everyone that mattered. Oh, she knew Mr. Lassiter was capable of protecting her, but she needed someone besides a bodyguard. She wanted Carver. And she wanted her father.

Lassiter asked her a question, but for the life of her, she didn't know what he'd said. She glanced up—he was looking straight at her. "You like him, don't you?" he said.

"What? What are you talking about?"

"Are you kidding? It doesn't take a clairvoyant to read the way you look at him. He kind of grows on you, don't you think?"

Cass thought back over the short time she had known Carver. Lassiter was right. He had sneaked up on her. In fact, he'd blind-sided her. She never saw him coming.

Lassiter tried to lighten up the feeling. "You know, you really don't have to worry about your father or Carver. You should be concerned for the kidnappers." He laughed. "What I wouldn't give to be there when Carver finds them."

"Tell me about Carver," Cass said. Maybe she could learn something about Carver from his best, and maybe only, friend.

She was surprised when Lassiter said, "Let's sit down over there and make ourselves more comfortable. I have a feeling this is going to take more than five minutes."

He took off his baseball cap and ran his fingers through his hair. "Carver is one of the most . . ." he searched for the right word, "noble . . . men I have ever had the opportunity to know. He's fearless in defense of what he believes to be right. He has natural uncanny instincts that govern his actions. He won't work with anyone, because he trusts himself and nobody else. He has survived because of his instincts, in situations no one else would have survived. Yet he was never brutal, nor did he enjoy his time in combat. He treats his enemy with the respect a great pitcher shows to a great hitter—admiration, but with determination that he will never get a hit off of him."

"What happened while he was in the military? He'll never talk about it," She asked.

"I guess I should have known. He's not one to talk about himself."

"Are you kidding?" she said. "He hardly ever speaks at all."

"It figures," Lassiter said. "Well, let me put it this way. He was the 3,464th person since the founding of our country to be awarded the Congressional Medal of Honor."

Cass looked dumbfounded. "Really? Isn't that the highest award you can get in the military?"

"That's right. And, including Carver, there are only 110 recipients of the Medal still living."

She found her voice, "But he never said anything."

"He never will. That's just him. After he finished his tour of duty, he retired from the military and vowed to never pick up a gun again. He refused a public presentation of his medal and never said why. He feels he did nothing to deserve such an award. He thinks the people that should be given the medal are those that gave their last breath for their country. He would hang me up by my toes if he knew I was telling you. He is the most private and humble person I have ever known. He's my hero."

"What did he do to earn the medal?"

"He single-handedly undertook the ground rescue of five downed Air Force crew members. Their plane had crashed in the mountains of Afghanistan. The Taliban was so strong in that area, command gave them no chance of being rescued.

"He disobeyed my orders and left camp on his own. It took him three days of traveling through hostile territory until he located three of the downed airmen. Once he found them, he had to get them back to base. That was a whole other problem. He traveled mostly by night and tried to avoid any contact or engagement with the Taliban. It didn't work out that way."

"Go on," Cass said softly. She had been right about Carver—he was something unique, something special. She felt a tear run down her cheek.

He continued, "Carver took a shot in the arm, and another in his leg. Once he reached our base camp and the airmen were safe, he turned around and left to find the other two downed men. He didn't even wait around to have his wounds treated."

Cass stood and started pacing. Carver was a real hero, not a comic book superhero. All this time she had mocked him and he had never said a word. Her mother told her many times she needed to learn to control her mouth. "What happened next?" she asked.

"He had obtained information from the rescued men where they thought the other two guys had hidden. It took him three more days traveling though enemy territory with a bum leg, but he found the two downed men. One was dead, and the other, seriously wounded. It took him five more days to carry the wounded airman back to camp. During that time, he evaded the enemy on numerous occasions until he had to engage and dispose of a squad of five Taliban fighters without firing a shot. Any noise would have brought a whole company of nearby Taliban fighters down on him.

"When he was only two miles from base, he was attacked by a full detachment and had to break radio silence to call in an air strike, which he directed on his own position. He was able to escape, using the suppression fire as a smokescreen. He staggered into our forward patrol, with his survivor on his back. They had to carry Carver to the infirmary, where he was treated for the two gunshot wounds as well as multiple other wounds. It was a miracle he made it the first time. The second, well . . . he had help from above. He is a living legend to the men of our unit as well as everyone that was stationed at our base."

Cass sat trying to get her head wrapped around what Lassiter was telling her. She remembered a quote from Uncle Remus: "There's other ways of learnin' 'bout the behind feet of a mule than getting kicked by him." She felt like she had been kicked by both feet.

Lassiter was watching her closely and when she didn't say anything, he continued. "I told him that I was putting him in for a commendation and he about tore my head off. He wanted nothing to do with it. But I was still his commanding officer, and he couldn't tell me everything."

"That would be so like him," Cass said. "Was it just by chance that he came to be involved in all this, or was he sent here on purpose?"

"When Carver left the Rangers, he never intended to be involved with trouble or weapons again. He came here to live the rest of his life 'away from the maddening crowd,' as he put it, where no one knew anything about him. All he wanted to be was a gentleman farmer."

"Now I want to tell you something I've never told another soul because I think you have a right to know. Besides, it might give you a little insight into our friend's reaction to this whole gold quest."

Cass moved forward in her chair because she was intrigued. She loved secrets.

"One time we were on a raid near a village in the tops of the mountains in Afganistan. It was very cold and there was a lot of snow. Carver, as usual, took the point and was shot. He fell down an embankment and we never would have found him if it hadn't been for a friendly villager, but that's another story. Anyway, when he finally regained consciousness, he spoke to me, alone, and told me he had a very unusual experience."

Lassiter got up and looked out the window. "He said he had a very real dream where he saw himself dragging an old metal box out of the ground. He didn't open it. He was afraid, and I've never seen Carver afraid of anything.

"After his recovery, he forgot about that experience until he found that metal box on his property. Then every memory came flooding back in vivid detail. The box he dug up was the box of his dream."

Cass was perplexed. It didn't seem to her that Carver exhibited any signs of fear ever, at least not about himself.

"He told me he never figured out the purpose or the meaning of his dream, but he knew he didn't want to expose anyone, particularly his friends to whatever came out of that box."

"So Carver called you after he found the box on his property, and that was the first you knew of this whole Rhoades Gold deal?"

"Actually, I'd been involved in this investigation for almost six months before Nash took the warning shot over the bough. I learned he was involved after the fact."

It all sounded a little fishy to Cass, almost like it had been a setup. "How could Carver have known a box was buried on his property? How could anyone have known he was going to be digging post holes that day? It doesn't seem like an accidental setting. In math, we would say there are too many coincidental facts to be an anomaly."

Lassiter continued, "The professional thugs somehow obtained a letter saying that Thomas Rhoades had buried a box on his property. They had no idea where to start looking for it, but they had been watching the property very closely. When Carver started digging post holes for his fence line, they saw him find the box. They apparently tried to scare him off and get the box for themselves. They hadn't counted on running into someone like Carver Nash. Now it appears that they decided Rylan was an easier target. That, or he just happened to be in the wrong place at the wrong time."

"Where is Carver now?" she asked.

"Good question—you probably know as much as I do. I trust he'll let me know what's going on when he knows something. Until then, we're just going to have to let him do his thing."

Carver knocked three times, waited, then entered the small log cabin. An old Ute sat in a rocking chair, flanked by two young men. Carver spoke with the young men in their own tongue, Navajo. He bowed to the gray-haired man and sat down cross-legged on the floor before him.

The old man spoke very good English and addressed Carver. "My Navajo friends came to me," he indicated the men at his side. "Forgive me but I do not speak their language. We can speak in English.

"They have asked me to help you. They say you have done much to help their tribe. They say you are known as, 'Fearless Walker.' My true name is 'He Who Speaks to the Sky,' but you can call me Jacob. What is it you wish of me?"

Carver told him he was seeking the people who invaded their land, looking for the Carre-Shin-Ob. He told them these men had taken a man he considered to be his father, and they would torture and possibly kill him. He suspected these men were now located somewhere on the reservation and had been involved in other murders.

"These evil men seem to be under the secret protection of a member of the Tribal Council." The old man thought for a minute and then said, "When the sun sets tomorrow night, come to my house again. I will see what I can do."

"Welcome, Fearless Walker. I have been told there is a cabin that has been abandoned for many years. Recently it seems it has been used. Anyone coming to the cabin has been told not to return. There are armed guards. No one in the tribal council knows anything about the cabin. It is in a remote location of the reservation. I have drawn you a map."

"Thank you, He Who Speaks to the Sky. I will visit the cabin."

"You should be very careful, Fearless Walker. These are not nice people."

"I thank you, He Who Speaks to the Sky. I would not have asked this favor except for the circumstances."

"Your Navajo brothers speak very highly of you, Fearless Walker. I have read your spirit. I would not have helped, except I know you are a man of honor. I trust you will use this information wisely."

"Peace be with you, He Who Speaks to the Sky."

Chapter Thirteen

Carver had been lying stretched out in the knee-high grass for hours. He figured he was about a hundred yards from the cabin with a clear view of anyone coming or going. The grass barely covered him, so it was necessary that he lie motionless. The cabin was situated at the base of a small hill. No timber grew in the area directly in front of the cabin, and the rear backed up to a hundred-foot sheer cliff. Anyone in the cabin had a clear view, or shot for that matter, of anyone approaching the cabin from the front while the rear was protected by the cliff. The location was ideal for holding off an army or for keeping a hostage.

He Who Speaks to the Sky held a place of honor in the tribe. He was a visionary man, considered to be holy. Because of his status, he had access to any information relating to the reservation. He had learned that the old cabin was under heavy guard, and it would be difficult for anyone to approach it. Someone could be holding Rylan inside.

He Who Speaks to the Sky had not been able to discover who in the tribe had control of the cabin, but he had given Carver an amulet and told him to show it to any Ute who stopped him. It would identify him as being protected by He Who Speaks to the Sky and allow him freedom to travel on the reservation.

Carver identified three guards stationed at strategic locations on the hillside surrounding the cabin. Each had in their possession fifty-caliber sniper rifles equipped with night-light scopes. The guards maintained contact with those in the cabin by two-way radios. Carver now had possession of the three radios and had listened to someone in the cabin trying to make contact with the outside guards for several hours. They were becoming more and more agitated and anxious as time passed because of their inability to connect. Carver expected they would eventually come out to see what had happened to their friends. Of course, if they had satellite phones, they could just call for reinforcements, in which case, he could find himself in the middle of a gunfight at the OK Corral.

He had located the cabin a day ago. It took him another day to locate the outside guards. Once he found them, he had silently taken them out of commission, one at a time. All three now lay in a cave, bound and gagged with duct tape. They wouldn't say what kind of communication those in the cabin had with the outside world.

None of his captives had ever been in the cabin. They had been shown their positions and given twenty-four hour shifts. That meant their replacements would arrive early in the morning. He needed to make something happen by then, or he'd have a whole new mess to deal with.

His prisoners didn't know who was in the cabin. They'd been paid by a courier and not told anything except to shoot anyone that crossed the killing field in front of the cabin without authorization. They knew once they took the money, they'd be dead if they didn't do their job.

Carver hadn't been able to find out how many people were in the cabin, or if Rylan was among them, but he believed he was there.

Carver had his sniper rifle trained on the cabin and would use it, if it came to that. In the dark, he used his own equipment. It was better than the night vision rifle sight. He watched as the door to the cabin opened enough for a man to slip out, dressed in dark clothing and moving like he had experience in night combat. He began moving slowly to the east, apparently towards the closest sniper position. Carver had him at a disadvantage because he had his night vision equipment, which allowed him to flank the man and intercept him as he slipped into the trees.

A cord went around the man's throat, immediately shutting off his breathing and ability to call out. He frantically reached with both hands to try to prevent the choking, couldn't, and slowly slipped into unconsciousness. Carver removed the radio from the guy's belt and quickly taped his hands behind his back and his ankles and knees together before putting a strip of tape over his mouth. He removed the pistol and threw it as far as he could into the long grass.

Shortly, the man came to and looked around. He stood on a log, held in place by a rope around his neck. Carver sat across from him in the moonlight, shaving a stick with a large knife, his rifle laid in front of him. The log moved as the man shifted his weight. Carver could tell he was awake by his movement, but didn't bother looking at him. He whispered, "I wouldn't move very much if I were you. If you fall off that log, you just might hang yourself before I'm able to help you."

The man tried not to move, but he shook. Carver again whispered, almost matter-of-factly, "Here's the deal. I'm going to remove the gag from your mouth. All I want to hear are whispered answers to these three questions: One, how many guys are in the cabin? Two, is Rylan Edison in the cabin? And three, who are you working for? If I hear anything but answers to those questions, in a voice above a whisper, I'm going to kick that log you're standing on and walk away from here. Do you understand?"

The man's eyes showed fear, and he nodded that he understood. Carver looked at him for a while, making sure he knew he was in deep trouble. Carver reached up and yanked the tape off the man's face, putting his knife against the man's throat. "Now, whisper the answers to me."

In a barely audible voice the captive said, "There is no one else in the cabin. I don't know the name of the man who hired me. It was a blind hire."

The man didn't say another word, but the fear still showed in his eyes. Carver waited and said, "What were you hired to do? Who do you report to when your job is finished?"

"I was supposed to hole up in this cabin until someone came looking for Rylan Edison. I was told to hire the outside guards and to tell them to shoot first and ask questions later. If someone looking for Rylan Edison were to get killed, I was to post a note on my blog. If I could not kill him and he got in the cabin, I was to give him an envelope. I left it on the table."

"How much were you paid?"

"I got $25,000 up front and another $25,000 when the job was completed, as well as money to hire the outside guards. Whoever killed the suspect was to receive a bonus of $50,000."

"Do you have any idea who hired you?" Carver pushed against the log with his foot.

"Hey, man, don't do that. I've answered your questions just like you said. I don't know. I only talked to him once. He had a funny accent. It sounded maybe Russian. I don't know."

Carver started to walk away before he heard the prisoner whisper to him, "Don't leave me here like this. I might fall off."

"I wouldn't do that if I were you. I figure it will take me about three hours to contact the Feds. They'll have someone here shortly thereafter. But they don't like people who are willing to shoot a man sight unseen. So, if I were you, I would hold real still."

The two guards outside the Edisons' house radioed Lassiter that they had apprehended an approaching man who said he was a friend. Lassiter instructed them to bring him to the front door.

"Bill," exclaimed Reber. "What's going on here?"

"You can let him go," said Lassiter. He invited Reber into the cabin just as Cass came out of the kitchen.

"Reber, what are you doing here?" she asked, drying her hands.

"I came to see you, and instead found a couple of guards who didn't respect my heritage and treated me like a gangster."

Lassiter volunteered, "Reber is my contact on the reservation. He was the one that first alerted us to the problem and requested our assistance. I've kept it a secret because we didn't want it to leak out. We worried he might have found himself pushing up daisies."

Cass gave out a sigh of relief. She had felt all along that Reber was just what he presented himself to be, an honorable man who was in this to help his tribe. However, she liked having her beliefs confirmed. She reminded herself to trust her instincts.

Reber looked at Cass and said, "That day, when we were riding and were shot at, I thought someone had figured out my connection to Homeland Security. Later I decided that whoever fired those shots may have only been trying to scare you and your father."

Lassiter asked, "Have you been able to learn anything about Mr. Edison?"

"All's apparently quiet on the reservation, but for some reason, I don't think I'm getting very good information from my sources. I still need to be careful until we identify the traitor, so I haven't really pushed any hot buttons yet."

"Does everyone still believe you have a romantic interest in Ms. Edison?"

"Well, everyone except Ms. Edison. I can't convince her I'm serious."

Cass was flabbergasted. "You mean everything between you and me has just been a put-on? You've just been using me to get information?"

Reber smiled. "No, Cass. Everything I've ever said to you is the absolute truth, including the fact that I fell for you while you were on your mission, and haven't stopped loving you since."

Cass blushed and quit speaking. She didn't like putting her foot in her mouth, particularly in front of Lassiter.

Lassiter added, "Well, for whatever reason, it worked. Everyone believes he's chasing you, and that enabled him to stay in the loop, since he could head this direction without any questions."

"Have you heard from Nash?" Reber asked.

"Not a word," replied Lassiter.

Reber reached over and took Cass's hand. "Your father will be okay. I know it. Is there anything I can do to help until we find him?"

The soft tone in Reber's voice broke through the barrier Cass had so carefully constructed around her fear, and she cried like a baby in his arms until she ran out of tears and her throat was dry.

Longbow tensed when he heard the footstep outside his cabin. His long fingers found his gun, but the voice stopped him before he picked it up.

"I would not do that, if I were you." A tall shadow filled his doorway, appearing as if from nowhere.

"What are you doing here?" Longbow asked, his voice cracking.

"I came to see you, old friend." The man smiled, his face showing no sign of mirth. "Why don't you invite me in?"

"Come in," Longbow said automatically.

"Thank you, but no." A flash of gunpowder and then the shadow was gone, leaving Longbow dead with his hand inches away from self-defense.

Early the next morning, Carver returned to the Edison home. Cass heard Carver speaking to Lassiter as she lay in bed after a sleepless night. She knew Carver would have some information about her father or he wouldn't have returned home, but she had not heard Rylan's voice. Carver hadn't brought him home—not a good sign. She had a sinking feeling in her gut. She hurried and dressed, although she took time to run a brush through her hair and check out her reflection in the mirror. What she saw made her do a double take. She needed some help.

Still, she was thrilled to hear Carver's voice. She didn't like it when he was gone, especially when he left to find trouble.

By the time she came out of her bedroom, Lassiter was just leaving. "I'll be in touch," he said, looking at Cass. "Will you be okay with him, or should I send in one of the guards?"

"I'll try, but tell them to be on their toes," she replied and managed a tense laugh. She looked at Carver—in fact, she had trouble taking her eyes off him.

Carver asked Cass, "Would you like some breakfast? Then maybe we can talk."

She would like to see his skills in the kitchen—the thought amused her. "Sure." She wanted to ask him about her father, but since he hadn't said anything, she was worried it was bad news.

Cass was amazed at the orderly and efficient manner in which he managed to start the bacon, put the eggs on a different burner, and put bread in the toaster at about the same time. He placed a glass in front of her and said, "Orange juice?"

"Sure," she said. He looked at her, and his eyes seemed to take in everything with just a glance, but he purposely avoided any sustained eye contact.

She finally couldn't take it any longer and blurted, "Did you find out anything about my father?"

"I didn't, but he's okay." He motioned with his head to an envelope on the counter. "I found a note he wrote. He was probably forced to write it, so don't read too much into it."

I'm supposed to tell you not to try to find me. If you continue to look, they claim they will kill me. They want you to continue to find the Lost Rhodes Mine. If you find it then contact them by placing a message on your Roosevelt blog, Cassandra. The message must provide the precise latitude and longitude of the valley of the mine. Then Mr. Nash is to get on a plane and fly to Paris. They say if you contact the authorities it won't matter if you find the mine, because I will not be around to see it. If you don't find it within two weeks they say they will dump my body

in your front yard.
Your dad

Cass read the note again. "He's trying to tell me something in code and there's something else. First, I don't have a Roosevelt blog. Second, he never calls me Cassandra, and third, he never refers to himself as Dad. Plus, he knows how to spell Rhoades."

Roosevelt might be where he was when he wrote the note—that made sense. She thought she had better set up a blog before someone started checking the site for her note. The other mistakes had something to do with his code. Maybe someone else had written the note while he dictated it, but it looked like his handwriting.

Then she saw it. He had written her a message by making certain letters bold. She started writing them down. "C – A – R – V – E – R L – O – V – E – S Y – O – U." He had to know this might be the last chance to say something to her, and he had chosen to tell her he thought Carver loved her? How could he even know that? And if he knew, why would he choose to tell her now? Unless, she thought, he knew something she didn't and he didn't want her to walk away from her superhero.

She didn't mention Rylan's secret message. Instead she said, "I think my father was in Roosevelt when he wrote this note." She walked over and sat on the couch directly across from the chair where Carver sat. He glanced up and met her eyes. She thought he started to blush as he turned his gaze away from her.

"I didn't like you being away," she said. She wasn't smiling.

He turned his gaze back to her, a questioning look on his face.

The silence was as heavy as a dense fog. "This is all wrong," he said. He was upset—she could tell.

"What?" she said. "It's wrong that I missed you?"

He wanted to say something, but seemed to struggle with the words. "It's all wrong," he said. He got up and began pacing. She waited for him to go on. "Don't you see, Cass, I can't do this to you."

"Do what? What are you talking about?"

"I've lived a life you can't even imagine, and I can't seem to avoid problems. I'm like a magnet. First, my parents both passed away. Then I went to war. . . . I have done things and seen things . . . that were horrific. I could never expect someone else to share that burden just because I can't escape it."

"Talk to me, Carver. Tell me about it." He had never been so close to sharing his life with her. He looked like he wanted to talk, to respond to her question, but couldn't. "Tell me what you were thinking, just before I sat down."

"That you are the loveliest woman I've ever seen."

She never expected him to say something like that. Her heart started to pound and the blood rushed to her head as she found herself at a total loss for words, a rare position for her.

"Don't you see," he said struggling to make his words heard. "I could never climb into your world. I would ruin it." His voice was soft and ragged, not filled with pain, but reality.

"Don't I get a vote? I might just like you climbing around in my world."

At that instant, his cell started ringing. "Talk about timing," she muttered, knowing the spell was broken.

Carver talked while her mind wandered. Had her father really known? She couldn't believe Carver actually thought of her as a beautiful woman. She really had been in the math department too long—she used to know if a guy had any interest in her.

"That was Lassiter," said Carver. "Right now they don't have any leads on Rylan's location. He thinks we should bring Reber in to consult with us and help in the search for the Mine. Reber can help us if we need to go on the reservation—besides, he's very familiar with the written and oral history of the Carre-Shin-Ob. What do you think?"

"I think," Cass said, "I think I want to go back to talking about our future. Reber complicates things. But if he can help, of course, bring him in."

Lassiter phoned ahead and warned Carver that he was on his way to the house with Reber. Cass told Carver she wanted to talk to Reber alone and went out on the porch to wait for his arrival. When the two men walked onto the porch, Cass was in a no-nonsense mood. She invited Lassiter to go in and talk to Carver, telling him she needed to speak to Reber. Lassiter shrugged and walked in the house, with Cass closing the door behind him.

Reber took a seat in one of the porch chairs, smiling. Cass wrapped her arms around her and leaned on the porch rail, looking across the yard. She wasn't looking forward to this little chat, but she had set her mind on it. Now all she had to do was figure out what she was going to say.

"Reber, we need to talk." She said it a little more forcefully than she wanted. She liked Reber, but only as a friend, and he hadn't been told that he had been relegated to the "just a friend" category. Carver, on the other hand, had been moved out of the "Superhero" category to "possible soul mate" status. Carver didn't know of this change, either. She still had to convince him it was a good move. But Carver wasn't as approachable as Reber, so she decided to practice on Reber. Besides, he was nice and might listen.

"We've been told we have to find the Lost Rhoades Mine within two weeks. If we don't find it, they've threatened to kill my father. On top of that, I know you still have feelings for me. I'm sorry, but that's not going anywhere, and there are a number of reasons for that, which I really don't want to get into right now. Just let me say this—"

She didn't know what to say and became more irritated as her mental debate raged on. Reber looked like he wanted to be anywhere but on the porch with her, but he seemed to sense it was not the time to interrupt her.

Finally she threw her hands in the air. "Just go in the house." Reber looked confused, but he got up quickly and fled into the house.

"What was that all about?" he asked Carver and Lassiter as he closed the door, before she could decide to invite him back.

Lassiter just shrugged. Carver said, "Probably some female thing."

Cass came in the house a few minutes later. "What? We're not going to find my dad or the mine if all the three of you just stand there gaping." She threw her hands in the air and walked into her bedroom, slamming the door. She was frustrated with herself, she feared for her father, Carver was being Carver, and she was helpless to do anything.

Lassiter sheepishly asked, "What did you do, Nash?"

"I don't have a clue," he responded.

Lassiter replied, "Well, I think I'll go out and catch a few bad guys. It's probably safer out there. You two can hold the fort down here, right?"

"Maybe I should go," replied Reber.

"No, you came to see her. You stay, I'll go help Lassiter," replied Carver.

"Umm, both of you better stay. I don't need any help, but it seems whoever stays is going to need some assistance." Lassiter chuckled as he closed the door.

Cass sat next to Reber, who kept his distance. Carver wanted to avoid her questions, and so avoided eye contact with her. They reviewed everything they knew about Rylan's kidnapping, which wasn't much. Then Carver stressed, "Essentially, we have to find the mine within two weeks or they may kill Rylan. I don't think they'd actually do it—as long as they have him, they have a bargaining chip. Of course, it might be easier to find Rylan and rescue him than to find the Lost Rhoades Mine." He paused, then added, "Cass thinks they were holding him in Roosevelt at one time."

Reber directed his next comment to Carver, staying clear of Cass. "We figured out who is the spy on the tribal council. It took a long time, but we simply kept following the money. His name was Longbow and it was his cabin where you found Rylan's note. They found his body yesterday. We don't know who was paying or controlling him. Now we never will, so that street is a dead end."

Cass suddenly spoke. "Reber, why don't you just ask the tribal leaders to tell you the location of the mine? Then we won't have to continue to chase down clues all over the county."

"Cass, I'm sorry, but no one in the tribe knows. The secret died with Chief Arapene. He didn't trust anyone with the secret. Not even Chief Tabiona knew. He let everyone think he pulled the plug and stopped providing gold because he was at odds with the Church. The fact is, he didn't know its location but didn't want anyone to know he didn't know."

"Well, that means we'll just have to find it for ourselves," replied Cass. "And we'd better get to it—time's running out."

Chapter Fourteen

Cass filled Reber in on everything they'd learned so far. Carver asked, "So, why do you think Thomas Rhoades, or Brigham Young for that matter, set up a series of hoops to jump through before allowing us to discover the location of the mine? I mean, why not just leave one box with a map that had directions to the Carre-Shin-Ob?"

Cass thought about Carver's query and was about to respond when Reber jumped in. "I don't want to avoid your question, but let me ask you this. If you had found a map in that first box which led you to the mine, would you still feel the same about the Carre-Shin-Ob and the people surrounding the legend?"

Cass felt Reber nailed it. "You're right. I felt I was going on a treasure hunt, hoping to find a pot of gold at the end of the rainbow. My father believed that finding the Carre-Shin-Ob would lend credence to his beliefs which others consider to be nothing but allegorical. He wasn't interested in the gold for the sake of gold. My interest was not quite so noble. But I feel different now."

Reber returned to Carver's original question. "Maybe the series of clues was meant to teach the seeker respect for the legend and history of the people involved, maybe even to discover how and why the mine's location remains a mystery even today." He paused. "It's almost like he wanted the seeker to earn his stripes."

Cass thought Reber was right on, and she saw Carver slightly nod his head. "In the first letter, Thomas Rhoades said he was told to create a hidden path by the prophet Brigham Young. Brigham told him that only the 'chosen' would be allowed to see the clues."

Reber smiled at Cass and queried, "So tell me, Ms. Edison, do you think you have been chosen? If you find the mine, what will you do with the gold?"

"That depends on whom it belongs to," said Cass. "It might make a difference if it's on the reservation, but then either way, it could belong to the Utes, the Church, or maybe the one who finds it."

Carver had climbed back into his turtle shell and wasn't speaking. She suspected he would only say something if he felt contrary to anything they said. Well, maybe . . . she decided to prod him, just a little. "So, Carver, we haven't heard from you. What do you think?"

To her surprise, he answered. "You know, I think there is a prophesy somewhere that says the Indian nation will one day rise up and become a powerful people. Is it possible that the gold could assist them to fulfill the prophecy?"

Carver wasn't through. "If there really are golden plates with a recorded history of Indians that lived in this area, just like Rylan suggested, have you ever thought of the implications? I mean, there could be references to historical events or places, maybe even some mentioned in the Book of Mormon. It could be additional evidence of the truthfulness of the Book of Mormon. But even if there were just golden plates, it would at the very least demonstrate that the inhabitants of this land kept a written record on plates, just like Joseph Smith claimed. It might not prove the Book of Mormon is true but it would tip the scales, for sure."

"Reber," she asked, "how is it possible that no one—no outsiders or even someone on the reservation—has ever discovered the location of the Carre-Shin-Ob? Is it possible it really doesn't exist?"

Reber responded, "Wakara knew where it was. So did Thomas and Caleb Rhoades. And apparently Isaac Morley also went there. Each speaks of the existence of the Carre-Shin-Ob. Thomas Rhoades said he had been there many times and the gold exceeded anyone's wildest imagination. We also have the agreement between Brigham Young, Chief Wakara, and Thomas Rhoades. Isaac Morley left his testimony that the mine existed, as did Jesse Knight. We also have several million dollars of gold that had to come from somewhere."

Cass became more insistent. "Then how is it possible that no one can find it? I mean, they have metal detectors and probably a slew of high-tech scientific instruments that are capable of locating large deposits of metal. They could over fly the area with such instruments to locate possible sites. Besides, prospectors have stalked the area with maps looking under every rock. They haven't found anything!"

Reber responded, "Well, I know more than one Ute who has taken an oath to keep gold seekers off the reservation. They are not against using any force necessary. However, I am also aware of a group of Utes who are trying to locate the mine. Most of the older Utes still believe it to be a sacred place and are against anyone even trying to locate it.

"I believe in the legend. I believe that the Carre-Shin-Ob is protected by Towats, the Great Spirit, and I believe no one will ever locate it without Towat's consent. It's so sacred, if anyone stumbled onto it by mistake they would not survive."

Cass was impressed by Reber's innate love for the Utes—their folklore, their unwritten history, and the intricacies of their way of life. He was proud of his heritage, legend or not, and he wasn't afraid to say so. Reber would be a force for good for the tribe.

Over the last hour, she had continually made comparisons between Reber and Carver. Both were honorable and committed to the right. Reber, while being a servant to his people, still managed to have fun. Carver, however, was still a little bit of a mystery, the strong, silent type. She just wanted to see into his heart or mind, to get some clue as to what was going on inside. Reber, on the other hand, was an open book and wore his feelings on his sleeve. Cass loved Reber like a brother, but she just wanted Carver to hold her.

Cass passed everyone a copy of the quit-claim deed and assignment that had been taken from the county recorder's office. "Look these over. I have also given you the cipher text, along with the decoded message using *Brigham Young* as the keyword. I have tried every other keyword I could think of and none decodes into an intelligible message. Am I missing something?"

They all spent time going over the documents. Each suggested keywords, but Cass usually responded that she had tried them, or, after trying them, said they didn't work.

Carver asked, "Is it possible that the keyword *Brigham Young* gives you a new message that must again be run through the cipher wheels with another keyword?"

Cass said, "I never thought of that. I'll try some of the other keywords to see if any of them work. While I'm doing that, you two look at these photos we took at the Lion House and see if you can find anything out of place."

The three had been working on the documents for about two hours when Reber got up to go outside and take a call. As soon as he was out of the room, Cass asked, "Carver, have you ever said anything to my father about me?"

She knew it was an off-the-wall question, maybe a little forward, but she still wondered why her father would use what might be his last words to tell her Carver loved her.

"About what?" asked Carver, looking dead guilty.

"About me."

Reber walked in and Cass knew Carver wouldn't fess up now, even if her father had said something, and now she had lost the element of surprise.

"None of the keywords I've tried even come close," said Cass. She was somewhat discouraged and didn't know which direction to turn next.

Reber asked, "I've been wondering about this photograph you have of the plaque on the front of the Lion House. Maybe they didn't have a very good method of casting signs in those days, but it seems that a lot of the characters are bolder or thicker than the others."

Cass took her copy and Carver found his copy of the photo. They all started looking at it. "There's no order or pattern to which letters are bold and which are not. You would think that all of the *G*'s, for example, would be bold if they had a problem with the *G* die," suggested Reber.

Cass remembered that her father had just sent her an encoded message. Maybe he had broken the code. She started writing down the emboldened characters and realized very quickly that she was barking up the wrong tree. The code was different than what Rhoades had previously employed. She started searching her mind for other well-known coding techniques.

Deep in thought, she felt a light come on inside her. She exclaimed, "I remember a cipher system that used groups of bold and non-bold characters to form a single letter. I've got to spend some time in my code books. Why don't you two go in and fix us something to eat. I assume you'll both fit in the kitchen at the same time."

An hour later, the guys finished eating a meal of spaghetti and garlic bread. They offered some to Cass but she muttered something unintelligible and went back to her books.

"I knew it was here," she shouted. "Sir Francis Bacon created a substitution cipher using bold and standard characters. His cipher text was broken down into groups of five characters where each such group represented one letter. To decode the cipher, you had to use the table in which each letter was assigned five characters. For example, *A* would be *****, *B* would be ******B**, *C* would be *****BB** and so forth. Give me a minute and I'll see what I can make of this plaque."

Twenty minutes later her face lit up. "I think we've just cracked the code. If I'm correct, it reads:

One hour twenty minute hike up ridge between Daniels and Center Creek
One half mile down from mine
Hieroglyphic granite rock fifty steps due east, a box is buried.

"Do you know the place, Reber?" she asked.

"I know the general location. The area has a number of stones with ancient carvings. I don't know specifically where this one is, but we should be able to find it. All we have to do is hike for an hour and twenty minutes."

"Yeah, but where do you start the clock?" asked Cass.

"Well, the creeks of Daniels Canyon and Center Creek join together not far from Highway 40. I assume the confluence would be as good as anywhere to start. Since everyone walks at a different pace, I don't assume that the hour and twenty minutes is a specific number—more like a general statement that will get us close. After we find the old mine, we'll head straight downhill about a half mile, another general number. We can estimate the distance and start looking for the ancient rock. I'm sure both landmarks will stand out like a sore thumb."

"Is it on the reservation?" asked Cass.

"No, this area is all National Forest land," replied Reber.

"The box should have the second map," Cass said. "At that point we should be able know the approximate location of the Carre-Shin-Ob. We don't have a lot of time left. Are we going to contact the Head Thug before we actually go to the mine? How are we going to be sure that we get my father back?"

Reber responded, "I think I'll leave the counter espionage planning to Carver—he's the expert. I've got a few things to take care of tonight, so I'd better run. I'll meet you in Daniels Canyon in the morning—I'll be in the parking area I've marked here at eight. Here's the map I've drawn."

"That sounds good," she replied. "We'll be there."

Cass closed the door behind Reber and walked over to where Carver stood, by the couch. "May I see your phone?" She held out her hand. He handed it to her. She pushed the off button and it made the sounds of dying, and then she gave it back to him.

Carver opened his mouth to protest, but she put a hand on his chest, pushed him down onto the couch, and said, "Sit." He sat.

"Okay, here are the rules. We're going to play a little game. It's similar to twenty questions, except I get to ask the questions. The purpose of the questions is to elicit an answer. A nod of the head, words like "umm," and silence are not acceptable. You may not choose to defer, or not answer a question. A verbally intelligible answer is required. Do you understand?"

Carver nodded his head. He wondered if Lassiter had been giving Cass lessons on interrogation. He may have even given her some questions to ask, which could make it even worse.

He thought back over the brief time he had known Cass. If he could have requisitioned a perfect woman, she would be it, but he couldn't let it go any further. He had to tell her there was no future for them—then he had to make her believe it. But he didn't lie very well, and she would most likely see right through him. He had avoided personal conversations with her for this very reason.

He knew that life, people, and relationships never lasted and that relationships took an incredible investment of self. He had given his heart and soul once and had never gotten over it. His first love forgot she promised him forever. He, well, he didn't know how to forget, and it still hurt. Survival for him meant never putting himself in that vulnerable position again—instead, he had given himself completely to his work, to whatever his next assignment was. He really hadn't cared if he lived or died. It just didn't matter. All he cared about was finishing his next sortie. He had seen things he could never share nor eliminate from his memory.

They haunted his nights and filled his dreams.

Cass had been talking to him and he hadn't heard a thing she said.

She threw one of the couch pillows at him, bringing him back to the present. "Are you listening?"

"Ummm . . ."

"Listen, Mr. Nash, we're going to get through this one way or the other. I'm not giving up until I get some answers. And I remind you that 'ummm' is not an acceptable response, so you need to try again."

"What was the question?" He wasn't being evasive—he just didn't have a clue what she had asked.

Cass looked at him like she had him in the crosshairs of her rifle sights. He squirmed. "Before I ask my question again," she continued, "you know, some people voluntarily choose to avoid life and hide in the shadows, afraid they might get sunburned. Some people think they can climb a mountain without leaving a little blood along the way. Others are afraid of fire because they got burned once. Some hide behind big walls because they're afraid of living and believe they're being noble and self-sacrificing by protecting everyone around them."

He was still squirming in his chair and not looking at her. She was right and he knew it.

"Let me tell you, Mr. Nash, and this is a fact, you miss every shot you don't take. You'll never be able to look down from the top of a mountain. You'll live a dismal, dreary life watching others fail, get up, and fail again. But you know, every once in awhile, someone will finally climb back up on that horse and stay.

"I thought you weren't afraid of anything. But I think you're afraid to live. You hide behind that wall, afraid to come out into the light. I understand that you're willing to put your life on the line for me, but what about your heart?"

She went silent, her piercing blue eyes penetrating his heart. She was right. He had never been afraid to die, but maybe he was afraid to live. He glanced in her direction and met her eyes, then quickly looked in the other direction.

"That was a question," she said.

He didn't know what to say, silenced by his own thoughts.

She continued, "What have you told my father about me?"

He flinched and thought back over the last couple of conversations he'd had with Rylan. He remembered only too well saying that he loved Cass, but he couldn't do anything about it. He had never told him why, just that he could never marry, and he didn't want to hurt her.

He didn't look at her. Finally his response came, muted, faltering, and charged with emotion: "Cass . . . it's been a long time . . . since I've let myself care about anyone or anything. You will be better off if . . . I'm not good enough . . ."

"I get to choose what's right for me. I get to make that decision." She got out of the chair, walked over, and sat on his lap. She put both arms around him and pulled him close.

It felt so good to hold her. He smiled and said, "Sometimes you talk too much." He wrapped his arms around her and kissed her, feeling a jolt of electricity race between them. She whispered in his ear, "My dad warned me about the strong, silent type." Then she returned his kiss.

After a minute, or maybe it was several minutes, he stood up with her in his arms and gently sat her back on the couch. "We can continue this conversation in the morning. You get some sleep. I've got to go out and check a few things. Just be sure you're ready by six-thirty in the morning."

She wouldn't let go and he wasn't complaining. His head and heart were pounding. He had known it for a long time—if he could fall for any woman it would be Cass and there was no doubt about it, he had started his descent when he first saw her at the airport. He loved her for her feisty, reactionary independence. She was someone he could trust and count on forever. She was willing to stick her chin out and wait for someone to try to knock her down. She was a fighter. He wondered what he had done right to deserve someone like her.

"Party pooper," she said.

He fled into the night to make sure she was protected.

Carver had breakfast ready when she walked out of her bedroom at six-fifteen, looking stunning. He had returned to the house to fix breakfast and was sitting at the table. He tried to concentrate on his food. Once he opened his heart, the flood of feelings came pouring in and he couldn't or didn't want to stop them, but he wasn't really comfortable expressing those feelings, either. He was way out of his comfort zone when he needed to focus on finding Rylan and protecting Cass.

She sat down and tried to break the ice. "Is this breakfast for me?"

"Yeah."

"That's it? You don't have anything else to say?" She was teasing him and he knew it.

"I'm a man of action, not words."

"Well, Mr. Nash, I know someone who teaches a speech therapy class that we need to enroll you in. What do you say?" She reached over and kissed him.

Later, she took his hand as he closed the door to the house. It was amazing what the touch of one human could do to the heart of another, he thought.

He had stocked the car for this morning's trip. He had a backpack loaded with his gear. He didn't know what they would be walking into, so he came prepared for anything. He hoped he could clear his mind enough to concentrate on the task at hand. He had to keep Cass safe—that mattered most. He had an array of firearms arranged in the car for quick access.

As he climbed in the car, he said, "I spoke to Lassiter this morning. He thinks he has a lead on the international thief he's been trying to catch up with. He'll keep us posted if anything breaks. Seems that this guy has a habit of robbing treasures of antiquity from around the world. Apparently he read some stories of the Lost Rhoades Mine and has been actively trying to decide if there is any truth to it. It seems as if, with all that's been going on with us, he's become very interested in the reality of this lost mine."

He strapped himself in and checked his revolver before putting it back in his shoulder holster. She watched him. He was extremely thorough and she felt safe with him. Soon they were heading down the highway toward Heber. She reached over and took his hand, squeezing it. He glanced over at her a number of times, but figured it would be safer if he kept his eyes on the road.

Without any warning he suddenly pulled the car into a turnout and threw on the brakes. He had his gun in his hand before she realized they had stopped. "Duck," he said. "Get down on the floor."

A car raced past without slowing. He waited for five minutes and kept her on the floor. "It's okay," he said. "I may have been just a little too jumpy."

The ride continued, but Carver was in another world, zoned in on everything that was happening around him. He scanned every car they passed.

"Umm . . . it would be better if you kept your eyes on the road too," he said. "I need to pay attention to something other than you right now."

"Albert Einstein once said, 'Gravition is not responsible for people falling in love.' "

"What?" he said. She was gazing out the window into the blue sky and seemed not to have a worry in the world.

"But then Lily Tomlin said, "If love is the answer, could you rephrase the question?"

"What?"

"I've also heard that love is like pi—natural, irrational, and very important. Which one do you think best describes love?"

"What? Do you understand where we are and where we're going? And oh, by the way, there are some very bad people that may be trying to stop us."

"That's your problem. So which one do you pick?"

By the time they left Heber, Carver was breathing again. On the way up Daniels Canyon, he pulled off the road twice, stopped, and waited. Nothing.

They had arrived at the GPS coordinates provided by Reber and slowed, making a left turn into a seldom-used parking area. After circling and surveying the lot, he pulled off the unpaved parking surface until his vehicle was hidden in a group of trees. He got out of the car and removed a camouflage tarp that he draped over the car.

He walked towards her and reached to take her hand. "That tarp is amazing. I wouldn't be able to see the car if I didn't know right where it was," she said.

He pulled her behind some trees. "We'll wait here for Reber." She sat in front of him with his arms around her—he felt like maybe he would be able to protect her if he could only keep her close.

Chapter Fifteen

The gray SUV circled the parking area twice, slowly. The passenger was definitely looking for someone or something. The SUV glided just past where they were hiding, almost coming to a stop, and then quickly proceeded on. Carver grabbed Cass's hand and said, "Follow me. Be as quiet as possible, which means, you can't ask questions."

She almost had to run to keep up with him. He led her straight up a hill to a ridgeline that looked down a small ravine. They got there just in time to see the SUV pull out of the parking area into the trees. The two men got out and started up the hill directly toward where Carver and Cass were now hiding. Carver handed her a gun and said "Don't use this unless it's absolutely necessary." He then loaded his rifle with darts.

They hid behind several large logs. The men looked like they knew exactly where Cass and Carver were hiding. Both men were carrying handguns, although it didn't look like they needed guns to inflict substantial harm to anyone in their way. They scanned the area as they continued their ascent. Maybe Carver had positioned them directly in their path for a purpose. He didn't run from a fight; she knew that. He knew what he was doing, even though she would have run the opposite direction. He squeezed her hand and motioned for her to hold still. He didn't move, but just watched and waited.

She had always heard that you should wait until you could see the whites of their eyes, and they were close enough for her to see white. She didn't know if she could hold still another second. Carver let her hand drop.

Then she heard a pop followed by whoosh, followed by the sound of the bolt action of the rifle. Another pop, and a second whoosh—it happened so fast, it could have been just one pop. She looked up and saw both men on the ground.

"What happened?" she asked.

She was shaking, but he appeared as calm as if were waiting in line to buy movie tickets; however, the tenseness in his jaw betrayed him. He tried to smile. "Nothing serious. It's just a dart with a quick-acting drug that affects the nervous system. It was developed by the military. Those two gorillas won't be able to move for about an hour. After that, they'll be fine."

He reached back, took her hand, and went over to the two downed men. She wasn't sure about that—what if the darts didn't work? Carver pulled out some handcuffs and chained them in an embrace around a tree. He ran a strip of duct tape around their mouths, allowing them to breathe, but not talk.

"That's so they can't eat through the tree," Carver said lightly. "That would be the only way they could escape. Come on, we've got to go find Reber." He flipped open his cell phone and spoke quickly, giving the coordinates of the location where the two thugs could be picked up.

Cass saw Reber approaching as they walked out of the trees.

"There you are. I thought maybe you started our little hike without me," he teased.

He looked at the weapons Carver and Cass held. "What is that strange-looking thing? Do you shoot charging elephants with it?"

"Just people you want stopped in their tracks, but not dead," replied Cass. "It works pretty well. I'll bet it would stop an elephant. There are two goons over there that'll vouch for it when they wake up."

Reber looked like he wanted some more information. Carver replied, "It's an experimental military gun. It shoots a tranquilizer dart, much like they use on wild animals, but it works faster. Did you make sure no one followed you?"

"Yeah, I rode my mountain bike cross-country to a friend's, borrowed a car, and then traded for another car partway here," Reber replied. Cass caught him glancing at her hand, which Carver was holding.

"Let's get started," she said.

"The two creeks come together right down here about half a mile." Reber pointed the way. A few minutes later, they crossed Daniels Creek and started their climb up the ridge.

Reber marked their time. They had hiked about a mile when Carver said, "You guys go ahead. I think I'll check our backs. If I haven't caught up when you get to the mine, go down and see if you can find the box without me."

Cass didn't want Carver to stay back alone, but then, it was obvious he could take care of himself. Reber already had a handgun and Carver had fitted a shoulder holster on her to carry the pistol he had given her.

"You've got one hour to go," he said. "I'll try to catch up with you, but I want to make sure we don't have any followers."

She wasn't worried about Carver but, she didn't like being separated from him. "Hurry," she said as watched him walk away.

The hill was steep and took some effort. It was beautiful pine-covered country. "So, you think he's the one?" asked Reber after they had put some distance between themselves and Carver.

"Reber, you're one of the best friends I have. I want to keep that relationship. But to answer your question, yes, I think he's the one. I'm not sure what he thinks. It's a little hard to know, since he and talking don't have a lot in common."

Reber glanced at his watch a couple of times before saying, "About another half hour up this hill and we can start looking off to the right for mine tailings. Tailings look like a big gopher dug a big hole and threw all the dirt out behind him. We have to remember this mine was dug about 150 years ago, so it's not going to stand out like a sore thumb." His voice was strained, not his usual jovial self. She felt sorry for him.

"Reeb, you okay?"

"I just want you to be happy, Cass." He looked at her while blinking his eyes. She didn't know what to say to him. She knew he was in love with her. She appreciated his words, but it was apparent that his feelings didn't match what he said, even if he understood. They walked in silence except for her strained breathing. She stopped and looked back from where they had come. She couldn't see Carver, but the scenery was spectacular. She rested her hands on her knees and bent over, trying to catch her breath and stall, hoping Carver would hurry.

"Beautiful, isn't it? You can see the whole Heber Valley from up here." After a minute he said, "Cass, he'll be okay. I've learned a lot about Mr. Nash. I was all wrong about him."

"Thanks, Reeb. You don't know how much that means to me."

The pines got thicker and the hike no longer followed a straight line. She tried to get a glimpse of the mine through the trees, but wasn't having any luck. She didn't know how they would ever find it. Even the tailings would have vegetation growing on them, making it hard to distinguish the tailing pile from the mountain. Besides, she could only see trees.

"If we walked as fast as Thomas Rhoades did, then we're about in the right area," said Reber.

"I don't know how we're ever going to see down the hill through the trees."

"What we need is to find a trail that starts down the mountain and follow it. However, the trail may have fallen into disuse over the years—unless some prospector has tried his luck recently," replied Reber.

"I wonder why Carver hasn't caught up with us yet." She kept looking over her shoulder to see if she could spot him, with no luck.

"Hey, Cass, look here." Reber pointing to a rock outcropping that had a groove worn in it. "This is a trail—let's follow it for a bit. I have a hunch."

"I don't see a trail," she said.

"You need to have Indian eyes for these kinds of things. Slide rules and calculators don't help here in the mountains," he said as he winked at her.

"I haven't used a slide rule for twenty years," she replied. "But hey, how do you know about slide rules? That's pretty high-tech for you guys on the reservation."

He reached over and put his arm around her, gave her a hug, and said, "I knew there was a reason that I liked you."

Another minute went by, then Reber pointed. "Look through those trees. I think we've found our mine," he said.

"I don't see a thing," she replied.

"Just trust me. The mine's right over there."

"Anybody tells me to trust them, I start headin' in the opposite direction," she replied, but looked over where he was pointing.

Five minutes later, they stood on top of the mine tailings. They looked around without finding the opening, but Reber believed they were in the right spot. "Hey, how's Carver going to know we took this side trail? I couldn't even see it. He could just go straight up the mountain and miss us completely."

"Don't worry, Cass. I broke a couple of branches where we turned off so Carver would know where we left the main trail. But if I don't miss my guess, Carver could track us without any help from me."

"Maybe we should wait for him," she said.

"No, we need to get down the hill and see if we can find the rock with hieroglyphics. It might take us some time to locate it. Carver will catch up with us."

Reber pulled out a compass and checked for a marker to fix his bearing. "See the rock cliff across the canyon? We just need to head for that. It should take us about fifteen minutes to be in the general area your letter described. Keep your eyes peeled for any large granite rock. It has to be pretty good size, maybe tall and thin, but then, it could have fallen over."

They made good time down the mountain and started looking for the granite marker, hoping that it would still be there and not damaged beyond recognition. Of course, it could have been taken away by anyone looking for ancient artifacts, or covered by vegetation or a landslide. It hadn't been more than thirty minutes before they heard a shrill whistle repeated in three short bursts. "That would be your friend," said Reber.

Cass wondered how Reber knew what was happening while she always seemed to be in the dark. Reber wasn't waiting and kept looking for the granite rock, so she stayed close behind him. She didn't want to get separated.

Carver sat next to a large granite rock that stood ten feet high and was about three feet wide. It looked like one of those carved monuments found in Central America. "I heard you guys turn off the main trail and start heading down the mountain. I came as the crow flies to intercept you and found this marker. You guys were right on target. Good work, Reber."

Carver pulled an Army-issue folding shovel from his backpack. Reber stood at the base of the marker, holding his compass, and said, "Okay, fifty steps in that direction." He started walking and counting: "forty-nine, fifty," and drew an X on the ground with his foot.

Carver came over and stomped on the ground, then started digging. "I don't hear anything to give me a clue where to start digging. I hope your stride is close to Rhoades', because our instructions didn't say how deep to dig. We might have to bring in a backhoe if we don't get lucky."

Reber sat down on the ground and pulled Cass down to watch. "We might spell you if you really need some help," Reber said, and smiled at Cass.

Twenty minutes later Carver had a hole about three feet deep. He was sweating. "It would have been a lot easier if they told us distance in feet rather than paces. How tall do you think Thomas Rhoades was?" he asked.

Reber finally stood up and offered to take over the digging. He expanded the hole away from the original mark. Cass came over and took Carver's hand, leading him over to the rock where she and Reber had been sitting. She liked having him close, although he didn't seem to be real interested in her at the moment.

"Did you see anyone behind us?" she asked.

"Nope. I guess they thought those two goons could take care of us and they wouldn't need any backup."

He called out, "Hey, Reber, I'm going to take a little nap. Let me know if you need some help—I'll send Cass over." She slugged him in the arm. He grabbed her hand and encircled her with his arms, pulling her close. Who cares about some stupid buried box, she thought.

"Hey, guys, I think we've found something," called Reber. Cass jumped up just as Carver's cell started to ring.

"How can you get reception up here?" she asked. "Most of the time, I can't even get it in Marion."

"Satellite," he said, and listened to whoever was talking on the phone.

Cass had enough of waiting and went over to help Reber. A metal box lay half-exposed, and Reber dug around to get it free from the earthen jaws. Cass jumped in the hole and started pulling to see if she could loosen the box.

Reber said, "Hang on. It will only take me a second and we'll have the box out."

Carver hurried over and said, "Hey guys, we've got to go. Those two goons we handed over to Lassiter this morning had more information than we thought. It seems that although they didn't know who hired them, they were given a rendezvous location in the upper Rock Creek area. Lassiter's international thug has been tied directly to them and he has now been traced by Interpol to a plane that landed in the small airport in Provo. Word is, that he thought his guys were getting close to locating the Rhoades Mine as they followed your progress. He wanted to be there himself when the jackpot was hit and he didn't trust anyone else to go into the mine."

"Have they caught him?" asked Reber.

"No, right now they just have the area surrounded and are waiting for our command."

"Any word about my father?" asked Cass.

"One of the guys they were interrogating thinks someone fitting Rylan's description may have been in the cabin."

Cass suddenly got a surge of adrenalin and shouted, "Let's get that box out of the ground now! We've got to go. Now!"

Reber finished digging and the box was free. It was heavy, maybe a hundred pounds. "How can something that small be so heavy?" she asked.

"It's gold," Reber answered.

Carver struggled, but was finally able to get it out of the hole and onto the ground. He put it into his expandable, and Reber commented, "Man! Don't tell me it's not heavy."

"It's heavy, but I've carried more weight than this," he said as he grabbed Cass's hand and headed down the mountain, Reber close behind.

"How come I have to sit in the backseat? This is discrimination," teased Reber.

"Tough it out," replied Cass. "The front seat's mine from now on."

They were getting close to the location provided for them by Lassiter. They had been driving just over an hour. They had to go through a road block and past a number of unmarked police vehicles, and then they saw it. The house was on fire and federal agents in well-marked vests with their guns drawn were standing all over. Cass felt her stomach tighten. What if her father had been in the house? She was sure Carver had the same idea, but was probably looking for Lassiter so he could get the straight scoop. They finally stopped by some of the armed agents. One called Lassiter and then let them pass through, giving them directions to Lassiter's location. Cass was the first to spot him and pointed him out to Carver, and they headed in that direction.

"We couldn't wait any longer," said Lassiter to Carver as he rolled down his window. "Someone was trying to leave, so we went into action and shut the place down. The shoot-out only lasted five minutes before they sent out the white flag."

"So you got everyone?" asked Carver.

"Well, no, we got everyone but the main man. He got away. He's a runner. Apparently the guy who's been orchestrating this whole thing is a guy by the name of Vincent Vargas. We've got some people after him."

"Can I talk to the guys you rounded up?" asked Carver.

"Sure. They're all bound hand and foot up there in that house."

"Cass, do you want to come with me? We might be able to get some information about your father."

"You want to race?" she smiled.

Up at the cabin, Carver took each of the men, one at a time into the bedroom and questioned them. They were all pretty much dressed the same; dark clothing, nothing distinct. All looked like they hadn't shaved in days. Cass watched from a chair in the corner. As the last man was brought into the room, Carver's phone rang. He said, "I'll be right back. I've got to take this call from Lassiter. Scream if he moves, and then put a shot right between his eyes. Okay?"

Cass rolled her eyes as Carver left the room. Suddenly the man looked like he went into convulsion, like he was having an epileptic fit. Cass hurried over to make sure he wasn't pulling a fast one but as she got within an arm's distance, quick as a cat the man had his handcuffed hands around her throat.

Carver stepped back into the room and dropped his phone. His gun was leveled at the prisoner's head, who was trying to hide behind Cass.

Cass raised her right foot like she was stepping backwards and brought it down as hard as she could on the instep of her captor.

He screamed out in pain. Almost simultaneously Cass drove her elbow into the man's solar plexus, with all of the power she could muster. At the same time Cass ducked because her attacker had loosened the grip around her neck. She didn't escape but she went down to her knees just as she heard a fist driven into her assailant's face. The man flew backwards. It was good she ducked because she felt Carver's entire body following the man over the top of her head.

It was over in a second and she felt him lifting her off the floor.

"Are you okay?" he asked.

She felt his eyes boring into her. She had never seen him afraid of anything and that was exactly what she was seeing. She smiled and threw her arms around him. He let out a breath he had been holding.

"I should have never left the room."

"Oh, come on, Carver. If you hadn't interfered he would have been pleading with me for mercy in a matter of seconds."

"Remind me to never sneak up behind you," he said.

Carver had conducted a search of the man and found a hidden compartment in his belt. It contained a riddle, written in old-fashioned script, on a torn and worn piece of paper:

"Look for the source of the rain from Heaven."

When the prisoner awoke, he was securely bound. Lassiter was in the room and was questioning him. They learned that the man sitting before them was indeed Vargas. Lassiter immediately contacted his boss at Homeland Security with the information. He had been advised that the man was wanted by several countries and that a chopper was on the way to take custody of Mr. Vargas, immediately.

"What about my father?" Cass asked Lassiter.

"We're not sure, but Vargas told me that your father escaped several days ago. Seems a medicine man, a guy called He Who Speaks to the Sky, or sometimes just the Sky Talker, orchestrated it after he promised to lead Vargas to the Carre-Shin-Ob. Vargas said he later learned from one of the Indians that he captured that the old Indian, the Sky Talker, had taken your father into the mountains on something they call a vision quest. No one knows where they are or how long they will be gone."

Cass turned to Reber, "Did you know anything about this little excursion?"

Reber shook his head. "Sky Talker doesn't check in with anyone, least of all me."

Cass was still concerned, "Okay, what's this vision quest stuff all about? Where would they go and how long will they be gone? And why didn't anyone call and tell us? You do have phones on the reservation, don't you?"

"One question at a time," replied Reber. "A vision quest is a special, deeply personal ceremony in which an individual goes off to try to gain a vision from the Great Spirit, which could help him find direction in his life. A vision quest, in the true sense of the word, is a process where one seeks to discover the highest within himself. Sometimes a holy man may choose to act as a guide. If the quest is successful, one or more 'helpers' from the four elements of fire, earth, air, and water will show themselves to the vision seeker and become the individual's sacred reflection of the Great Spirit. These guardian spirits will remain with the person all their life and protect them as long as the heart remains pure."

"Where will he take him? Is he safe? I need to find him." Cass persisted with the questions.

Reber continued, "Usually they go to a high mountain. It could take days or even weeks. It just depends on what happens. As long as Rylan is with He Who Speaks to the Sky, he'll be safe. You would never find them, even if you knew where to start looking."

"Someone must know," she said more assuredly than she felt. "And what about that phone call?"

Reber answered, "Cass, your father is safe. He escaped, and he wouldn't have gone if he didn't trust the Sky Talker. Vision quests are only pursued after serious contemplation. Your father wanted to go, or the Sky Talker wouldn't have taken him. So you need to just cool your jets. He will return when he returns."

"And he hasn't been gone long," Lassiter chimed in, climbing out of his car. "There wasn't time to call you."

She was frustrated, but greatly relieved that her father was safe, well—kind of safe. She had to go find Carver, who had walked away with Lassiter. He turned when she approached and she folded into his arms.

"What's this all about?" asked Lassiter, looking at Caver holding Cass.

"Lois Lane finally broke through the wall," she said to Lassiter, and she smiled up at Carver.

Lassiter slapped Carver on the back and said to Cass, "Yeah, but what are you going to do with him? You know he's not house broken."

Reber suggested they go to his house, only a half hour away, to open the box. Now that Rylan was safe, he wanted to pursue the search for the Carre-Shin-Ob. Cass wasn't sure she cared if they continued the quest. She knew her father was alive and that was all that mattered.

Once in Reber's house, Carver extracted the box from his backpack. It had a locking mechanism like the first box, and before long, Carver lifted the lid.

Inside the box were about eighty pounds of early Mormon gold coins, similar to what Carver found in Rock Creek cemetery. When Cass saw the coins she said, "Rylan did some research on the value of these coins. He figured there was close to $10,000,000 in the box we found earlier, and this looks about the same."

Carver looked over at Reber and said, "We want you to take these coins, Reber, and use them for the tribe." Cass heartily seconded the motion.

Reber was flabbergasted and asked, "But who owns them?"

"Near as we can figure, the coins belonged to Thomas Rhoades. In one of his written documents, he directed the finder to use the gold for whatever purpose he deemed best. We figure the best use is for the tribe. However, we have a condition. Do not disclose to anyone where or how you acquired the coins, or how much you have."

Reber thought for a moment and said, "Maybe I can set up some kind of a trust or foundation that I control for the benefit of the tribe. I can say it came from a rich benefactor who chooses to remain nameless."

Cass retrieved a pouch from the box similar to the ones they had previously found. The first document she pulled out of the pouch was written in the Deseret Alphabet.

"Great," she said. "It will take me an hour or two to decode this message and I can't do it until I get back to my father's house and my computer."

The next document was the second map that apparently took up where the first map left off.

Surprisingly, there was one additional document. The paper was yellowed and the writing hard to decipher, partly because of the penmanship and partly because of the faded ink. It appeared to be a note from Chief Wakara.

In my youth I was shown a vision of the Carre-Shin-Ob.

I was taken there by Towats.

He made me the guardian of the Carre-Shin-Ob.

I was told that the riches were to be used to assist

the Tall Hats.

I was also told that in the days to come that my people would become like a young lion among the whites and the Lion shall move through the flocks with power and none shall stand in their way. And my people would assist the building of a new city and new temple where the Great Spirit shall come and dwell.

Since that vision I have been to the Carre-Shin-Ob many times. I have done all that Towats said.

I leave my mark that these things are true.

Chief Wakara, 1856

Cass read the document out loud. Reber seemed most effected by it. In fact, she was surprised when he got up and started pacing the room.

No one wanted to break the spell that had been cast by Wakara's note. Finally, Reber said, "The thing that sealed the deal, as far as me joining the Church, Sister Edison, was reading the Book of Mormon."

Cass replied, "I remember that after you finished reading, you were somewhat shaken, although you would never admit what happened."

"I remember it like it was yesterday. I was reading 3 Nephi, Chapter 21. It speaks about my people. It spoke to me. I have never felt anything as powerful as when I read that chapter. I memorized those verses. Verse twelve says,

> And my people who are a remnant of Jacob shall be among the Gentiles, yea, in the midst of them as a lion among the beasts of the forest, as a young lion among the flocks of sheep, who, if he go through both treadeth down and teareth

in pieces, and none can deliver.

"Sounds familiar right? Look back to what Wakara said."

Cass was flabbergasted. She had read the scripture before but didn't realize the possible implications. She addressed Reber. "Do you think the gold in the Carre-Shin-Ob could be the means to help your people become the young lion?"

Reber went on. "And verse twenty-three says,

> And they shall assist my people, the remnant of Jacob, and also as many of the house of Israel as shall come, that they may build a city, which shall be called the New Jerusalem.

"Wow," said Cass. "Did Wakara read the Book of Mormon before he wrote this note?"

Reber said, "He didn't read or write in the white man's language. In fact, this note could not have been written by him—someone had to write it for him, and then he placed his mark. I've seen his mark many times and this is an original."

Chapter Sixteen

"Listen up, you guys, I've got the message decoded. It's another message from Thomas Rhoades." Cass handed both men a copy of the decoded message, then read aloud from her own.

The gold and artifacts contained in the Sacred Church Mine are under the control of the Great Spirit and are to be used only for his purpose. At the appropriate time Towats will choose which of you will be allowed to enter the sacred mine.

In order to complete your quest you must have:

1. map 2, found with this note;

2. map 1, found at the county recorder's office;

3. directions to the mine entrance from the X on map 2.

If you are missing any of these you will not be able to complete your quest.

Thomas Rhoades, 1856

Carver was perplexed. He read and reread the document. Finally he asked, "Do we have a document that has the directions to the mine entrance? Because apparently the second map only gets us close. I don't remember seeing anything like that."

"You're right," replied Cass, as a cloud of doubt passed over her newfound optimism.

Mumbling to herself, she walked over to the copies of documents Rylan had accumulated since their quest had begun. Carver watched her leaf through them one by one, shaking her head. When she finished, she sighed. "I don't see anything like that."

She handed the documents to Carver. "You take a look at these and see if you can find anything. I've suddenly developed a mild headache." Cass passed them to him and rubbed her head.

Carver muttered to himself, "I don't understand. We have all the documents. Where are we supposed to find the directions Rhoades referred to? It's got to be there." Carver flipped through the pages, looking for some kind of anomaly, something different. Nothing jumped out at him.

"I know it's here. It's another of those clues that is hidden in plain sight. We're just not looking at it from the right direction. I'll keep going—you take a break," Carver replied.

Carver knew something else was bugging Cass. The lines around her eyes tightened and the corners of her mouth turned slightly down. He wondered if she got the same look when she was stumped with a binominal quadratic equation. She was stubborn and she would chew it like a dog on a bone until she found a solution. In this case, maybe he could help her find the missing piece.

"I'm going to look through those documents again." She took them from Carver and went over to Rylan's desk. Soon she became lost in her own little world as she pored over the documents.

When Carver's cell phone rang and he wandered into another room to answer it, Cass didn't even bother looking up. She was involved in her search, and he knew she was wondering how they could have missed something that was probably so obvious.

No one had seen or heard from Rylan or the Sky Talker in the week since they left. Reber went home to Roosevelt, leaving specific instructions with Cass to call if anything at all happened. He wanted to be with them on their trek to the mine, if they found the directions, but he would not enter unless he was invited by a guardian of the mine. "Not even Wakara would enter the place without a specific invitation from Towats," he had said reverently.

Carver knew Cass was upset and worried about her father, even if she wouldn't admit it. She never initiated conversation about her father, but she was usually quick to jump whenever the phone rang or a car pulled into the driveway. Oh, she repeatedly told Carver she knew Rylan would be all right, but she would ask questions that were an obvious attempt to reassure herself that the feelings were not unwarranted imaginations of hope.

Carver tried to stay close so she could lean on him. He was within arms' reach all the time except at night, when he slept somewhere outside. He still wasn't convinced that all the bad guys had been rounded up. He wondered if there were still some renegade Utes that might be involved in this whole mess. He had been vigilant, day and night. Nothing was going to happen to Cass, not on his watch.

Finally, Carver ended his phone conversation. "Cass," he said. "I need to talk to you, and no, it's not about your father. No one has heard anything from him yet."

She looked up, marking the spot where she'd been reading with her finger.

"That was Lassiter. It's a long story, so try to hold your questions. I'll do the best I can to tell you everything."

Cass sighed and said, "Okay, I'm listening."

Carver continued, "At this point, the story is a bit sketchy. Within the last two days Reber was called to a secret meeting with the Sky Talker. He didn't return from the meeting, and apparently went with the Sky Talker directly into the mountains. He did speak to his mother before he left and asked her to tell you he was safe, that he would try to see your father, and that he would be back when he got back. He emphasized that you were not to worry about him or your father. No one knows exactly where they went or why."

He took a breath. "Lassiter thinks it might have something to do with the vision quest, but he has nothing to substantiate that feeling. I don't know if there is a tie-in to your father and the Carre-Shin-Ob, but then I don't believe in coincidences, either. Three people have voluntarily vanished—your father, the Sky Talker, and now Reber. It seems a little bit peculiar that all three men have gone on a vision quest to a region where the Carre-Shin-Ob could be located. It's just too coincidental."

Cass asked, "Did Reber say anything else to his mother?"

"Not that I know of," he replied.

Cass went silent, deep in thought, and then Carver continued, "Unfortunately, there's nothing we can do but wait."

Cass had listened without interruption, which was unusual for her under the best of circumstances, but she finally said, "I think we need to find those directions to the mine so we can find our three missing persons."

"I'm not sure we should continue the search," replied Carver. "Not until we have heard from your father or Reber."

"Well, you can do whatever you want, but I'm going to find the mine if it's the last thing I do. I want to find my father."

"What if he doesn't want us to find him right now?" asked Carver.

"I'm not going to sit around on my hands doing nothing," she replied. She got up and went back to her desk. "I'm going to find those directions; you can help if you want."

Cass knew she had taken her frustrations out on Carver earlier in the day. It wasn't his fault her father was missing, yet he had taken her verbal onslaught without flinching or arguing with her. Of course, it wasn't unusual for him to keep silent. She appreciated his quiet understanding. He had given her the space she needed. After her blowup, she had retreated back to her search for the missing directions. Now she could almost repeat from memory every word of each document. Still, she hadn't found the clue she knew was staring her in the face.

Out of the corner of her eye she watched Carver walk out to the front porch and sit in the swing. The sunset was magnificent. It was time to go tell him she was sorry, something she was not very good at doing.

She brushed her hair and attempted to restore some kind of order to herself. She knew she had neglected her appearance lately, and wondered if Carver had noticed. She slipped into some clean clothes and checked herself over one more time in the mirror before heading out to the front porch. She looked passable—not great, but passable, especially on such short notice.

Carver seemed lost in his thoughts and didn't acknowledge her, although she was sure he knew she had crossed into his field of vision. She sat down on his lap, put both arms around his neck, and held him. Slowly, he reached his arms around her without saying a word. She felt safe, cherished. She wondered if he could feel her heart rate increasing.

She came out of her fog bank and realized he was talking very softly to her. She didn't want to break the spell and just listened while he continued with his tale.

"Everyone thought I was a hero for what happened in Afghanistan. I didn't do anything that any other GI wouldn't have done for his buddies. I hated all the publicity. The only reason I got the medal was because the military needed someone to be their poster boy, and I was nominated. They wanted me to go to the White House to receive the medal in front of every camera and reporter they could assemble. I flat-out told them no. My commanding officers weren't real happy about my attitude, well, except for Lassiter. He understood. We had a job to do and we did it, nothing more."

He was opening the door to himself and all she had to do was walk right in. Maybe the Great Wall wasn't so solid after all. "I told you how my fiancée married my friend. I didn't think I would ever recover, but I threw myself into my missionary work to forget. When I got home from my mission and went into the military, I got to utilize those skills of focus and hard work. Nothing else mattered, just the next mission."

He gently caressed her back. "I was fine until you showed up. I had my own little world, and no one ever entered. I didn't need anyone or anything. At least, that's what I told myself. But you wouldn't let me be. You sparkled like a star in the night, like a ray of sun breaking through the clouds."

He went silent. She found herself stroking his hair, hopelessly in love with this big lunk.

"It was the day we finally solved the cipher in the Lion House plaque. Remember, I asked you about the bold and non-bold characters. Oh, I knew I was in trouble before, but that day I couldn't resist the light any longer."

He laughed. "You were so headstrong, a bull in a china shop. When you sat down next to me at lunch you tried to squeeze me into the corner, just to get my reaction. It was hard then not to put my arms around you and say uncle."

Suddenly she jerked away from him and exclaimed, "That's it! That's what we've been missing this whole time. I've looked at it a zillion times. The deed didn't have just one message, it had two. The legal description is a Bacon cipher. I'd bet the house on it."

"What are you talking about?" he asked. The spell was broken, but then she kissed him and knew it really wasn't.

"Let's go," she said. She jumped up, grabbed his hand, and pulled. He was heavy, but he was smiling.

"Okay, okay. Is it always going to be like this, having you around?" he asked.

"What are you talking about?" she asked as she pulled him into the house.

She went over to her desk and pulled out her Bacon coding pad and the legal description on the deed from Rhoades to Timpanogo. It didn't take long before the message appeared.

300 steps due east thence north 1000 steps; bearing 290 degrees to slide at base of cliff

She jumped up and threw her arms around him, kissed him and exclaimed, "I love you, Carver." Her heart was racing. She felt dizzy and happy.

He crushed her in an enduring bear hug from which she didn't ever want to escape. She reached up and kissed him again. After she caught her breath she said, "You're getting better. You just need a little more practice."

Carver's phone started buzzing. He reached in his pocket to find out who was calling. Before he answered it, she asked, "Did you have someone call on purpose? You really do need some more practice, you know." She kissed him again as it rang and said, "Are you sure you want to answer that now?"

"It's Lassiter. Maybe he has some information about your father."

Cass heard Carver's side of the conversation and tried to put the pieces together, but she didn't have much to work with. He listened more than he spoke, and she never heard her father's name mentioned.

As soon as he folded his phone she said, "Okay, tell me everything, don't leave out anything, and come sit right over here while you talk." She patted a spot on the couch right next to her.

"The U.S. Attorney has taken over the prosecution of Mr. Vincent Vargas. Apparently, three other countries want to talk to him about the theft of antiquities. I don't think he's going anywhere for a while. They have enough evidence to charge him with arranging for three murders on the reservation. Seems they worked a plea deal with two of his henchmen to testify that he hired them to kill tribal members. One of the dead Utes was Longbow, the guy who was on the tribal council that could have testified against him. They have also traced the money paid to Longbow to a Swiss account that belonged to Vincent Vargas."

"Has Lassiter heard anything about my father or Reber?"

"No, but he still thinks they're safe. He thinks now that they have Mr. Vargas, the rest of the hoodlums will evaporate. He doesn't think the tribe will have any further trouble. In fact, he pulled all of his men out of the area and he returned to Washington."

"So what do you think?"

"I think he's right, but I have this nagging feeling that all of the loose ends haven't been tied up, just yet."

"Why do you think that?"

"If you remember, there were a few killings, besides the Indians, that took place on the reservation prior to the time I found the first cache. They could have been related to Vincent Vargas, but why would he take out a couple of old, harmless gold miners?"

"And your theory is?"

"I don't know, but it just doesn't add up."

He put his arm around her and drew her closer, then leaned down and kissed her. When she came up for air she murmured, "See, I told you. If you keep working on it, you might make my top ten."

"It's time for you go to bed. I'll see you in the morning," he said as he stood to leave.

"Hey, it's early. The clock just struck midnight. We still have time to practice."

He smiled and said, "I had a missionary companion that had three rules when you were with a girl. He said you could violate any two of the rules but never all three at the same time. The rules were: alone, for a long time, and stationary. We are alone, stationary, and it's been a long time. I'll see you in the morning."

"But don't I get a vote?" she said as he closed the front door. "Dang!"

Chapter Seventeen

The next morning Cass stumbled out of the bedroom, looked around, and found Carver at a work station he had established on the kitchen table. He had several large maps scattered across the table, as well as copies of both Thomas Rhoades' maps, which he studied. She knew he was intentionally ignoring her. She decided she needed to put herself together before she made her grand appearance. She wondered how he looked so good in the morning, while she felt like she had just walked through a tornado.

After a quick shower and grooming she made her entrance. Without looking up, Carver offered her a bagel and a glass of milk. She tried to engage him in a conversation, even though she was doing most of the actual speaking. After several minutes of her one-sided conversation and in the midst of a sentence, she paused, then continued on without stopping for a breath. "I made a major decision last night."

Yesterday, they had spent the entire day trying to locate topography that would come close to matching either of the Rhoades maps. They were using the best up-to-date USGS maps. The Rhoades maps, however, were so general, they could depict any number of locations in the vicinity of Rock Creek-Granddaddy-Lakes Basin, which is where Carver believed the Carre-Shin-Ob was located. Carver had been searching the USGS section maps for landmarks he could key into either of the two Rhoades maps. He had narrowed the area down but it still took a lot of guesswork. They were missing a key piece of the puzzle. They needed a better starting point.

Cass had the scrap of paper they had taken out of Vargas' belt and was fingering it. "What if this is the missing piece of the puzzle?" Carver had wondered about the note and responded, "But we don't know if the note has anything to do with Vargas or his search for the Carre-Shin-Ob. If it does apply, it's like having a single piece of an incomplete puzzle. It doesn't help."

Cass said, "I think it's your missing piece."

"Maybe," he said.

Apart from protecting her, he had to deal with the logistics of getting them on the reservation without permission. If they got a permit, a whole flock of people would know of their presence and he didn't want to parade around with banners, announcing that they were looking for the Rhoades Mine. He wasn't even sure they could get on the reservation legitimately, considering the recent problems. He also knew the Tribal Council wouldn't outwardly support their investigation. There could still be some renegade Utes who were sworn to keep any white men out of the area.

After listening to Carver, Cass suggested, "I could call Reber's mother. I believe she had some influence with certain older tribal members. Maybe she could help us get access to the reservation."

"If she knows we're looking for the Carre-Shin-Ob, then others will also know, and we don't know which side they're on. We can't risk the wrong people finding out. We'll just have to rely on stealth and secrecy. If we get in trouble, I always have this amulet the Sky Talker gave me," replied Carver.

"What about the guy on the Tribal Council? Reber said his name was White Rocks or something like that. Maybe he could help."

"That's a good idea—I'll think about calling him. If he grew up on the reservation, he might know a back door we could use," Carver replied.

Cass had told him she'd made a decision, but she hadn't told him what. He asked, "So, what is it that you decided?"

She didn't respond so he added, "Does it involve me?"

She glanced over at him with that little sly smile and said, "Umm, well," and then paused.

"Okay, I give," he said.

"Yes! That's my answer to the question you should be asking me right now."

The lights came on, flashing like neon. He got red in the face and stuttered, "Right now?"

"Can you think of a better time?"

"Well . . ."

"We don't have time for all that romantic stuff. I'm almost an old maid, so right now would be perfectly acceptable. But," she smiled, "You'd better be sincere, and make it good, buster."

He groaned.

"Hey, this isn't supposed to be painful. You didn't get started very well. Do you want to try again?"

He got down on one knee while holding both of her hands, and said, "Ms. Edison, would you be willing to change your last name?"

"That depends on who's asking and why," she responded, playing like she was totally bored, smiling all the time.

She was going to make him say the words. He couldn't avoid them any longer. "Cassandra, would you consider being my wife?"

She pulled him up and threw her arms around his neck. "I never knew you were such a romantic," she teased, and kissed him.

After a long moment, she released him and he asked, "Was that a yes, or do I need more practice?"

"We'll have plenty of time for that. By the way, where's my ring? If you're going to ask a girl to marry you, you should at least have a diamond to give her."

"Cass, let me ask you a question, hypothetically, of course," said Carver. "Let's say the Carre-Shin-Ob really does exist." They were driving towards the reservation the next morning. "Let's say it really is a sacred place containing mountains of gold. Do you think the Great Spirit or God would allow us to just waltz in, walk around, and take as many samples as we want?"

Cass thought about the question and responded, "Do you think He had anything to do with us getting to this point?"

"Do you always answer a question with a question?" he asked.

"I don't know what I think. If I remember my Church history correctly, however, people dug everywhere on the Hill Cumorah for years, looking for the gold Joseph Smith claimed to have found there. The digging was so extensive that almost all of the trees were stripped from the hill. Some of the searchers found a few trinkets, but no one ever found the golden plates or the cave Joseph said he was taken to by the angel. And he said the cave was filled with golden records, the sword of Laban, and other artifacts."

Carver asked, "Yeah, but Joseph had an escort, an angel, and I haven't seen any around here lately."

She thought for a minute. "Maybe we've had an angel following us around for the last month. I believe we have been protected by someone or something."

"Maybe Towats won't like the fact that we intend to enter his cave," Carver responded.

"Are you suggesting that we not go into the Carre-Shin-Ob, even if we find it?"

"I don't know. I'm just asking."

"Well, I think if we find it, we go for it, at least until someone or something tells us not to, and that someone better look like he could stop us if he wanted," she responded.

"Somehow I knew you were going to say that," he replied.

"By the way, Carver, I don't mean to change the subject, but what do you intend to do with the gold you got out of the first cache?"

"Well, since your answer was yes, I guess that means you have an equal say in what happens to the gold," he replied.

She echoed his former statement. "Somehow I knew you were going to say that. It presents me with some very nice options. There are a number of stores I've been dying to visit, but I never had the time or money."

"Okay. After you get tired of shopping, what do you think we should do with our remaining gold?" he asked.

"You think there's going to be some left when I'm through?" He could see the sparkle in her eyes and the sly smile appeared, the one he loved. "Reber's idea to use the money you gave him to help the tribe was good, but it was way too general."

"From the tone of your voice and that crooked smile, I'm willing to bet you've not only spent some time thinking about it, but you have a very specific plan for spending a hundred million dollars," he said, as he leaned back to listen to her plan.

"We both have spent a lot of time on reservations. I don't know what you observed, but I found some very intelligent people, but it was impossible for them to break out of the mold. If the Indian nation is going to rise up in the last days and be a mighty people, they're not going to be able to do it with bows and arrows. They are going to need some leaders, some educated leaders, but the younger generation believes it's just not cool to go to the white man's school and learn.

"If we found a few of those bright kids, the future leaders, and teach them, motivate them to learn how to deal with the rest of the world, they'd create some examples, some superstars, which the younger kids would look up to and try to emulate. We need a school, but not an ordinary school; a special school just for them."

Carver thought she was brilliant, besides beautiful. "Maybe, he said, "we could add some athletic teams to the mix. I've seen some terrific athletes that just need a field and someone to teach them how to throw a ball."

"It will be a hard sale, because we're going to have to turn their thinking upside down. We can ask other American Indians who have been schooled and become successful to give seminars or even teach at the school. The key is to convert a couple of superstars to our plan, and then the rest will follow."

"I'll bet you have already selected a few kids to go after, haven't you?"

"As a matter of fact, I have. How did you know?"

"I suppose you already have some teachers chosen as well?"

She smiled. "Well, right now I only know of two, me and you. We should really be able to attract some kids once we tell them you are a Medal of Honor recipient."

"Cass, you know I'm not going to let you tell anyone about that, but I will volunteer to coach some of the teams—boys' teams, that is. I'll leave the girls to you."

"Come on, it's for the cause."

"No!" he said and quickly changed the subject. "What I really want to know is, how many kids you think you can convince to take differential equations and applied physics?"

White Rock had given Carver directions to where he would meet them. It was, he said, a true back door to Rock Creek Canyon that almost no one knew about and it was very isolated. He had quickly agreed to meet them, once Carver used Reber's name. Carver had used the code words, "Rifle Rim Pass," as Reber had instructed him.

The two-track Carver followed was deeply rutted and got worse with each mile. The road almost became a trail and slowed their progress. It didn't show a lot of recent use, and Carver hadn't seen any signs of human habitation for over an hour.

He had continued to try to talk Cass out of going with him on the initial sortie, but it was like talking to rock. He insisted it would be safer if he checked out the area first, but that didn't fly. She believed if they found the Carre-Shin-Ob, they had a chance of finding her father, and she wasn't waiting in the car.

Carver didn't have a good feeling about this little adventure, and with Cass determined to go with him, he would have to prepare for every eventuality. It was futile to try to talk her out of going. She would probably go without him if he told her she couldn't go. They had the two maps and the directions—if the canyon they were headed to was the canyon described in the Rhoades maps, they had a good chance of finding the Carre-Shin-Ob.

Finally, they spotted a black Jeep parked inside the tree line near the entrance to a box canyon. White Rock was leaning against the front fender, waiting for them. He appeared so casual, it seemed he was out for a Sunday hike in the woods.

Carver shook hands with White Rock, also called Peter, and introduced himself, then Cass. He hadn't told Peter why they wanted to secretly reconnoiter this part of the reservation, and Peter hadn't asked—a gentleman's agreement.

Peter looked at Carver's rifle and handgun and said, "I forgot to tell you—I can't let you take any firearms onto the reservation. I'm already putting my neck in a noose, and if you take guns, it could create a whole different set of problems." He looked at Carver and said, "That's not a problem, is it?"

Carver didn't say anything, but went back to his car and left his handgun and rifle. When he returned, Peter spoke up. "The area you want is just over that hill. It's not a long hike. The head of the trail is over there by that draw," he said, pointing towards the rear of the box canyon.

"Okay, we'll follow you," said Carver. He made sure Cass was in front of him and he brought up the rear. Peter talked loud enough for anyone within a mile to hear them. Carver was about to say something about secrecy when Cass dropped back and put her hand in his. He didn't have a great feeling about Mr. White Rock. He needed to pay close attention to him.

As they rounded a bend, Peter turned around. He had a pistol pointed at Carver. Carver immediately moved in front of Cass. He quickly scanned the area and saw three armed men as they stepped out of hiding, with rifles pointed directly at him. He had one bandit on each side, one at his rear, and Peter in the front.

So, White Rock was the inside guy. He somehow knew Carver had maps leading to the Lost Rhoades Mine and wanted them. Carver knew that once White Rock had the maps, he and Cass would no longer be of any use. These guys meant business and he only hoped his preparation would suffice. He had two paralyzing darts that could be thrown by hand, one up each sleeve which he released by pulling on the cuff of his shirt. They dropped into his palms without anyone noticing. He then bent over to tie his shoe lace.

"Hey, stand up," shouted Peter.

"My shoelace came undone," responded Carver as he pulled the lace on his right shoe.

"Hands up," shouted Peter. "Go search them," he said to his henchmen.

"I get the girl," said one of the guys, laughing as he approached Cass and Carver.

In one fluid motion, Carver kicked the shoe off his right foot. The shoe flew towards a tree not more than five feet from where they stood. At the same time he threw a dart with each hand at the men approaching from the sides. He quickly grabbed Cass and fell to the ground on top of her.

The explosion sounded worse than it was, but it immediately produced a dense cloud of black smoke that filled a fifty-foot radius. Both darts found their marks and the men instantly fell to the ground, paralyzed. A rifle sounded, and Carver felt the slug pass just above his head.

He whispered to Cass, telling her to belly-crawl to their right, downhill. He heard a few more shots go off, but it wasn't in their direction. The smoke bomb also continued to send off loud bangs that covered the sound they made crawling along the ground. Carver found a rock outcropping, put Cass behind it, and said, "Don't move, I'll be right back."

She looked up at him, pulled him close, and kissed him. "Hold that thought," he said, and he was gone.

These guys were amateurs, but still dangerous. Apparently, the guy bringing up the rear had circled the smoke and found his partner. The bomb stopped exploding and Carver heard them talking nervously. Peter tried to talk his partner into going into the smoke to see if he could find Cass and Carver. He even promised him more money, but the man wasn't having any of that.

Peter put his pistol against his friend's head and said, "If you leave before this is over, I'll come looking for you, and then your wife, and last, your kids. Understand? Now you go that way and watch your step."

Peter turned and went up the hill. His partner turned and went down. A quarter mile down the hill, Peter's partner ran into a tree branch the size of a baseball bat—a homerun swing was all it took to knock him out. Peter's buddy wouldn't be moving for some time. Carver quickly bound his wrists around a tree, picked up his rifle, and went to look for Peter.

"Cass, it's okay," said Carver as he walked towards the rock outcropping. She stood up and ran to him. "I was so worried," she cried as she threw her arms around him. He felt like she was never going to let go. He kind of liked that.

"It's okay," he said.

"What happened? Where are those creeps? I didn't hear anything except a tree branch breaking, or something like that."

"It broke over one of their heads. I think he's going to have a headache when he wakes up."

"What about the rest of them?"

"I've got them assembled just up the hill a ways."

Three men were tied around trees, not moving. Only Peter was awake and he faced them, his hands tied behind him around a tree.

"So, they came peacefully?" she asked.

"You might say that," he replied.

"What's this all about?"

"Remember how everyone thought there was a bad guy on the Tribal Council? Well, it turns out there were two of them. Peter was not involved with Vincent Vargas. Peter's been operating his own little squad that intended to find the Carre-Shin-Ob by themselves. Apparently, he doesn't believe in the legend that the gold is sacred and protected by Towats."

"Are any more of his friends around here?" she asked.

"Not according to Peter, but then I don't know. I have his two-way radios and I haven't heard any chatter, so he's probably telling the truth."

"Well, then what are we waiting for?" she asked.

"What do you mean?"

"Let's go. I want to find my father."

"What about these guys?"

"It doesn't look to me like they're going very far. We can always call our friend for a pickup after we've finished."

"You forgot, he's in Washington."

"Big deal. He can always call someone. It doesn't bother me if these guys sit here for a day or two."

Chapter Eighteen

In the midst of guns, smoke, and mayhem, Cass had felt amazingly calm. Well, maybe calm wasn't the right word, but at least she wasn't terrified. She knew it had something to do with the handsome lug holding her hand. He never seemed to get rattled, except around women. She wasn't sure what they would face around the next bend, but she wasn't worried. She knew he could handle whatever it was. It was nice to have someone to carry the load. She had relied upon herself for too long.

"So where did that little smokin' shoe trick come from?"

"We got in a lot of sticky situations overseas and we had to be a little creative. I've used it on more than one occasion."

"Did you just happen to be wearing your smoke bomb shoe today?" she asked. "Or is it part of your everyday apparel?"

"No, not usually. But after I talked to Peter, well, things just didn't seem to add up. So I decided to prepare for anything."

"And why didn't you tell me?" she asked.

"I wasn't sure there would be a problem, and I didn't want to unnecessarily alarm you. I mean after all, Peter was one of Reber's trusted friends."

The walk hadn't been very long and they were enjoying their little trek. Carver pointed to their left and excitedly exclaimed, "You were right, the Vargas note was the missing piece. The water from heaven was a waterfall and there's the waterfall. It's almost hidden from view by the foliage and the cliffs of the box canyon."

Cass was looking where he was pointing, "I can't see anything."

"You'll have a better view once we get out into that clearing."

Cass continued to look without any luck. "Can you hear it?" he asked.

"I think I can hear something, but it doesn't sound any louder than water running out of my faucet."

"The canyons and foliage dampen the sound. Besides there's not a lot of water in the stream right now."

"Oh, there it is. It's beautiful—green, so it blends in with the background of the box canyon. Can we get closer?"

"We need to stay to the left if we are going to get to the top of the spillway. At least it's good to know Vargas's notes were accurate." He said. "I don't think many people know about this waterfall. Besides, Vargas probably never figured it out."

Just as they were about to crest the top of the cliff, Carver nudged Cass and pointed to a large rock just ahead of them. Sitting on the rock with his legs dangling over the side was He Who Speaks to the Sky.

"What took you so long?" he asked as they approached. He didn't look at them, but concentrated on his whittling. Almost nonchalantly, he added, "We've been waiting for you."

Cass looked around and couldn't see anyone but the smiling Sky Talker with his knife and stick. "You said 'we.' You wouldn't be including my father in 'we,' would you?"

"Around here, we call him Brother of the Winds. He is now a revered teacher to our people. He speaks with the power of the Winds and all listen. He speaks of things that are to be."

"My father?" she asked incredulously.

He ignored her question and continued, "He was called to a vision quest. First he went through the purification rights in the sweat house. Then he made himself ready to receive his vision. After finishing his purification, he did something very unusual. Some wanted to ban him, but when he spoke none could lift a finger against him. Then he read to us from his book. His voice was like the gentle wind yet all heard and all listened. All believe he is a holy man."

"You're talking about my dad?" Cass said.

Carver put his hand on her shoulder, "Cass, remember the rockslide? He was called to serve this people."

"That's real nice but if you don't mind, umm . . . I would like to see him and even talk to him if that's permitted. I have a few questions for the Wind Talker and sooner would be better," Cass said, smiling.

"Impatient one, isn't she?" Sky Talker said, smiling at Carver. He got up, motioned and said, "You two follow me to that little fire pit over there and he'll be along soon."

"What about Reber? Have you seen him?" She asked.

"She asks a lot of questions, too, doesn't she?" Sky Talker noted, chuckling to himself.

"Just don't get her started," warned Carver, placing a hand on the old Indian's back. "But at least she has good intentions." Cass jabbed him in the ribs.

As they sat, Sky Talker knelt in front of Cass and took both of her hands. He looked into her eyes for what seemed like forever and said, "Your true beauty comes from your heart." Without turning to look at Carver he said, "Do not let this one get away. She is the pearl of great worth that you should go sell all you have to purchase."

Cass had never had anyone look into her soul like that. She turned to Carver and asked, "Well, what are you waiting for? He just told you to go sell everything you have so you could marry me."

"He didn't say marry," teased Carver.

Sky Talker laughed out loud.

"See what I told you?" said Carver.

"She's spunky too," said Sky Talker.

Cass glanced up the hill and saw a man and an Indian maiden

walking towards them. Cass rose and looked, and as they got closer she recognized her father, but he looked different—dignified like the Sky Talker. She started walking, and then ran towards them. Rylan greeted her with a warm embrace. She cried and hugged him. "I've been so worried about you," she said.

He helped her back to where Sky Talker and Carver waited. The maiden followed close behind.

It was getting towards evening and Sky Talker lit the wood he had in the rock fire pit. As the fire flamed, the group watched.

Cass heard a noise and looked up to see Reber walk over and stand by the beautiful maiden. She could see that Reber may have just forgotten all about her.

Rylan interrupted the silence, "Well, I guess you want to know where I've been and why I didn't tell you I was going."

Cass said, "Why do you think we're here? But first, I want to know what happened to you."

Rylan laughed. "What do you mean? I'm just me but Sky Talker taught me a few things. It kinds of suits me doesn't it?"

"Well, I'm not sure that's exactly the word I would have chosen," she said. "Okay, start from the beginning and don't leave anything out. I know how men are—they skip all the details."

Rylan started speaking in low whispers. "Only in stillness can one hear the whisperings of the spirit." He spoke softly but she heard him—no it wasn't like hearing; it was like feeling.

"Cass, I was called on a vision quest by my brother, He Who Speaks to the Sky. I learned that such a quest is the inward journey to understand my innermost self within the harmony of the Four Balances; fire, earth, air and water.

"The purpose of the vision quest was to realize a oneness with all life and creation. Sky Talker told me that only those of exemplary character can prepare themselves to receive the vision. I wondered why he had sought me. In time, I learned that to progress, one is required to forget one's own needs and dedicate oneself to the Great Spirit."

Cass wondered if her father had forgotten who he was.

"Cass, I was told when I almost died in that rockslide that if I continued to be faithful that I would be able to lead many of my Lamanite brothers to the truth, to the gospel."

"There is only one God. He is truly the Great Spirit.

"After I was made ready by my brother, Sky Talker, I went to the top of a mountain where I was filled with the spirit of the Holy Ghost. Later, much later when I could see again, I turned and saw Sparrow Hawk," he nodded his head to the woman standing by Reber. "I knew that I was supposed to follow her."

Rylan stopped speaking and appeared to contemplate what or how to continue. Cass knew this was not the time to start with the questions, even though she had a million of them. Her father would get around to his story in his way. "Patience," she said to herself.

"Cassandra, I was taken by Sparrow Hawk to the entrance of the Carre-Shin-Ob. There standing in the entrance was Reber."

Reber spoke, "Cassandra, I was called by the Great Spirit to be the guardian of the Carre-Shin-Ob. I have beheld the sacred treasures contained therein. I was told to show your father because he would assist me in helping to bring my people to the power and position described in the Book of Mormon."

Rylan couldn't contain his excitement any longer. "The sacred mine is beyond imagination, not only for its wealth in gold, but because of the value of the records and artifacts contained therein. I was permitted to leaf through the records and to touch the golden artifacts and sacred objects that have been saved for generations. The mine is filled will gold of all kinds and has been protected to be used for His righteous purposes.

I have been called to help start those plans in motion. It will not be long until some of the plates in the Carre-Shin-Ob will be known throughout the world. There is more gold than one can imagine. Some of it has been worked into intricate artifacts of ancient design, some into golden murals."

Again he stopped speaking. To Cass, he seemed to glow during the telling of the story. Finally, he continued, "I was allowed to see other things that I am not privileged to speak of today.

"After my excursion into the mine, I fell into a trance much like King Lamoni and I couldn't move for a day. He Who Speaks to the Sky and Sparrow Hawk nursed me back to health. I was allowed again to enter the Carre-Shin-Ob. When I entered the outer chamber, I again encountered Reber standing as sentinel near the entrance."

Cass looked over at Reber. He, too, had changed. He looked more refined, more ennobled. She had been right—he would be a key person to assist his people into the light.

Rylan continued, "I have been allowed to tell you and Carver of my vision, and none other. You are not to tell anyone of my experiences. The gold treasures contained in the Carre-Shin-Ob are sacred and are to be used as the Great Spirit, who is God, directs."

"Reber, have you known where the mine was this whole time?" Cass asked.

"Are you kidding? I was brought here just the other day."

They talked into the night—Reber, Cass, Rylan, and Carver. Sparrow Hawk always stood close to Reber. Reber never let her get far away.

He Who Speaks to the Sky brought them all something to eat while they continued to speak. Rylan told them that he did not yet know his part in the plan but he trusted that in time, he would learn.

Finally Rylan showed them the Inca Sun Mask. It was the one artifact he had been allowed to bring with him from the mine. Cass was stunned by its brilliance and antiquity. It was pure gold so bright it almost appeared white. The craftsmanship was extraordinary, the details exquisite.

"This," Rylan said, "was worn by nobility when they worshipped in the Temple of the Sun. It is pre-Columbian. The Inca believe that one couple was sent to earth to bring civilization to humanity. They were sent by their father, the Sun god Inti. Inti was honored and depicted as a formidable face surrounded by blazing rays. The Aztecs, a tribe similar to the Incas in many ways, told that the Sun was home to the great god Quetzalcoatl."

"It's beautiful," said Cass.

"You know what this means?" asked Rylan.

Carver replied, "It could mean that Montezuma may have

brought some of his gold this far north to escape Cortez."

"You're right, Carver. However, you notice that some of the Inca legends parallel the Bibical stories of Adam and Eve and the legend of Quetzalcoatl is really the story of Christ coming to the Americas as told in the Book of Mormon."

"Dad, umm could we skip the history lessons right now." Some things never change, she thought.

"By the way," said Rylan. "I believe congratulations are in order, Carver. I knew that you would find her as irresistible as I do."

"How did you know?" asked Cass, surprised.

"I have my ways. I was called on a vision quest, you know."

She looked at him in wonderment, "Just kidding," he said. "All you have to do is open your eyes and see the way he looks at you. Or maybe you tipped me off because you haven't let go of his hand since I got here."

"I couldn't be happier," said Cass.

Reber teasingly added, poking Cass, "And all this time I thought you were really waiting for me," he said as he reached over and put his arm around Sparrow Hawk's shoulders.

Appendix

A Brief Description of Some Coding Techniques

Throughout history, codes have been used to keep and pass along secret messages. Coding techniques employ well-known symbols to communicate something other than their ordinary meaning. Any word or letter or series thereof could be a cipher. In order to decipher the message, you must know the coding technique and the keyword or symbol used to create the cipher.

Cryptography has been in use throughout the history of mankind, and has been a decisive factor in a remarkably large number of military and political campaigns. The substitution cipher of Julius Caesar is one of the most well-known cipher substitution methods. Many different methods were later developed and continued to be used until the 1900s.

In the novel you have just completed, several different cryptology methods were used to create secret messages. They were briefly explained in the text. For those of you interested, this appendix explains some of those methods in greater detail.

Definitions

Plain text: the message that is to be encrypted.

Cipher text: the message written in code; the encryption.

Encryption key: the word or symbol used to help decipher the encryption, using one of numerous techniques.

The Vigenere Cipher

The Vigenere cipher is a simple substitution cipher technique. It was first used by Blaise de Vigenere in the Court of Henry III in France, in the sixteenth century. It uses a table of alphabetical characters arranged in a tabular form. Below is shown the entire alphabetical table to encrypt a message.

In this cipher substitution method, each row contains the entire alphabet. The first row starts with A and ends with Z. Each following row is shifted one letter.

```
    A B C D E F G H I J K L M N O P Q R S T U V W X Y Z

A   A B C D E F G H I J K L M N O P Q R S T U V W X Y Z
B   B C D E F G H I J K L M N O P Q R S T U V W X Y Z A
C   C D E F G H I J K L M N O P Q R S T U V W X Y Z A B
D   D E F G H I J K L M N O P Q R S T U V W X Y Z A B C
E   E F G H I J K L M N O P Q R S T U V W X Y Z A B C D
F   F G H I J K L M N O P Q R S T U V W X Y Z A B C D E
G   G H I J K L M N O P Q R S T U V W X Y Z A B C D E F
H   H I J K L M N O P Q R S T U V W X Y Z A B C D E F G
I   I J K L M N O P Q R S T U V W X Y Z A B C D E F G H
J   J K L M N O P Q R S T U V W X Y Z A B C D E F G H I
K   K L M N O P Q R S T U V W X Y Z A B C D E F G H I J
L   L M N O P Q R S T U V W X Y Z A B C D E F G H I J K
M   M N O P Q R S T U V W X Y Z A B C D E F G H I J K L
N   N O P Q R S T U V W X Y Z A B C D E F G H I J K L M
O   O P Q R S T U V W X Y Z A B C D E F G H I J K L M N
P   P Q R S T U V W X Y Z A B C D E F G H I J K L M N O
Q   Q R S T U V W X Y Z A B C D E F G H I J K L M N O P
R   R S T U V W X Y Z A B C D E F G H I J K L M N O P Q
S   S T U V W X Y Z A B C D E F G H I J K L M N O P Q R
T   T U V W X Y Z A B C D E F G H I J K L M N O P Q R S
U   U V W X Y Z A B C D E F G H I J K L M N O P Q R S T
V   V W X Y Z A B C D E F G H I J K L M N O P Q R S T U
W   W X Y Z A B C D E F G H I J K L M N O P Q R S T U V
X   X Y Z A B C D E F G H I J K L M N O P Q R S T U V W
Y   Y Z A B C D E F G H I J K L M N O P Q R S T U V W X
Z   Z A B C D E F G H I J K L M N O P Q R S T U V W X Y
```

The Vigenere Cipher uses this table with a keyword to encode a message. If, for example, the keyword is "TOWATS" and the message is "Rhoades Mine," the technique that is used to create the cipher is as follows: write the keyword and plain text as shown below, and then create the cipher text using the above array.

Keyword: T O W A T S T O W A T
Plain text: R H O A D E S M I N E
Cipher text: L V L A W WL A E N X

The letters of the top index row are used for the keyword while the letters of the first index column are used for the plain text. For example, the first letter of the keyword "T" is found on the first index row, while the letter "R" is found on the first index column. The letter at the intersection of "R" and "T" in the table is the first letter of the cipher text, "L" in this case. The remainder of the cipher text is created in the same manner, letter by letter. You can see how the keyword becomes critical to decipher the coded message.

If your task is to decode a cipher, then you have the cipher text. With the keyword you can simply work backwards to decipher the message into plain text.

Francis Bacon Substitution Cipher

Bacon used two typefaces of alphabetical characters, slightly different in weight or boldness. He broke up his cipher text into five character groups, each group representing one plain text character. Using the keyword table and cipher text, one could search for the bold characters and find the plain text letter.

In the following example:
- "*" is any non-bold character in the cipher text
- "B" is any bolded character in the cipher text

So each letter of plaintext is represented by five letters in the cipher text. In the example below, the cipher text for each plain text letter is:

A: *****	G: **B**	M: *BB**	S: B**B*	Y: BB***
B: ****B	H: **BBB	N: *BB*B	T: B**BB	Z: BB**B
C: ***B*	I: *B***	O: *BBB*	U: B*B**	

D: ***BB	J: *B**B	P: *BBBB	V: B*B*B
E: **B**	K: *B*B*	Q: B****	W: B*BB*
F: **B*B	L: *B*BB	R: B***B	X: B*BBB

As an example, let's assume the cipher text reads:

"To be or not to be that is the question"

To decipher the coded message, you break the characters into groups of five letters each. Using the cipher text key above, you can find the plain text

"To be o / r not t / obe th / at is t / he que / stion"

The plain text is then "M E E T M E"

Cipher Wheel Substitution Cipher

This substitution cipher method was used extensively in the Civil War. It uses a keyword (or series of words), a plaintext, and a cipher text. The substitution is accomplished by using two concentric circles (one smaller than the other), each having the alphabet around the outside. The inner wheel (alphabet) can be rotated to be aligned with characters on the outer wheel (alphabet). In some versions, one or both of the alphabets is arranged in a random order rather than alphabetical order. See the example on the next page.

Using the substitution method, except substituting the cipher wheels for the tabular alphabet as used in the Vigenere method, you can code or decode a message as follows:

Keyword: T O W A T S T O W A T
Plaintext: R H O A D E S M I N E

Using the outer ring for the keyword and the inner ring for the plaintext, the cipher text can be determined.

The keyword first letter on the outer wheel is aligned with "A" on the inner wheel. The first letter of the plain text message "R" is found

on the inner wheel and the first letter of the cipher text is found by noting the letter on the outer wheel that aligns with the "R," "O" in this case. The sequence is followed for each letter of the plaintext message aligning with the adjacent keyword letter until the entire message is encoded.

The Deseret alphabet displayed on the next page was implemented by Brigham Young and used in the novel.

Brigham Young believed that the alphabet was designed to reform the representation of the English language, not the language itself. It had several advantages, including that it: 1) Demonstrated cultural exclusivism, 2) Kept secrets from curious non-Mormons, 3) Controlled what children could read, and 4) Eliminated the awkward problem of phonetic spelling.

It fell into disuse for a number of reasons. David Bigler in The Forgotten Kingdom proclaimed "On some things, the people of Utah quietly overruled their strong-minded leader." Practically speaking, however, other reasons for its failure were: 1) Its introduction into public schools was not accepted, 2) The tailless characters, and the monotonous evenness of the lines, made the words difficult to distinguish, 3) It was found impossible to ensure uniform pronunciation and orthography, and 4) It was extremely expensive to typeset.

LETTER	NAME	SOUND	LETTER	NAME	SOUND
⟨glyph⟩	e	FEED	⟨glyph⟩	OO	GOOD
⟨glyph⟩	Z	ZIP	⟨glyph⟩	F	FAN
⟨glyph⟩	WH	WHALE	⟨glyph⟩	G	JACK
⟨glyph⟩	WOO	WAG	⟨glyph⟩	N	NIGHT
⟨glyph⟩	K	KITE	⟨glyph⟩	ENG	SING
⟨glyph⟩	GA	GAB	⟨glyph⟩	i	PIE
⟨glyph⟩	FE	FEW	⟨glyph⟩	H	HAT
⟨glyph⟩	OO	BLUE	⟨glyph⟩	UR	RAT
⟨glyph⟩	O	OVER	⟨glyph⟩		BURNER
⟨glyph⟩	AW	CAUGHT	⟨glyph⟩	CHE	CHEW
⟨glyph⟩	FO	FORT	⟨glyph⟩	m	MIST
⟨glyph⟩	D	DIP	⟨glyph⟩	THE	THEN
⟨glyph⟩	ESH	FISH	⟨glyph⟩	YE	YET
⟨glyph⟩	ZHE	VISION	⟨glyph⟩	A	WAIT
⟨glyph⟩	S	SIP	⟨glyph⟩	AH	ART
⟨glyph⟩	SI	SIT	⟨glyph⟩	V	VAN
⟨glyph⟩	BO	BOY	⟨glyph⟩	B	BIKE
⟨glyph⟩	CO	COT	⟨glyph⟩		MAT
⟨glyph⟩	b	BIKE	⟨glyph⟩		CUP
⟨glyph⟩		BEG	⟨glyph⟩	P	PIKE
			⟨glyph⟩	T	TIP
			⟨glyph⟩	ETH	THIN
			⟨glyph⟩	i	LIFT

Author's Note

The Mystery of the Carre-Shin-Ob

Speculation runs rampant as to the existence of the Carre-Shin-Ob. No one that is in a position to really know has ever admitted to its reality or that the Mormon Church benefited from gold that was removed from the Carre-Shin-Ob. Many legends exist, in which Chief Walker (Wakara), the purported last guardian of the mine, allowed Thomas Rhoades, Brigham Young's agent, to remove gold from the mine for the benefit of the Church. Neither the Church nor Brigham wanted rumors of gold being found in Utah. Brigham did not want a second California gold rush nor the type of people that would come prospecting. Chief Wakara likewise did not want rumors of a sacred gold repository to become known. So there is no actual confirmation from those who would have known.

However, there are numerous facts that simply won't go away. Thomas Rhoades became one of the wealthiest of the early Utah settlers. It is no secret that he acquired his wealth from Spanish gold. Early Mormon gold pieces have the same chemical composition of Spanish gold.

Isaac Morley was a poor farmer who somehow saved the Mormon Church from bankruptcy following enforcement of the Edmunds-Tucker act. Prior to assisting the Church, he claimed to have had a vision of the Carre-Shin-Ob.

The architect of the Salt Lake Temple admitted to using Rhoades' gold to cover the angel Moroni and possibly the twelve golden oxen holding up the baptismal font in the temple.

It is also well known that when the Mormons, when they entered the Salt Lake Valley, had less than twenty dollars in combined wealth. Yet within just two years, they had paid for land, for emigration of sixty thousand Saints, and built an expanding metropolis. It has been estimated that these costs would have eclipsed three million dollars; a king's ransom in those days.

So if the Mormons didn't get gold from the Carre-Shin-Ob, where or how did they acquire sufficient wealth to pay the huge expenses they incurred?

If the Carre-Shin-Ob does exist, why hasn't anyone been able to locate it in over one hundred and fifty years? Is its location protected and hidden from men by Towats, the Great Spirit? Is the key Towats, the Great Spirit? There are records, testimonies and diaries of individuals who claim to have visited the Carre-Shin-Ob in vision or in person. It is described in many ways, but generally it is described as a cave containing many artifacts fabricated from gold bullion. Are these documents simply made up figments of imagination, or in reality, testimonies?

Chapter Notes

Chapter 2

1. George A. Thompson, *Faded Footprints: The Lost Rhoades Mines and Other Hidden Treasures of the Uintahs* (Salt Lake City: Dream Garden Press, 1991), 177.

2. Thompson, *Faded Footprints*, 179.

3. Ibid.

4. Kerry Ross Boren and Lisa Lee Boren, *The Utah Gold Rush: The Lost Rhoades Mine and the Hathenbruck Legacy* (Springville, UT: Cedar Fort, Inc., 2002), 11.

5. Kerry Ross Boren, http://abouttreasurehunting.com/treasure/AA032099.HTM, in "The Lost Rhoads Gold Mines," The Lost Rhoads Gold Mines@Everything2.com, http://www.everything2.com/index.pl?node_id=1389039 (accessed June 4, 2007).

Chapter 6

1. Thompson, *Faded Footprints*, 18.

Chapter 7

1. Thompson, *Faded Footprints*, 101.

2. Ibid.

3. Ibid.

4. David Horne in Thompson, *Faded Footprints*, 24.

Chapter 8

1. Manti Temple Centennial Committee, *The Manti Temple* (Manti, UT: Community Press, 1877), 4.

Chapter 10

1. Boren and Boren, *The Utah Gold Rush*, 13.

2. "The Mormon Gold Mine," Where Brother Brigham Got The Gold to Build Up His Zion, http://www.angelfire.com/trek/forthetruth/brighamyoung.html (accessed September 29, 2008).

Appendix

Information supplied in the index was pulled from these internet sites:

Cryptography: starbase.trincoll.edu-crypto/historical/gronsfeld.html.

Cryptography defined and brief history: www.eco.utexas.edu/faculty/norman.bus.for/course.mat/ssim/history.html.

The history of cryptography: cse/stamfprd/edu/class/sophomore-college/projects-97/cryptography/history.html; www.wolframscience.com/reference/notes.1085c.

The deseret alphabet: at www. utlm.org/onlinresources/deseretalphabet.htm.

The secret language: www.exploratorium.edu/ronh/secret/secret.html.

The Vigenere Cipher: starase.trincoll.edu/-crypto/history/vigenere.html.

Book Club Questions

1. Do you think the Carre-Shin-Ob really exists or is it just another mystical legend? If not, how do you explain how the Mormon Church was able to pay such fantastic debt when it had no visible means to acquire such wealth.

2. Cass has decided to give up on marriage. What brought her to this decision? In what ways do you agree with Cass and in what ways do you disagree?

3. The Carre-Shin-Ob is rumored to be guarded by a spirit named Towats. Do you believe in spirits? Do you believe they have been given jobs to do on the earth? Do you think Chief Wakara was appointed by Towats to be his earthly guardian? Why or why not?

4. Carver doesn't like to talk about his feelings. Why do you think this is? Did his experience in the military help or hinder his ability to share his feelings? And do you think he'll ever find it easier?

5. Cass is attracted to Reber, even while developing feelings for Carver. In what ways are these men the same, and in what ways are they different? What do you think attracts her to each of them, and what did you think of her choice?

6. Did Carver, Rylan and Cass unnecessarily put themselves in danger while trying to locate the Carre-Shin-Ob. Do you feel they were justified in their quest or should they have sought help? Did the outcome balance the danger?

7. What do you think of Brigham Young's decision not to discuss the Carre-Shin-Ob or his relationship with Thomas Rhoades? He could have confirmed or dispelled the rumors. Why did he chose to do neither?

About the Author

Dennis Mangrum grew up in Salt Lake City. At age fourteen he won a prize for his oil painting, his first creative endeavor. Later he attended West High School in the days when if you didn't beat then during the game, you did after. At West his teachers considered him a jock who dabbled in academics. He attended the University of Utah on a football and wrestling scholarship and continued to fiddle around with academia, graduating with a master's degree in civil engineering. He worked as a structural engineer for a few years before taking a job at Boeing Aircraft in the computer interface structural engineering department. He later returned to Utah to attend law school at the University of Utah. His law practice commenced with Spensley, Horn, Jubas and Lubitz, a patent law firm in Century City, California. He left that firm to start his own practice in Thousand Oaks, California where he worked for twenty years. He then returned to Utah and the private practice of law in Utah, earning enough in the day to support his real love of coaching baseball, which he has done each and every day that there isn't any snow on the ground.

Dennis now lives with his wife Liz in Sandy, Utah. His wife was coincidently his girl friend in sixth grade and later at West High. He is the father of seven children and hangs up on any of his children's kids who call him "Grandpa." He thinks that title is for old people and he lives by the words of Dylan Thomas who taught to "rage, rage against the dying of the light." Dylan coaxed each of us to "not go gently into that good night."